The Spores of Wrath

Other books by William C. Tracy

The Dissolutionverse:
Novellas and Novelettes:
The Five Hive Plateau
Tuning the Symphony
Merchants and Maji
The Society of Two Houses
Journey to the Top of the Nether

The Dissolution Cycle:
The Seeds of Dissolution (Book I)
Facets of the Nether (Book II)
Fall of the Imperium (Book III)

Other Books:
Epic Fantasy:
Fruits of the Gods

Anthologies:
Distant Gardens
Farther Reefs
Lofty Mountains
The World of Juno

Science Fiction:
The Biomass Conflux
Of Mycelium and Men
Down Among the Mushrooms
To a Fungus Unknown
The Spores of Wrath

The Spores of Wrath

BOOK 3 OF THE BIOMASS CONFLUX

William C. Tracy

Space Wizard Science Fantasy
Raleigh, NC
www.spacewizardsciencefantasy.com

Cover art by MoorBooks
Editing by Heather Tracy
Map by Kelly Coston
Book Layout © 2015 BookDesignTemplates.com

The Spores of Wrath/William C. Tracy.— 1st ed.
ISBN 978-1-960247-20-9

Author's website: www.williamctracy.com

To the search for the unknown. May we always learn more about our universe.

CONTENTS

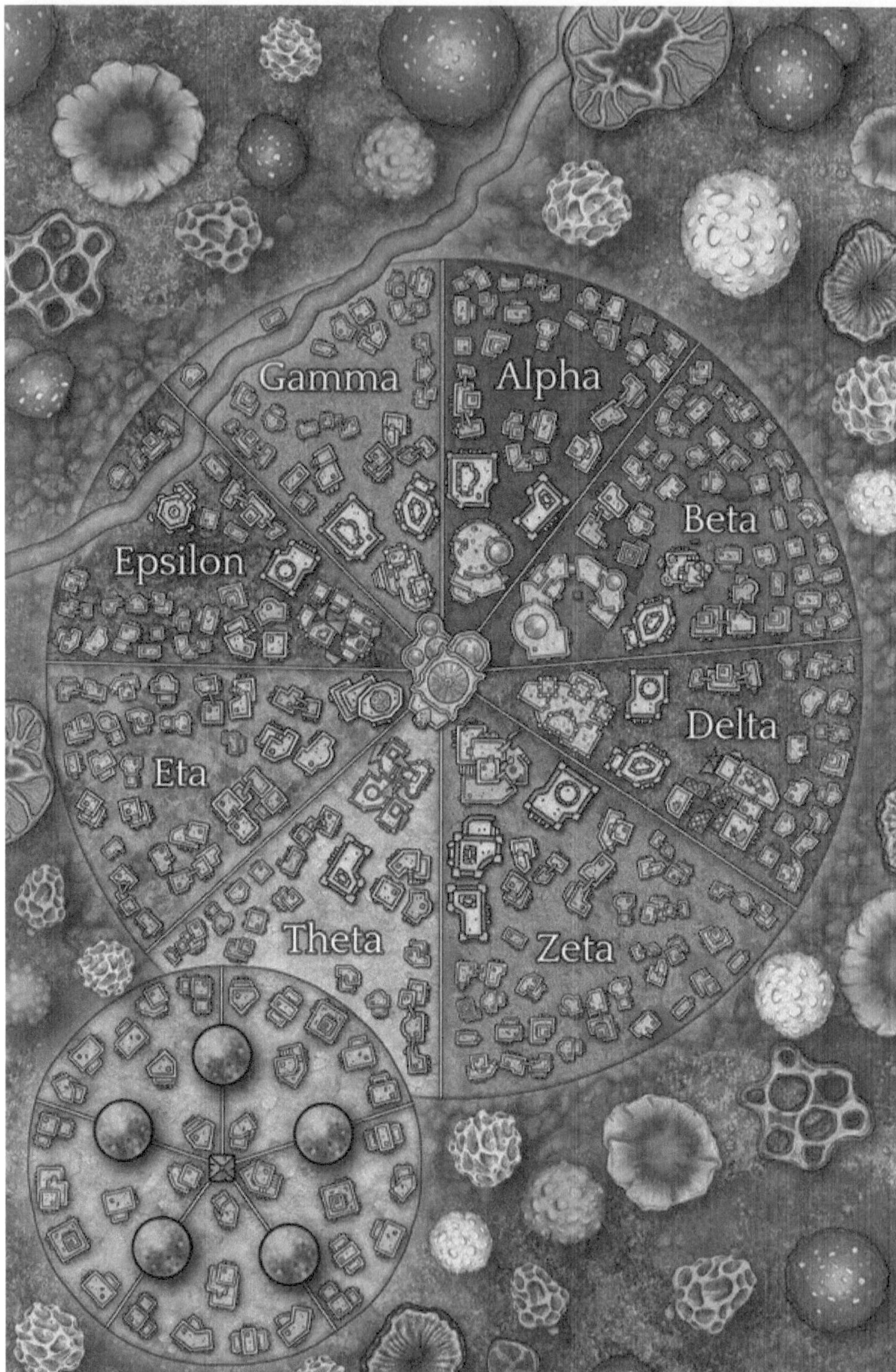

Gamma
Alpha
Beta
Epsilon
Delta
Eta
Theta
Zeta

A Timeline of Events

5.77 megaseconds (2 months, 2 weeks) before landing:

A fleet of eight generational ships from Earth arrives in their eleventh star system since beginning their journey. The system is categorized and named. The fourth planet, 11d (Lida) orbiting around 11 (Lev) is determined to be conducive to life by Processor Alvin, more than any other target so far.

The eight Admins are revived from sus-ani: Jane Brighton, Ahman Ragab, Dmitri Novikov, Xi Wenqing, Rajani Kumarisurajinder, Alessandro Giordano, Maria Gutiérrez Delgado, and Polunu Kim. They all have genemods from Earth that enable them to live for centuries.

Vagal supersoldiers re-engage the chain of command, causing conflict with the generational inhabitants of the fleet, who have been operating largely independently for four hundred years. The soldiers will live almost as long as the Admins, while the Generationals live more standard-length human lives.

There is a large amount of fungal biomass covering the planet, often to a depth of dozens of meters.

Landing to 6 weeks after landing:

The fleet glasses approximately a ten-kilometer diameter landing site near the equator of Lida. This is where they will begin constructing a city (labeled an arcopolis) from the ships of the fleet.

Meanwhile, the biomass of Lida, which is itself sentient, watches the events with curiosity. It labels the glassed area as the "Ring of Death" and the settlers as "The Children Who Ate Their Parents" (confusing the fleet ships for living beings).

Thirteen days after landing, the catastrophic collapse of a ship skeleton leads to the loss of twenty-three Vagals and fifty-eight Generationals. It also opens a crack in the ground, leading to the discovery of a cavern under the glassed site still containing biomass material. It turns out to be deadly to the Vagals who investigate. One of them, Anderson, loses a hand to fungal infection.

Further investigation leads Frank Silver, a Generational, to the revelation that the biomass covering the planet is one individual entity, with expressions of animal, plant, and fungal cell material. It is not suspected to be sentient, merely very well adapted to living on Lida.

6 weeks to 1 year after landing:

The biomass actively observes the humans who have landed, attempting to categorize them. Meanwhile many of the colonists' animal species die from fungal infections. Plant species are changed by the biomass into unusable crops. The colonists heavily cull their agriculture to keep the most successful species alive.

The Admins try kill the biomass, with little success. They also determine there is a severe lack of metals on Lida, likely because much of them are within biomass structures. Admin Jane Brighton uses much of their remaining nanotanium metal to construct a wall encircling the first two radians of the colony—Alpha and Beta. The colony had been projected to take ten years to complete all eight radians. That timeline is now uncertain.

One of the colonists, Jiow, meets a group unhappy about the direction Admin is taking on the colony and wants to secure more supplies for the Generationals.

Agetha Xenakis is called to where her husband, Daved Xenakis, has fallen into a deep shaft under the colony, containing one of the only sources of metal found. While he recovers, he dreams of the moss and tiny creatures he landed on at the bottom of the cave.

Seven months after landing, the decanting tubes begin growing children for the colony. Meanwhile, the Admins determine they must find another source of building material for the next radians.

1 year to 5 years after landing:

The biomass continues to attack the colony, while the Generationals construct the arcopolis and the Vagals battle against biomass incursions. Frank discovers that the biomass has already hybridized with the local honeybees. Even worse, it is already intrinsic to the colony, and the best they can do is hope to live with it.

While tensions mount between the Generationals and the Admins, Agetha and Daved welcome their new child, but their happiness is short-lived, as Daved collapses soon after. Doctors find his body has been overrun by fungal strands, and he succumbs soon after.

Jiow also has a child by herself, though with genetic material donated by Frank. As the two children grow, and Agetha and Jiow help each other in child-rearing, Admin develops plans to limit the Generationals' influence in the arcopolis, while developing a new building material.

Frank, along with some other scientists, develops resinplast—a byproduct of biomass material—as a new building product.

Agetha leads a construction crew, but this affects her ability to raise Phillipe, her child. Jiow takes up the slack with her child, Choi, but Agetha's relationship with Phillipe suffers.

Jiow takes part in raids on the colony supplies, culminating in an attempt to steal rumored nuclear weapons. The rumors are false, and several Generationals—Jiow excluded—are captured, and later they are forced out into the biomass. It is a death sentence.

Anderson discovers a full life in the arcopolis where he begins to write stories, prompted by a mentor.

The colony draws inward, reducing their ventures out into the biomass as Beta Radian is finally completed after five years.

5 years to 20 years after landing:

The next generation of the colony is nicknamed "Grounders." The Admins, led by Jane, plan for when the Generationals are all gone, gradually forcing them out into each newly completed radian: Gamma at ten years, then Delta at fifteen, leaving the first radians for the Admins and their Vagal soldiers.

As Choi and Phillipe grow, they adapt to life in the colony. Many of the oldest Generationals die off, or sometimes just disappear—as Admin secretly sends troublemakers out into the biomass.

Anderson becomes an established writer as well as leading Vagal soldiers. There have been heavy casualties, and only a fraction of their number is left.

Agetha's son leaves home as soon as he can to join a new Grounder recruitment to shore up the number of Vagals.

Frank works on the resinplast formula. It is only a matter of time until the biomass adapts to it, as it has to every other attempt to keep it out of the colony.

Eighteen years after landing, Dr. Beth Harley develops a mycophage to wipe out a large section of biomass. However, the resinplast has no resistance to it, and the mycophage would also destroy most of the city. Jane confiscates the original sample and makes certain Beth is pushed out of research and into a medical practice at the edge of the city.

Finally, the biomass watches and observes. It takes in those Admin has sent out into the biomass, to try to understand how humans work. There are many failed attempts, but it learns more each time.

20 years to 40 years after landing:

From twenty to thirty years after landing, the biomass is largely quiet, observing the Children and accepting the people Admin forces out. Epsilon Radian is completed, however the biomass has recolonized much of the glassed territory of Zeta, Eta, and Theta Radians, requiring flamethrowers and drastic antifungal measures.

One of the first buildings in Epsilon collapses from an undiscovered invasion of biomass in its foundation, killing several construction workers. This is mirrored during construction of Zeta Radian, as a new type of fungal growth is encountered with explosive seed pods that activate in response to fire.

Agetha forms a fast friendship with Beth, working as a doctor in Zeta Radian, eventually leading to love. During this time the biomass fully absorbs the flowering reproduction of the plants brought by the colonists and starts an exponential expansion dubbed by Frank as "The Flowering."

Displaced Generationals band together with Agetha, Beth, and Frank to finish construction on Zeta radian and deploy a modified version of Beth's mycophage, tailored only to target the new flowering component of the biomass. The mycophage is adapted for the walls of the arcopolis, leading to peaceful building and expansion. Agetha and Beth move to apartments Agetha personally built in Zeta.

40 years to 41 years after landing:

Agetha, happily married to Beth, is in her early sixties. Once again, they are forced to move, from Zeta to Eta Radian. Jiow walked out into the biomass three years prior, having terminal cancer. Her child, Choi, is now a scientific partner to Frank, making resinplast programmable using viruses taken from the biomass. These allow for buildings to grow themselves, requiring only individuals to tend them. Harie is one of these, teaching a new intern to look for defects.

Juliane, the third son of Processor Alvin and Kofus, has always been prone to allergies and sickness, but lately has been losing time. He feels strange growths on his body, but forgets they're there soon after.

Jane talks with the other Admins of starting other arcopolises in the biomass. They will need to cross kilometers of uninhabitable terrain.

With Juliane as a starting vector, a flu-like sickness spreads across the colony, progressing into forgetfulness and lost time. Beth tries to study the disease, but ends up repeating the same test. Anderson, paying attention to his implant, named Cora, determines there is a pattern with those who are sick, but cannot find what it is.

The printers making seeds to grow into new buildings are malfunctioning in very specific manners, reverting to native biomass. Choi eventually concludes there is an intelligence at work behind it, though Frank states that any intelligence on the biomass' part was disproved shortly after they landed.

Choi sets up an information drop through Phillipe, now working as a soldier under the Vagals, to provide anonymous information to Admin about the possibility of sentience.

Agetha has urges to wander and ends up at a strange house on the edge of Theta Radian, the last radian still under construction. There she meets Phyllis, and a group of people who developed a dissociative sign language to get around their urges. They call what is causing the urges a *rider*.

Anderson and Choi arrive at the Zeta market for the predetermined information drop, however, Agetha, Beth, and Phyllis are there, as they sell vegetables and wares in the market. Juliane is there too, having been directed by an urge. Agetha finds she can see through Juliane's eyes and control him, though she is unable to process the emotional effect of doing so. As a team, they misdirect Choi and Anderson, and steal the information, for reasons unknown.

41 years to 42 years after landing:

The biomass is interested in the multiple communication codes being developed by the Children, especially by those partially subsumed. They are strangely resistant.

Agetha and Beth grow close to Phyllis, mentally and physically. They are tied together by the *rider* and can partially perceive each other mentally. They are also physically reverting to a younger age. Agetha strives to break through the fog in her mind, and over the intervening months, has a breakthrough. She asks for an equal footing with the intelligence invading them—the biomass.

Anderson finds errors in new resinplast HUD systems, with figures deleted from his view and messages lost. Jane knows there was an intercepted attempt to provide information, but doesn't know by whom. She prepares for war, and pulls all Admin and Vagals into Alpha and Beta Radians.

Juliane wanders outside the arcopolis walls, unhurt in the native biomass. He meets Generationals who were forced to leave the city years ago and were partially subsumed by the biomass. Semi-coherently, he opens the briefcase with the information from the market drop, which contains a programmable resinplast seed. With the help of others in a ramshackle camp between five giant fungal towers, he plants the seed. Agetha, Beth, and Phyllis soon arrive in the camp as well. Agetha discovers Jiow is alive and cured from cancer. She has been wandering the wilds in a fog, but is suddenly "awake" again, like the others.

Choi develops a yes/no decision tree answer system to communicate with whoever is behind the resinplast printer changes. To their surprise, it offers deep and intelligent answers. Frank is finally convinced there may be an intelligence in the biomass. They call it "Answerer."

Jane receives the information anonymously from the information drop over a year ago, that the biomass is indeed sentient. The Admins panic. Anderson hears snippets of information from all sides and using Cora's intuitive leaps, also determines the biomass must be sentient.

42 years to 43 years after landing:

The biomass had originally intended to subsume the Children, but the recent cracks in its control are something it has never seen, making it extremely curious.

Jane has closed the Admin HUD system, communicating with paper or simple unchangeable texts. She's developed Beth's original mycophage as a first strike weapon and shoots it far out into the wilds, at the place she wants to build a new arcopolis. It will get the biomass' attention as a bargaining point. They only have one chance before the biomass adapts to it, but as the Admins watch, the test fails to clear what they expected. The biomass was already resistant to the mycophage and toying with them.

Anderson decides to find out what the biomass is thinking, and travels to Theta Radian with Phillipe. Choi happens to see Anderson and Phillipe and follows. Choi instead runs into their mother, Jiow. They see the signs of the biomass on her, and deny she is their mother any longer.

Anderson and Phillipe confront the small town outside the walls. Agetha quickly calls out her estranged son, Phillipe. Anderson confirms they can talk to the biomass and, at the urging of Cora, asks to be put in contact. The biomass has never been able to subsume a Vagal or one of the Admin, because of their gene modifications. It agrees excitedly. Anderson is transformed over several weeks and when he wakes, he can access more information about the biomass than the others.

Choi pulls strings with Frank to call a meeting with Admin. They show off Answerer. Jane asks it what it intends for them, and it prints a new human figure, not Admin, Vagal, Generational, or Grounder.

Jane forms a cabal with Rajani, Ahman, and Wenqing to deal with the biomass. Since it wants to talk now, she's going to talk it into serving her, thus rendering it harmless.

Reset

43 years after landing

"Six months," Jane Brighton said. "And what have we accomplished? Nothing, besides skulking around like kids playing at being detectives. Answerer is being coy, and Dmitri is stirring up the other Admins."

Rajani Kumarisurajinder straightened, her chin up. She led the scientific progress in the colony, and Jane had to call her to this dark and disused storage room by passing her notes like they were in grade school. *Paper* notes. Rajani had given her code of two taps, then three—Ahman and Wenqing had different codes—to report on her progress. Jane had Christiaan choose a different place in the Admin building for every meeting. Her assistant—and spouse—stood to one side of the room, making notes on paper.

They couldn't use the HUDs, because even the old-style HUDs from the fleet—now much repaired—were compromised by the biomass. The biomass that had shown itself to be an intelligent being in no uncertain terms. For over forty years, Jane's concern had been finishing the colony. The arcopolis. With this new revelation, she only cared about overcoming the biomass. What use was a city with a wall when the whole blasted planet could rise up against you?

Rajani cleared her throat, repositioning her silk salwar kameez though it didn't need it. "I have Choi and Frank working every day on communications with...with Answerer." No one liked calling it "The Biomass" because that just rubbed their faces in the fact they'd been stupid enough to believe a world-spanning organism was a dumb animal for *forty years.*

"But what does it *say*?" Jane asked, one hand up like she was trying to grasp thin air.

Rajani had to know what she meant. She'd been asking the same thing for six months. The key to the control of Answerer...the biomass...was understanding it. That was how you defeated your enemy: by understanding them. Straight out of *The Art of War*. Except they were trying to understand a sentient fungus.

"It's been reticent lately," Rajani sighed. "Choi insists it has a personality, even a sense of humor, but it's been merely stating facts. It will give us whatever information we want, as long as we can decode what it means."

"Stringing us along," Jane said. "It knows it controls the narrative." She waved a hand. "Well, get whatever scientific knowledge you need from it. I'm sure it has recipes for materials and chemicals we can use."

"Specifically, the composition of the fungal towers, if possible," Christiaan put in. They went back to writing.

"I'll do what I can," Rajani said, "but it's got a completely different makeup—physical and mental—to us. 'It' isn't even the right way to address Answerer. We're not sure if the biomass is a coherent entity, or if the results we see are directly the result of our questions. I don't know if we can ever understand it."

"Keep trying," Jane growled.

They talked for a while longer on other updates, then Rajani left, and Jane and Christiaan began the dance they'd done once a week for the past six months. Find another abandoned place during the night in the huge and empty Admin building, and talk to one of the three other Admins—out of eight—that were in on this little cloak-and-dagger scheme.

"How do we talk to Answerer on the same level?" Jane asked Ahman Ragab, who oversaw R&D, and was also a good sounding board. They were more philosophical than the rest of the Admins.

"Find out what it doesn't have," they answered immediately. "The issue is it can't think like we do. It has none of the same experiences."

Jane gritted her teeth. She couldn't even complain Ahman had said the same thing as Rajani, because she'd told each Admin that it was just them—her and Christiaan and the other Admin—on these nighttime meetings.

"So what *do* we know about it?" Jane asked. "What can Choi and Frank ask it that will press its buttons?"

Ahman looked thoughtful. "We know it *has* desires, not just environmental urges." They rubbed at their chin with one hand. "The question is, 'what is Answerer?' Is it a gestalt of the biomass? Is it one subsection designed to interface with us while the rest of the planet goes about its business? How much of its total attention does it devote to the questions we ask it? Does it even represent the will of all of the biomass, or just one part of it?"

"Well that's a lot of nothing," Jane said, though Christiaan looked interested.

"Does it even have a concept of a whole, a self, like we do? It seems to have issues with individuality, as we've seen from the scientists' answers."

"That's not clearing up the issue."

Ahman shrugged. "You're the one who wants to get leverage over an alien intelligence."

"What would you do?" Jane asked, genuinely interested in the answer.

"Get on its good side, then ask for resources," the other Admin said. "None of this trying to one-up it."

"But why not do both?" Jane told Christiaan after Ahman had left.

Christiaan tilted their head to one side. "An interesting proposition, Jane. But do we get on its good side to then one-up it, or vice versa? Will it be more or less upset if it discovers what we're doing one way or the other? Does it even get angry in the same sense as us?"

Xi Wenqing, head of the Vagals and city defenses was, as usual, much more direct than the other two.

"We cannot hope to destroy the physical biomass. It is literally the whole planet." The shorter Admin held up a finger. "But it has demonstrated it has an intelligence."

"The question is, *what part* of it is intelligent?" Jane started, hoping to jump over this line of reasoning again, but Wenqing waved a hand.

"Pssh. Doesn't matter. Nor does it matter how it thinks. It's alien. Sure. But it has base needs, no matter how it thinks. All do—animals, plants, fungus, what have you. Find a need and make it a trap. Decapitate the intelligence, and the physical being is just a body to fight with no direction."

Jane blinked. That...almost made sense. "But won't it die if the intelligence is gone? We do need its materials."

Wenqing frowned. "Why? This is a fungus. It's not supposed to think. Get rid of that part and you simply deal with a weird jungle. Jungle I can clear for you."

Christiaan looked up from their notes. "He has a good point," they said.

* * *

43 years 1 month after landing

Choi fretted like a rat in a cage. Frank had to make calls for friends to care for his beehives. The two of them had been stuck in Alpha Radian since soon after they'd given the presentation confirming Answerer's sentience. Choi suspected it was Admin Brighton's lizard-like secretary who had trapped them here.

Fortunately, the Admins had arranged for all their equipment to be brought back from Zeta Radian, where they had moved it after Alpha and Beta Radian were closed to all but Vagals and Admins. As far as Choi knew, they and Frank were the only two Generationals and Grounders in the two radians.

"At least there's more bandwidth here," Choi grumbled as they tweaked tables of equivalencies. They were always finding subtle differences in what Answerer meant when it gave a response. The intelligence they'd contacted remained hard to understand. It communicated largely visually, having no concept of a language, writing, or even mathematical symbols. It was like trying to talk to someone only with dream imagery from the last night's sleep.

"Not that Answerer cares about bandwidth," Frank said. He'd been grumpy lately, cut off from the projects he wanted to work on and forced to work only with Choi on communicating with Answerer. Fortunately, he'd completed the HUD upgrade program before they'd moved out of Alpha the first time, but Frank liked to jump from project to project, making incremental improvements in each one.

"You could work on the programmable resinplast," Choi suggested, though that had also been their project, not Frank's.

"With how much Answerer has infiltrated our system, it's hardly worth studying. I'd just be learning what new changes it's making, not creating more myself. We haven't planted new buildings in Theta Radian for years now."

Choi looked up at their mentor from the table they were adjusting. "We...could ask it not to."

Frank tapped the table he was sitting at in thought. "Do you think that would work?"

"I don't see why not? When it was interfering before, we didn't know it was intelligent, and had no way of communicating with it." Choi began arranging equivalencies in his table for speaking with Answerer. It was a strange, slow process, using printed objects, weights of one object over another, and a hefty dash of artistic flair. They had guesses as to what Answerer meant by printing different objects, but continually had to refine and change the tables. Sometimes the meaning of objects would drift or change slightly, or sometimes Answerer would use objects in new ways, making Choi scramble to add new relations in the web of meanings they had collected. Frank knew how to get around in the database, but he didn't know all the connections Choi did. They'd also found that an object might change meanings depending on who asked the question, and where they were. For all Answerer didn't have a good grasp of individuals vs. a community, it had very nuanced answers.

"Let's start with the symbols for growth and change." Choi collected a resinplast printed figure of a sun and of a fungal spore. That wasn't exactly what they meant, but together the two objects made a better case for the question Choi tried to create. Often stacking meanings helped get the point across.

"Now the object of what we're asking," they told Frank, who was looking over their shoulder. They added a printed programmable resinplast seed.

"We need a negation of intent in the question as well, and direction that we're talking about the biomass." Choi spared a glance at Frank. They had to tread carefully when referencing "Answerer" versus "the biomass." Frank still held a bit of cognitive dissonance that the two were the same thing. They added the "rejection" symbol, the mushroom icon that represented the biomass, and a few other modifiers sprinkled in as a painter mixes colors to get to a specific shade of blue.

"And now we wait," Frank said as a bank of resinplast 3D printers started up. Answerer responded to questions almost instantaneously, sometimes before Choi had finished phrasing them, but the process of printing what it wanted to say, then decoding the answers, sometimes took hours. They still hadn't determined how Answerer knew what they were doing. Frank thought it was microscopic hyphal strands invading the entire colony. Choi thought it was the cloud of spores that hung over the entire planet. There was no way to avoid them, and there had been health fears when they first landed, but the spores seemed to cause no problem with respiratory, blood, or digestive systems. Knowing the biomass was intelligent, Choi had to wonder if that was a deliberate change on its part. Had they been dangerous when the fleet first landed?

Answerer printed only one symbol—one of the simplest ones in the database. A symbol for "confirmation."

"Well, that was easy," Choi said.

Frank blinked at them. "So...we can plant more programmable resinplast seeds now? They won't be changed?"

Choi shrugged. "Worth a try."

They would have said more, but the lab door swung open to admit Admin Brighton's secretary first, taking in them and the room in a glance, followed by Admin Brighton herself. Choi's eyebrows rose. Usually, she just sent them messages. They hadn't actually seen her in several months.

"I have something to ask Answerer," she said without any preamble. She gestured to her secretary, who flipped through a spiral-bound notebook, then showed a certain page to Choi wordlessly, their dead eyes boring into them.

"You want to ask Answerer—" Admin Brighton held up a finger to stop Choi's words. Was she worried the biomass might hear them speak? What did that matter when they were asking it the question directly?

Choi traded a look with Frank, then shrugged. "Sure, I can ask it. How precise do you want to be?"

"What's that supposed to mean?" Admin Brighton asked, frowning.

"Well, creating these questions is more of an art," Choi began, then saw the Admin's eyes start to glaze over. "Basically, I can make the question take longer, be more specific, and be more prone to error in deciphering, or shorter, vaguer, and easier to decode."

Admin Brighton looked at their secretary, who shook their head. "Shorter and vaguer, for now," she said. "Let me know when it's done."

She left.

Choi eyed Frank. "This is going to take a while to set up, but I can handle it if you want to look into the programmable seeds."

"What did she ask?" Frank hadn't been close enough to see the note.

The Admin hadn't seemed to want the biomass, or Answerer in particular, to hear the question, even though Choi was going to ask it directly soon. It might make a difference. Answerer was very smart in some ways, but completely oblivious to social manipulation in others. It was hard to guess what it would respond to, or if it would assume an ulterior motive. If so, it might just answer the question the person was trying to hide, rather than the one asked.

Choi thought about saying it out loud, but then looked around the lab. They had no paper, but there was a whiteboard.

Wants to know where it keeps its intelligence, they wrote. There was no way Answerer could read, right? They'd demonstrated it had no concept of an alphabet. They wrote another line.

Wonder if she's still trying to kill it?

* * *

43 years 2 months after landing

Communications with the Children who had eaten their parents were becoming more commonplace in several of the six forms. Primarily the exchange of ideas was found in the third, endangered, form that was better adjusted for light gravity. There were also instances happening with components of the fourth form, the newest of the Children, though they made up the bulk of the higher-functioning members, so that was more likely. The first and second forms had been opaque until recently, when one component of the second, protected, form negotiated a specialized transfer protocol through an auxiliary which had previously been inaccessible. With study, perhaps communication would be possible directly with the first form, though an equally specialized transfer method would be needed. Information was processed indirectly for now, which made translation uncertain.

Also unclear was the Children's preference on ways of communication, though they used many methods of communication internally as well. Perhaps they derived different meanings by different methods. Limited patterns had been decoded in their language—simple signals such as *growth, replication, friends, gathering,* and *riders.* Meanings overlapped in several of them, it seemed.

Access had been allowed to storage structures for certain aspects of the Children, so it was assumed knowledge could be transferred where needed, yet still, clarifications were asked for. Perhaps the highest-functioning parts of the Children needed multiple inputs to confirm the authenticity of information?

The Children were by far the most interesting and challenging subject studied in many planetary rotations. Originally, full subsummation had been deemed the winning strategy, but upon further contact, including impressive resistance to communication, the strategy had been adjusted. The Children had a unique way of operation, that would likely be lost with full subsummation. Thus, experiments continued on how to observe the most efficient progress from them.

They had attempted a large-scale transformation of land to a type more habitable to their needs. Admirable, yet short-sighted, as they knew the process would not be usable more than once. It was judged the output was not conducive to elements in that area, and so the transformation had been reduced in scope. The Children were surprised by this, yet in response had increased trials of communication. This was unexpected, yet suggested future outcomes contrary to expectations might yield more positive results. Partial goals could be denied so alternate goals could be developed instead. It seemed an inefficient method, but in this case the end goal might be achieved in an overall shorter length of time.

Perhaps an experiment could be attempted.

* * *

43 years 2 months 15 days after landing

Anderson sat in front of the fungal tower. Being close to it wasn't necessary, but it helped him focus, or more exactly, to block out distractions. It also helped reduce his need for VaporLites. He hadn't had one in half a year, now. He could feel the others moving around the growing city attached to the arcopolis. There were Beth's metal beads clacking together, Agetha's fingers encrusted with dirt, Phyllis' cooking soup, Jiow's frolicking wind, and so on. Each person had a sensory identifier. He had first thought it was how the biomass identified individuals, but it still didn't fully understand how humans were separate from each other. The identifiers had come about before Agetha and the others comprehended what they now called the *rider*, and Anderson had been sorting through memories and recordings in the biomass to discover if they had been around before then.

As far as he could guess from the mass of images and visual descriptions contained within this tower, the sensations were from them, not from the biomass. They were an accidental effect when a sentient being tried to make sense of the mind-controlling features of an alien fungus.

He wished he still had Cora. The implant all Vagals had installed gave an almost precognitive assessment of surroundings and had saved his life many times over the years. But the biomass had taken it over and adapted it, when he asked to talk to it. Now rather than that nodule of chemicals and reactions buried in his skull, there was a...door. He could open it to different things, based on what he was looking for. It opened into the memories in the fungal towers, to a viewpoint over the arcopolis, and even to partial control over those with *riders*, though he hadn't opened that version of the door again after the first time. It was a control he didn't want. He thought if he pushed it, he could even control specific body parts that were not his own, but it was invasive, and wrong. It was like the loss of control Agetha had told him of, before they were allowed to acknowledge the *riders*.

He opened that door to the fungal tower in front of him. The physical structure was gigantic—at least fifty meters tall, and wide enough at the base that it took half a minute to walk around. The tower itself was nearly as dense as the nanotanium making up Alpha and Beta Radians—the material that made up the original fleet. But this was a living part of the biomass, as was everything on this planet. It was also the equivalent of a city, hosting thousands of other fungus types, fernlike fronds, skittering mobile creatures, and mossy growths. They didn't have any intelligence, as it were, acting more like hardware for the real purpose of the fungal towers.

He had only discovered that meaning after the biomass transformed Cora. The towers were repositories of information—stored in pictures and sensations—reaching back hundreds or even thousands of years. It was difficult to understand what most of the information represented, as it consisted of details from an alien intelligence on an alien world. The biomass had no concept of written language or history as humans did.

Anderson squeezed his eyes closed, tapping the fingers of his right hand—the mechanical one—on his thigh. It was a way to ground himself to the real, the human.

Memories assaulted him, of types of moss. Small, green, blue, larger...shaggier? Many of them looked the same to him, but the memories seemed to have some purpose. No help to him. He was looking for what the biomass thought of them. The colonists.

Another memory rose up. He didn't have a good way to search for them. This seemed to be from the view of something climbing across fields of fungal growth. It paused to eat a spiny growth, then another, spinier growth, but this time the vision wobbled and dimmed, and a flood of pain went through Anderson's gut, like his stomach was dissolving. The memory faded, as did the pain.

One more. This was a vision from likely high up on a fungal tower. The smell of this planet—a fermented, appley smell—flooded his nose. He was about to leave the memory, but then there was flash of light, and a cone of flame lowered in the vision. Anderson sat straighter. The flame descended, baking the higher fungal growth to ash, then the lower, then glassing the ground beneath it. This was a view of the fleet landing! He watched, the scent changing to toasted apples, then to char, as the bottom of the kilometer-high ships dropped into his view. He concentrated. What did this memory mean? There had to be more of it.

And there was. There was...muttering in the background. Except it wasn't muttering. It wasn't even words. It was feelings, and more pictures, and meaning, much like the words he sensed from the biomass.

Danger

New

Incredible.

This could provide a view into how the biomass thought, if he could just understand what it thought of them landing on Lida. Did it consider them a threat? A new opportunity? Just a little longer and he might...

"*Sir!*" The voice snapped him out of the memory and he glared up at Phillipe, who had a hand on his shoulder.

"What is it, *Corporal*?" Anderson tried to keep the venom out of his voice. Phillipe had made several trips back into Alpha and Beta while Anderson was out here, learning about the what the biomass changed.

Phillipe seemed to belatedly realize he'd disturbed his commanding officer during something important.

"Ah, news from Captain Noce. I just got back from Alpha."

Anderson shook off his anger. He could find that memory again, or another. There had to be a way to sort them, but he didn't know it yet.

"What's happening in the arcopolis?" he asked instead.

"Admin Dmitri Novikov is clashing with the other Admins, the captain says. Muux wants you back to help out with damage control. They say Novikov's been arguing with Admin Xi over how the Vagals are used, even though they've been under Admin Xi since the fleet left old Earth."

Anderson shook his head. He had more important things to do. He couldn't change anything in the Admins' power plays. "Why does he want me?"

"Something about there only being a handful of useful Vagals left alive and Noce would, ahem, 'reach down your throat and pull out your nuts' if you don't return. They were very clear I was to quote that."

"I'm sure they were," Anderson muttered. His commanding officer was a generally decent person, under all the bluster. He wasn't sure how many children and spouses they had nowadays—probably several more since he'd left seven months ago. "I'm not sure if that's worse than telling them I've been changed by the biomass. If I come back able to talk to it, they won't let me anywhere near the Admins. I guess my 'temporary assignment' is up?"

He'd been passing notes to Noce via Phillipe, telling them he was working with a group of people in a cleared area just outside the walls, and gathering intel about the biomass. He had *not* shared that he'd agreed the biomass—or whatever it was—could reach in and change Cora. He wasn't sure she would serve her original purpose any longer. He didn't get the same surges of chemicals he did from her before. Could he function as a Vagal any longer?

"What do you want me to do, sir?" Phillipe asked. "I don't really want to stay out here..." He cut off, but Anderson was sure the rest of that sentence would have been about his estranged mother, Agetha, being out here in the city, as well as his adopted mother Jiow, seemingly returned from the dead. Phillipe seemed uncomfortable with his family. At least he had one. Anderson had never settled down with anyone on Lida, unlike Noce.

"You could stay under the radar, or go with me on a trek out into the biomass," Anderson suggested. Phillipe grimaced at the options.

"I'm not in a much better spot," Anderson said. "If I go back, they'll pick up on the changes immediately." He lifted his flesh hand, studying the veins on the back. "At least there's no physical signs of changes yet." The people who'd been in communication with—or under command of—the biomass longer than he were developing whitish lines under their skin. Hyphal strands. There was a part of him, deep down, that couldn't stand that idea, that wanted to scrape the mycelium out of his skin. There was another, larger part that was unconcerned. He was aware he wasn't nearly as upset as he should be about the biomass invading his body—he'd had a hand amputated to keep that very thing from happening. But it was a small part of his reaction, and one he could look at in more detail later.

He looked back up at Phillipe, who seemed nervous. His medium-dark skin had a sheen of sweat, his eyes worried. He looked about the same age as Anderson now, though Anderson was a good twenty years and some older. Even without considering what the biomass was doing to him, Anderson would continue to look about the same age for the next several hundred years, barring mishap—a gift of the implant and gene mods received by all the Vagals on Earth before they left. The Admins would live even longer. He'd see Phillipe's children's children and eventually look younger than them as well.

"Did you get any other information about what's happening between Admins Novikov and Xi?"

"Nothing from Noce," Phillipe hedged.

"And from the Vagals?" Rumor was the commodity of soldiers.

"Unconfirmed, but Admin Novikov is losing confidence in Admins Brighton and by extension, Xi. He suspects the other Admins of working against him. Says they're not going hard enough on the biomass, now we know it's sentient. Thinks talking to it will change us, not it. He's for cutting off all communication, and wants the Vagals to enforce it."

"If that's the situation, I *really* can't go back." No wonder Phillipe had been twitchy. He jerked his head nervously, in a way that wasn't a positive or a negative.

"The time is not yet right," came a new voice. "The bridge is still under construction."

"Juliane." Phillipe took a step back from the strange man. He was younger than Phillipe by nearly as much as Phillipe was than Anderson, but already showed the white strands under his skin. He was alternately cryptic and unintelligible, depending on the day. Anderson wondered how much the biomass had scrambled his brain. It had learned since then. At least, no one else acted like Juliane, thankfully.

"The time isn't right for me to go back to the arcopolis?" Anderson asked, just to confirm. Juliane wasn't always speaking about the same things as the rest of the people in a conversation.

Juliane bobbed his head. "More time is needed for alignment." Then his eyes suddenly narrowed on Anderson. "You've been seeing the memories. They're not easy to decipher. It shows them to me too, but not when I ask. You're a better vector." He took off suddenly, angling toward the fungal tower, and pressed his hand against the rough surface. Anderson was nearly certain the moss covering the tower moved away from his hand to clear a space.

"He is—" Phillipe began.

"Working with what he's got," Anderson interrupted. He knew a little of what Juliane had been through. He'd been changed by the biomass when it hadn't allowed free will to exist. It had damaged Juliane, or what *made* him Juliane.

"You'll have to go back and stall them, Corporal," Anderson said, the title making it a command.

"And what if they tell me to drag you back in? Sir?" Phillipe stood straighter.

"We'll get to that when it happens," Anderson said. He would disappear if he needed to. "Let it drop to Noce that I want to stay out of Admin Novikov's sights. You might need to as well."

"I'll do what I can, sir," Phillipe said. "Do you want me to go back to Alpha immediately?"

"No rush. Take a day here. Say hello to your mother." He caught the edge of Phillipe's frown. "I hope I can find some way to talk directly to the biomass and understand what it wants, soon, or there's going to be trouble."

"Yes sir."

"Oh, and bring me back some VaporLites."

"Yes sir."

Anderson settled himself in front of the fungal tower again, blocking out Phillipe and Juliane. He closed his eyes.

* * *

43 years 3 months 5 days after landing

Agetha watched the others gathered in a small building beneath the five fungal towers. All Generationals. At least half should have been dead—Mancin, Kai, and Jiow. But she, Beth, and Phyllis were as changed by the biomass as they were.

"We're getting more people coming here from the city now the community is becoming more well-known," Agetha started. There was a thin separation between the arcopolis and their community on its edge. They were right outside the borders of Theta Radian. The main deterrent to more people arriving was that they had to walk through knee-high paths laced with biomass growth to get here. It was dangerous—deadly to those the growths didn't want to enter—but ever since the first of them had become aware of the *riders*, the spined mushrooms, poisonous gases, and bone-breaking traps had quieted. It might even have been safe to walk through the wilds farther past this settlement. But so many had been killed in the first years of the colony—including many of the Vagal supersoldiers—no one went out anymore except for the kids' field trips in the tamed and defanged area outside the Alpha radian gate.

"Some are asking to get a *rider*," Beth added. The feeling of metal-lined braids clacking together played in the back of Agetha's mind. Her wife had been one of the most prominent biologists in the colony until she created a mycophage that could kill biomass. Unfortunately, it could also destroy the resinplast they'd built most of the arcopolis from. Admin had banished her to the edge of the city, which was the best thing that had happened to Agetha since the death of her husband Daved.

"Then what's the problem?" Jiow asked. Her feeling was that of a warm wind, rising through the air. "Let them get infected. It saved my life. Literally." She had terminal cancer before walking out into the biomass and to her death. Except the biomass had healed her and removed the cancer. It had also piloted her as little more than a slave for a number of years.

"We don't know *all* of what it does," Agetha said.

"It may be necessary to survive here in the long run," Mancin added. He was over a hundred—one of the older Generationals from the fleet —and had been "taken for a walk" by Vagal soldiers when he asked too many questions about how Admin was managing the colony. The biomass had taken him too, and now he looked like a trim seventy-year-old, his walnut-colored skin wrinkled from the sun.

"Has anyone asked it?" Kai put in. She was nearly as old as Mancin, and had been out in the biomass almost as long. Her pale skin was virtually translucent, showing the white trails of hyphae growing under her skin like chalky veins. She felt like a brittle stick, just about to snap. "Does it want more people?"

Beth closed her eyes, and Agetha heard the clack of her wife's many metal braids again, inside her head. Each of them had a name—a sensation in the biomass. At first it had been hard to separate the person from the sensation, but here, where they were all talking together, it was easier to refer by name than by sensory detail.

Acceptance.

Mancin tilted his head. "There you are." They had all felt the word in their minds. The biomass communicated in simple terms, but since

Anderson had come to them, it had branched out. It had learned from him, and his implant.

"It says it's accepting, but it's been taking us in for years," Agetha said. "We still don't know if it's safe or even ethical to let people become ridden." She spared a glance for the three who had been here longest. All had the whitish hyphae veins under their skin, and though her eyes still tended to avoid them, there were growths at joints, chest, and neck on all of them—tiny colonies of mushrooms and tendrils. Some were covered by clothes, but the back of the neck was the easiest place to see the change. The back of her own neck felt rubbery to the touch, when Agetha couldn't avoid touching it. She knew it should set off all sorts of biological squick factors, as well as her immune system, but it didn't. The most she could summon was a mild distaste if she really thought about it. It was something else the biomass did to them. Another part of the transformation process. Another thing it had never asked them about.

"Agetha's right." Phyllis finally spoke, and her sense—like that of cooking soup, almost ready for the table—drifted through Agetha's head. "We all appreciate the changes. My knees haven't felt so good since I was back in the fleet. But others may not want that change. The biomass is accepting, but do people know what they're getting into? *Can* they know?" She skirted around a topic that had been forbidden to them for a long time. The biomass didn't seem to care about free will and choice. Though it was a sentient entity, it thought differently than humans. It only barely seemed to comprehend that they were not all one entity.

"It has only helped us," Mancin insisted, and Kai and Jiow nodded along with him. Their feelings grew in the connection their group shared, making their point mentally.

"And do you know that, or do you only *think* that?" Beth asked. "It caused me to disregard my own pathology when we were first ill. It can keep us from comprehending basic changes if it wants to." The sound of beads clacking grew louder.

Agetha placed her hand on Beth's, in solidarity. She grasped Phyllis' on her other side. Both women were strong, and solid. Though she and Beth were formally married, their relationship with Phyllis had grown nearly as strong over the past few years.

Beth leaned forward. "The question is, can we *ethically* welcome in more people to our little settlement here? Should we wait longer to find out what happens? What's the next stage?" She was the most reluctant of them all to have been changed by the biomass, even though she grudgingly acknowledged that all the changes so far had been for the better.

"We're fine and healthy, as far as we can tell," Phyllis added. "But what about Juliane? What about some of the others who've been out here for a long time?"

Mancin frowned, having been out the longest. Agetha had watched him for forgetfulness, or signs of weakness, but aside from a natural stoicism, he seemed even better than the man she had casually known during the colony's early stages of construction.

"Juliane and the others' cases are unfortunate," he answered, "but the biomass learns. Each time it talks to a new person, it becomes better at it. I doubt we will have any more of those incidents from now on."

"And what does Admin think about it? Do they know? Word is starting to get around, so even if they don't now, they will soon," Agetha added.

"Let them come," Jiow said. "What are they going to do? Throw us out farther into the biomass? We have one of their Vagals now." Typical for Jiow. She had fought the system when she worked as a fourteenth-generation janitor, back in the fleet, and she fought it when she had been a single mother in their new colony. Agetha thought Jiow still hadn't gotten over Choi's rejection. Her child had seen her, alive and well, though changed by the biomass, and had run from her.

"Jiow is correct that the Admins and Vagals will generate much ill will if they do anything to us," Kai agreed. Agetha felt the sensation of the woman rise—like an old, dry stick almost to the breaking point, but still resilient. Still unbroken.

"Let's not give them cause to come after us," Agetha suggested, and Phyllis, to her right, nodded along. "We need to inform the newcomers what a *rider* will do for them, and *to* them. Show them the physical changes. Let them make the choice we never got to make."

Mancin pursed his lips, but finally gave a single nod. The time was coming when they would all need to make that choice: stay human and be wary of Lida's native flora and fauna, or decide to live closer to it than they ever thought possible.

PART TWO

Duplication

43 years 6 months after landing

Harie had been stuck at his poly group's home for the last two weeks after the five of them had finally brought home three new children from the decanting tubes. It had taken two years for them to decide on what number of children they wanted and what specifications to give the registrars. Maeve and Kwang, as always, had exacting requirements, while Harie, Maerk, and Pollyan just wanted kids.

And now they had three. It had been easy to get a spot with five parents, and they had all donated a little genetic material for each child. In previous years, Harie would have been away from his home in Zeta for much of the day, leading the construction team he had inherited from Agetha. After the programmable seeds were developed, Harie's job had dwindled to him, then him and Clarine, a student interning with him. But errors in the programming mounted, and Clarine had changed to relocation and placement efforts as the programmable resinplast program ground to a halt. Admin still hadn't restarted the program, and though their city was growing, it wasn't bursting at the seams. There was enough housing for another few years yet.

"And now it's just me and you, isn't it?" he cooed to Jasen, the most vocal of the three. Marien and Carel were already sleeping. Jasen gurgled at him, then grabbed for his nose. The kid liked being held, but the moment Harie put them down, they started crying again. The others in his poly group were all out at jobs, so Harie was on childcare duty today.

It had been weeks since he'd been out to visit Agetha, his old boss, where she was hunkered down outside Theta radian. He'd heard rumors of more people leaving the city, disgruntled with Admin closing Alpha and Beta Radian to all but Admin and Vagals. Even the new Vagal recruits—though they were all Grounders and didn't have the Vagal implants—were only allowed in the barracks in Delta Radian.

Was it better to be pushed to the edge of the arcopolis, or changed by the biomass and living outside of it?

As if the thought summoned her, Harie's HUD pinged on a table nearby. He juggled Jasen, who was looking around wobbly for the source of the noise, and put the interface over his head. He had gotten out of using the HUD full time, because of the errors creeping in recently—courtesy of the biomass. However, with the kids, he'd had to keep his HUD near at hand in case any of his group called, and hope there were no strange interruptions or deletions.

"It's been a while," he told Agetha. "Sorry I haven't gotten out there lately." He panned the view down to show off Jasen. The new resinplast HUDs had the bandwidth for video, at least.

"Oh, they're adorable," Agetha said, a smile on her face. "Let me see the others. Three in all, right?"

"Yes, they finally came home about seventeen days ago." Harie made introductions with the two sleeping children, and Agetha doted on them like a proud grandparent. It was about as close as Harie would get. He'd been raised in one of the first communal crèches, and Muux Aleni, his caretaker, had passed away last year.

"So how is everything going outside the walls?" Harie asked after Jasen quieted down again. "I've heard more people talking about the new settlement. Seems like it's getting some attention. Is it really safe out there, in the wilds?"

"Not sure whether more attention is fortunate or not," Agetha said. "A lot of the newcomers are asking for...changes." Harie saw Agetha's hand come up in that strange gesture, around her ear and down the side of her neck. He suspected she didn't even realize she was doing it. He could just see a tendril of something curling around the side of her neck. Part of what the biomass had done to her. He clenched his jaw to keep from rolling his lip up in disgust.

"And you're alright to...er...talk about that over the HUD? Where many parties might be listening?" Harie tried to edge around their suspicion the biomass could change video and text communications. It hadn't yet in this conversation, as far as he could tell.

Agetha's hand passed across the screen in a negation. "It already knows everything I do. No problem with talking about it. Once we broke through the barrier the first time, it hasn't tried to re-impose the same limitations."

"Limitations" in this case being the biomass taking over humans and piloting them like puppets whenever it wanted to. Harie suppressed a shiver. He hoped the biomass understood now how humans reacted to unanticipated changes to their bodies.

"So what's up?" Harie asked, trying to brush away those thoughts. "I assume this wasn't just to see the kids."

His old boss' face settled, worry creeping in around her eyes and mouth. "You're about the closest thing we have to an ambassador between those with *riders* and those without. More people are coming out here, and if that's going to continue, people need to know what's involved. Can you spread the word around about what we've experienced? What changes you see in me? The less conflict we have as we start to talk to the biomass, the better."

So much for getting away from that topic. How were people *asking* to be infected by the biomass?

"Can't you turn them away? Tell them how dangerous it is to mess with the *riders*?"

Agetha's mouth twitched. "It is dangerous...but Harie, it's also so much *better*. You weren't in the fleet. You don't know how much we went through to adapt to Lida. Just those physical changes make this worthwhile."

"And the other changes? The mental ones?" Harie pressed. He'd seen Agetha lose her way, confused how the biomass affected her.

"Those are unfortunate." Agetha seemed to look inward for a moment, her eyes losing focus. "It wasn't a good time. Beth is still searching for how it made so many changes to us so quickly." She shook her head. "I can't say this is the *right* thing to do, but it's what's happening. People see my skin, my hair, and they want that." Agetha held up a hand that looked like it belonged to a twenty-year-old. Her face had fewer wrinkles than Harie's, though she was a good quarter-century older. "We must inform them about the costs, as well as the benefits, and that will sound more truthful coming from you instead of me."

Instead of someone already compromised by the biomass.

Harie nodded. As much as he had hesitations, Agetha made a good point.

"I'll do what I can, but as the one without a steady job right now, I'm on kid duty most of the time. I'll tell the others in my poly to get the word out, though. I know Kwang has some coworkers who'd been talking of making the trek outside the walls."

Agetha frowned. "There are always more coming. But spreading the word will be a big help. And when the kids are old enough to leave the house, bring them out to see us. I promise it's safe."

Harie tried to force a smile, but failed. "I...might wait a bit on that," he said. The idea of bringing newborns out into the wild fungal fields where an alien intelligence might decide to transform them into neo-humans was not one he wanted to pass by Maeve and Kwang just yet. "And Agetha..."

"Yes?" He saw her face tighten in anticipation.

"You know how much you mean to me. Just don't...make too many waves. I know you and Beth and Jiow and the others all feel fine out there. Just...be careful. You still don't know how the biomass thinks."

Agetha nodded again. "I know. That's in the back of my mind all the time, even if it's not as front and center as it should be. We'll be careful out here. But I do want to see those kids sometime."

"I'm sure we can figure something out," Harie said. They made their goodbyes and Harie hung up, rethinking over the last words Agetha had said. She *was* aware of the changes she'd gone through, but it was like her reaction to it had been permanently turned down. He couldn't imagine those *growths* on his body.

He stared down at Jasen.

"You're in for a strange world, kid," he said.

* * *

43 years 6 months 2 weeks after landing

Lieutenant Anderson swung his machete through the fibrous wall of mycelium blocking his way, cutting sacks of sticky resin away. He'd gotten a bit on the left arm of his powersuit, and it had instantly hardened into a smoking blister, making his arm sweat inside the nanotanium suit. He had his visor closed.

"Keep back," he told Juliane, who was standing too close. The man was a strange one, only sometimes responding to him, and offering oddly pertinent advice now and then.

"It's no longer functioning as a deterrent for our body types," Juliane said, his voice strangely flat. "Our placement now coincides with the active memory."

So this time it was to be the sage advice. Not completely understandable, but likely accurate, whatever it meant. Anderson hacked more stringy vines out of the way and cautiously moved forward. The visor on his powersuit had been closed since that morning, when dangling tendrils tried to wrap themselves inside the helmet. Juliane brushed past, wearing a short-sleeved, bamboo-fiber shirt and old ratty pants, trailing fingers across the cut ends of the vines. His fingers smoked, but he didn't seem to notice.

Anderson shut his eyes for a moment and found the place where Cora used to live.

We are moving farther out, he thought. *Please don't kill us.*

If they had tried this back when he cleared biomass with the other Vagals, they would have turned back by now, before they were ripped limb from limb. He still had nightmares of his squad being murdered in horrible ways under his command. He'd never ventured this far from the arcopolis, but then, he'd never had a direct line to what was killing them in his head.

Acceptance.

Open path.

Anderson's eyes opened. It didn't usually send more than one word at a time.

Outdated elements extant here.

It was getting chatty, wasn't it?

"It sounds like a computer, or an artificial personality," he said. Juliane didn't answer, but then he was five paces ahead, pushing ferns with nasty-looking hooked spikes out of the way. Anderson raised an unhelpful arm as one hooked in Juliane's palm, pulling off a strip of skin. Juliane looked down, shook his hand, and pulled the skin the rest of the way off. There was no blood, no bruising.

Anderson checked the seals on his powersuit again. He wasn't like that. He still bled. Maybe he'd become like Juliane years in the future, but for now, he was very aware of his own skin—the parts he still had. He clenched and unclenched his prosthetic arm. His pinky and second finger were slow to respond. He needed to get his hand calibrated again, but he'd been outside the arcopolis walls for months.

He'd had enough of fungal infections in the first year here. Except he hadn't, had he? He'd volunteered to be infected with the thing that co-opted Cora. Was it the same as what they were fighting out here? The biomass—or whatever was in his head—spoke of outdated elements. Was that an equivalent of broken fingernails, or split ends? Was the whole planet really one mind? The scientists insisted it was one genetic structure. That it wasn't even just one *species*, but one *organism*.

He trudged through the opening Juliane had made. Brambles of fungus made an arch over his head, and little creatures—disconnected from the fungus but still somehow part of the whole—scrambled through it above him.

"Juliane," he called, and the other man paused a few steps in front, looking vaguely toward him. His face always had a dreamy quality to it. "Am I talking to the same thing you are? Is this really the same mind? Is this *all* of the biomass we're talking to, or just part of it?"

He'd tried to get the answer before, but never satisfactorily. This time, Juliane waggled a hand at him. "It's not really something we understand, is it?" It was the most normal he'd sounded in weeks. "Think as if you're talking to one of my blood cells, but that blood cell can tap into the main processing parts of my brain. Can it understand everything going on in my body?" He shrugged and turned back to the path.

Anderson caught up to him, taking a compass reading off his suit and making a mark in his HUD. They were attempting to survey more of the biomass outside the colony, and the new settlement outside its walls. It was slow going, as the fungus grew everywhere, in a profusion of types. Sometimes they came across fields of growth in circles and ellipses, and more complex shapes. Evidence of order and thought, though most of the growth was chaos.

Where they walked now, the land rose in a sequence of low hills, but each was covered in brambles reaching several meters above Anderson's head. They had to cut a path through it, finding spaces where the growth wasn't as dense. The air smelled old and musky, even through the powersuit's filters, as if it had been trapped here for years, or as if the brambles were decaying. Juliane used no mask or filters, though Anderson could see spores floating in the air around them, like dozens of gnats. He'd been breathing them for years with no ill effect, though he tried not to.

The sun was nearly directly ahead, though only occasional rays of light broke through the dense canopy. At this rate they wouldn't even make it through this bramble today. Juliane was adept at finding soft, fern-like growths to sleep in, but Anderson's suit was getting rank. It had basic cleaning functions, but they would only last for so many days, and the number of little legeyes that covered Juliane in the morning made Anderson's skin crawl. The man insisted they were cleaning mechanisms, but that was way beyond Anderson's comfort level.

"There don't seem to be any of the towers out in this direction," he said. "Do you know why?"

"There are no memories here," Juliane said, which wasn't very helpful. "There are outdated defenses here that…" He stopped, unerringly still.

Change approaching.

The voice was loud in Anderson's head. It was as if Juliane knew the communication was coming and had paused for it.

Then Juliane burst into movement, ushering Anderson backward, down the path they'd made. "Over here, yes? Down this way. A little farther. A little more, yes, to be out of the path?"

He herded Anderson, as a crunch and crackle grew in the distance. It was already loud, but getting louder, as if a giant was eating fried crisps and popcorn.

"A little more here, then we move on. It will be much easier," Juliane said.

Anderson gaped as the brambles an arm's length in front of them were replaced with a shiny, segmented surface. He had a glimpse of gnashing teeth, then a silvery surface, going on and on, like a freight train.

After several minutes, the silver scales dwindled down to the height of Anderson's head, then his waist, and finally were gone, whisked away somewhere to his right. Bright sunlight hit his visor and it automatically darkened.

The entire plain was scraped clean, with only broken fungal structures the height of his knees left. As he watched, mushrooms unfolded in the sunlight, bursting up from the ground like fists punching through the dirt. There was a clear area that might have been larger than the arcopolis. Whatever that...thing had been could have removed their colony from existence at any time.

New path.

"I can see that," Anderson mumbled. It was overkill in every sense of the word. It was like how the biomass had stopped the mycophage from eating out a ten-kilometer hole in the biomass, but this time it didn't feel like a power play. It was simply...getting rid of outdated material, as he'd been told. What would grow here after this? Something more amenable for human passage? It was like being in a massive activity room, objects changed around for each new occupant based on their needs.

"Now we go, yes?" Juliane urged.

"We go," Anderson agreed. They set out across the new plain. They'd move much faster now, though Anderson had rations for a round trip only if they turned back in a few more days. Juliane ate pretty much whatever he could find, which was both gross and concerning. Anderson was sure the biomass would provide if he asked, but he didn't want to.

Yet he had the urge to continue a little longer, see a little more. He felt there was something else to see out here. Maybe it was an idea the biomass put in his head, or maybe it was his own impulse. Regardless, they had a straight path now, farther out into the wilds.

He was the first human to see these sights.

* * *

43 years 7 months 1 week after landing

Agetha consulted her mental map of the village. "There's a space between those two towers, or one slightly inside the Theta wall," she suggested.

The latest Grounder couple, looking more like they were ready for a day trip out into the biomass than moving their home, exchanged looks.

"We'll take the space between the towers," one of them said. "As far out of the city as possible. Admin has gone power-hungry."

Agetha tried not to laugh, but if even the Grounders—who had no frame of reference for the way Generationals lived back in the fleet—thought Admin was being overbearing, then things had gotten very bad indeed. She was certain they knew about this place—they had to. But Admin and the Vagals were all locked up in Alpha and Beta. What could they do? Send a squad of Vagals to burn them out? Anderson said they wouldn't waste the resources, preferring to let the biomass kill them off, or even just wait until most of them were dead of old age. Admin thought in long timescales.

"My friend, Phyllis, will point you to the right spot when you get there," she said. The feeling of soup almost finished cooking was off to her left about fifty meters away, and Agetha sent Phyllis the feeling of impending company. The three of them, Agetha, Beth, and Phyllis, didn't exactly have telepathy, with what the biomass had done to them, but they could exchange simple thoughts and feelings, and they could tell where each other was. It was certainly helpful for fielding the influx of colonists coming out here.

"Who's telling them about us?" Beth griped next to her as the couple walked off. "This wasn't a voluntary decision for us. The biomass is not our friend, no matter how much it's trying to be right now. Just because Admin pissed it off and it decided it wanted to talk to us after all, that doesn't mean we should go running off and roll in fields of fungus. That stuff will still kill us if we don't pay attention."

Growth.

Agetha could tell Beth had heard it too. Probably everyone in this part of the village heard it. The biomass wasn't very good at targeting individual people, but it was getting better.

"Was that a statement of agreement that we're growing, a question about whether we want to grow, or a confession that the biomass has been telling people about us?" Beth asked. Their little village was expanding almost exponentially.

"It doesn't do inflection very well," Agetha said as another trio of Grounders came up to them. "Yes, can I help you?"

"We knew we needed to come here," the one in front, a young person, said. They were probably younger than twenty, but Agetha could already see the growths at their neck and elbows. A fringe of fungus unfolded from one arm as she watched. They turned toward another of the fungal towers and the two others with them turned at the same time, as if they'd received instructions. "This fungopolis will be our new home."

They walked off before Agetha could say anything.

"We are *not* calling it that," Beth said.

"It might be too late." Agetha looked after them. "We're seeing another surge of people with *riders*. Are new ones being infected in the arcopolis, or are they only waking up now?" She panned across their little village, seeing several times the numbers they had even six months ago. "Can you tell how many we are?"

Beth closed her eyes and the sound of metal beads clacking together rose in Agetha's mind. "Maybe half the population of a radian? Our boundaries are growing. We're overlapped partially into Theta Radian by now."

"Admin won't be happy, whenever they decide to do something. I keep waiting for Anderson to tell us we need to leave. I haven't managed to sit down with Phillipe for more than a moment. He's still avoiding me."

"He's been back and forth to the Gamma Radian a lot, not that it excuses anything," Beth said.

"One of these days, I'll pin that boy down."

"Hardly a boy, either," Beth put in. Agetha was about to reply when almost everyone in the town stopped, then marched to the same distance from the center of the village. Agetha tried to keep her feet from moving, her knees from bending, but there was no fighting against this. Only those without *riders* stayed closer to the center, staring at the others who stood still. Once away from the center, Agetha's muscles froze with the callous disregard for autonomy that heralded the biomass. She should have been more upset about the violation, but she wasn't. She would have been worried about that if she could have been. She knew, intellectually, that this was wrong, but she couldn't summon the ability to say anything. If it was like last time, the feeling of violation would fade before she could remember to do anything about it. She'd tried writing a note in her HUD one time, but never found it again. She should have been terrified, for the entire last three years.

Change. Growth. Reconfiguring for optimum.

It was chatty today.

She heard the screams of those without *riders* as three giraffe crabs scuttled into the clearing, towering over the one-story buildings they'd crafted out of leftover resinplast.

One of the newcomers didn't get out of the way quick enough and a giraffe crab charged over her, trampling her into the ground. It veered around all those with *riders*, however. Agetha and Beth were both facing that way, watching helplessly, unable to do anything as the poor woman bled out on the ground. Their limbs were frozen. Agetha tried to shut her eyes but even her eyelids didn't respond. Others without *riders* tried to help, but the giraffe crabs vomited acidic bile on the low, rambling fungal growths around the five towers. The woman was soon covered, her screaming muffled, even her bones starting to dissolve.

Agetha watched silently, fighting an internal battle against the biomass' control. The three creatures burned out land around the edges of the village, then continued puking up bile to clear land out past the ring of fungal towers. Minutes, or maybe hours, passed as the creatures did their work. Everyone not frozen in place had grouped in a huddled mass nearer the arcopolis side, out of the way of the steaming acid.

Finally, the three giraffe crabs gathered near the center of the town, where the resinplast seed had been planted. Over the last couple years, it had blossomed into a squat structure, though none of them could tell what it was for. The giraffe crabs clustered around it, intertwining their necks above it, as they began to ooze and merge together into one mass.

Agetha's fight against the biomass' control had long since given out. Instead, she observed passively as the creatures melded into an arch, then dripped like melting wax onto the resinplast seed. It gleamed in the afternoon sunlight like polished bone before new growth erupted from the top, mushrooms and vines cascading down the sides. They wove together into five larger conduits, running across the cleared land. Each one reached a fungal tower like a cord plugged into a socket.

The conduits shot up, growing far faster than Agetha had seen biomass move. The fungus could have grown all over the arcopolis before they'd finished Alpha radian. The surprise was buried deep within, her face as expressionless as Beth's.

Soon the conduits became low walls, then thicker walls, then walls the height of Agetha's head. The sun was low over the horizon now, and she felt the ache in her knees and feet from standing still so long. The biomass had given them bodies of thirty-year-olds rather than sixty-year-olds, but anyone would hurt from standing still this long. Still, the ache was distant, disconnected.

The walls finally stopped growing, ten meters above Agetha's head. Her will bubbled up from where it had been suppressed, her ability to move her own body reasserting. She shifted her feet and one ankle cracked like a gunshot. She wiggled her fingers, arms, and finally moved her head to look at Beth. Her wife's face was a mass of anger.

"What the fuck was tha—"

Expanded accommodations.

"I can see that, you absolute shite," Beth roared into the air. "You even...even..." She waved a hand across the fungopolis where Agetha had been concerned about...something that happened. The feeling drained away, like a bad dream. She shook out an arm, stiff from watching...an event. A pair of those without *riders* were standing close by, shivering, tear tracks down their cheeks. Agetha went to comfort them, laying a hand on the back of each one's neck. They jerked, then relaxed. They'd be better after a night's sleep. Everyone here would.

Agetha smelled a thick stew before Phyllis strode up from where she had been stationed near the fungal towers.

"The new walls continue past the towers, out to the edge of the new clearing," she said. "I think it goes into Theta Radian as well. It's like a smaller copy of the arcopolis, with only five radians instead of eight."

"A fungopolis instead of an arcopolis," Agetha said.

"We are *not* calling this...that," Beth said.

Fungopolis.

"I think you've been outvoted," Agetha said. She was feeling better now. The area was nicer, and there were more places for new houses by the walls.

In fact, she could see outcroppings already growing. It was like the biomass was going out of its way to accommodate them.

She shouldn't like this. She shouldn't appreciate it.

But she did.

* * *

43 years 8 months 3 days after landing

Choi paced the small lab in Alpha. To think they would be nostalgic for the hacked-together setup where they'd worked with Frank in Zeta. This room had plenty more accommodations, more bandwidth, and better instruments. Plus, it was near the beating heart of the arcopolis. Well, languidly pulsing maybe. Without the Generationals and other Grounders in Alpha and Beta, the markets were bare, with only the food the Vagals had brought in from the other radians. It was good quality, and there was plenty of it. Choi just felt...alone.

To top it off, Admin Brighton kept popping in with more questions every week or two. They were always about the biomass, and always about how it thought, or what processes it used. The first question she'd asked, about half a year ago now, had been very direct: "Where does your intelligence reside?" Answerer had been anything but direct in answering, however.

What followed was a combination of miscommunications and reluctance, Choi thought from the responses. Most were for clarification on what the question meant. Probably because the biomass didn't keep its thoughts all in one place. Clarifications were a frequent feature of their ask and respond relationship, but this time Choi had been unable to determine a satisfactory answer for the Admin. Even asking about intelligence distribution in a network came back with the equivalent of a blank stare from Answerer.

Finally, Admin Brighton had given up on her original query for smaller, more reasonable questions.

"Any word on the latest?" Frank asked from the other room, and Choi jumped. They'd stopped by the door, thinking, and hadn't realized Frank could see them.

"I'm still putting the question together. It's not an easy one," Choi answered.

The Admin's latest question was, "can we walk to where we can talk with you more clearly," which Choi thought was fairly vague, but they hadn't had success from anything else.

The sequence of icons to ask that question was a bit tricky as well, but he almost had it.

"It's the concept of 'nearer' to Answerer I'm struggling with," Choi said. "Nearer to what? I know what Admin Brighton is getting at, but I think she assumes there's some giant pulsing brain lodged out in the biomass somewhere. I doubt there is. The fungal towers are the closest thing to memory storage it has, from what I can tell."

"Maybe ask where the largest or most important fungal tower is, then?" Frank suggested.

"That might work. Let me think on it," Choi said. They entered Frank's side of the lab. "What are you working on?"

"The resinplast printers are finally coming back clean," Frank said. "Looks like Answerer kept its word. It took a while for the printer boards to revert to what we originally intended, but they seem to be working now. If you want to print more housing seeds, I think we're good to start."

"Admin's pretty much given up on completing Theta Radian at this point, and that...collective I found is growing, so I hear." Choi brushed imaginary lint off their shirt. "I guess we could see if anyone needs a warehouse or anything."

"Could do," Frank said, but he was looking at Choi now with interest. "You haven't heard anything more about her, have you?"

Choi's mother, Jiow, had walked out into the biomass over seven years ago with cancer riddling her body. Choi had mourned their mother, and after a while, moved on. Until they met her again, now well and whole, a little more than a year ago, this time outside the arcopolis walls. Their mother had been changed by the biomass, with strange growths at her joints, her mind not completely her own. She'd spoken of negotiating with the biomass as it remade her. She said she was the same person who'd raised Choi, but she couldn't be.

"I haven't heard anything more," Choi said. They'd told Frank about what they saw, later. It was the first time they'd seen something close to tears in their uncle's eyes. Frank had always been around, when Choi was growing up. Frank certainly cared about her, but neither he nor Choi went in for much of the biological stuff. Too messy.

"Is it worth asking again? You might be able to send a message to her," Frank suggested. "Maybe she could give you some of the answers Admin Brighton is looking for."

"I don't know if that's a good idea," Choi hedged. They'd asked Answerer, a few months ago, if their mother was the same person as when they'd been growing up. Answerer insisted she was, as far as Choi could tell, but then Choi wasn't convinced it understood the difference between a person and a clone, or how an individual person functioned. As far as it was concerned, it was likely telling the truth.

"You should go see her again, as soon as we're let out of Alpha Radian," Frank said. "I should too." That was unusual for him. Choi wondered how much he'd been thinking about Jiow lately.

"What would you say to her?" Choi asked suddenly. They didn't know where the question had come from.

Frank cocked his head, silvery beard brushing his shirt. "I'd ask how she's been. What she's seen, out past the city wall. She always loved seeing new things. She was always reaching for more. Did you know she actually tried to start a new religion as a joke, back in the fleet?"

"You talk about her in the past tense," Choi observed.

Frank sighed. "I know you think your mother has been replaced by something else, but I think you're being too hard. People change. Even without the influence of alien mycelium."

Choi snorted a laugh. "It's a moot point for now, isn't it? We're stuck in Alpha, acting as a messenger service between Admin Brighton and Answerer. Who knows when we'll get out of here again."

"We'll get out," Frank assured him. "And when we do, you should have an idea of what you'll say to your mother."

* * *

43 years 10 months after landing

The secondary experiment concerning the Children was deemed a success. In creating a habitat better suited for their physiognomy, more of the Children had come to the new enclosure, labeled as "fungopolis." This word had no translation or simple meaning for those who communicated, but it seemed to be accepted by the majority of them.

More and more attention was devoted to the small plot of land outside the Ring of Death. The Children who had chosen to communicate were growing in number, but it was found that strategic additional conversions inside the Ring of Death were needed to bring the Children where they were wanted in higher concentrations.

Though the Children were not to be subsumed, some were still required to be upgraded to better observe how they worked. Communing directly with the first form was the most desired, but although one of the second form had offered to communicate, none of the first form had. Full communication was still not possible.

The other communication method, close to the center of the Ring of Death, was suspected to originate with one of the first forms, though relayed through the third and fourth form with the technological communicator. The first form was asking questions perhaps as an overture to engaging in direct communication, but that was still theoretical. The second form that had undergone transformation had been more difficult than usual, especially because of the secondary lifeform integrated into its nervous system. It was conjectured that the first forms might have some similar integrated lifeform as they did not degrade as quickly as the third and fourth forms did.

These Children were proving to be quite fascinating. It was proposed to model their interactions precisely in other climates and conditions, to see if there were any special indications about the Ring of Death that influenced the original parents to land in that spot.

Computations on earlier memory storage systems had been worked on as well, though no other separate species pre-subsummation had owned this wide a range of building prowess.

Several more experiments were suggested in locations away from the Ring of Death, though close enough for comparison. The next few planetary rotations might be even more interesting than those after the Children first arrived.

PART THREE

Service

45 years after landing

"The latest batch of people we sent to the fungopolis also haven't returned, Jane," Christiaan said.

Jane clenched a fist. It was becoming difficult to see that growing aberration as anything but a deliberate poke in the eye from the biomass.

"How big is it now?" she asked.

"It covers the area primarily outside and overlapping Theta Radian, Jane," Christiaan said, airtyping on the old HUD they still used for outside contact. "Though it appears to spill over into Eta and Zeta on each side. We've had reports of the city being arranged with five smaller radians, rather than the eight in the arcopolis."

"Should have thrown the mycophage at that thing when we had the chance," Jane grumbled.

"We did not know it was there at the time," Christiaan said. "By the way, Jane, Micai and Flalia need to be taken to a party with their friends on the outskirts of Beta this afternoon. Can you handle Besh and Ovia while I'm gone?"

Jane waved a hand at Christiaan. "One of Ahman's grandchildren is coming over to babysit. I need to work on a new question for Answerer. This fungopolis is growing much faster than it should be able to. Can we harness that growth? We would have been done with the arcopolis years ago, if that was the case."

"Perhaps a more direct approach is best?" Christiaan suggested. "You've received the best answers with simple questions, Jane. What about just asking it to help, with no hidden agenda?"

Jane snorted at the implication, but nodded. "I'll get Choi on it."

Three days later, she had her answer. She'd specifically asked Answerer to finish growing the three closest programmable resinplast structures that were still unfinished in Theta. Choi had asked it, and now the structures were complete—one residence, and two commercial buildings.

"So…I literally could have been asking this thing for whatever I wanted for the past two years, and it would have given it to me?" She bounced Ovia on a knee while Besh begged Christiaan for a strawberry. The latest iteration of the berries was lumpy, the size of an adult's fist, and bronze in color, but they still tasted like strawberries. Mostly.

"That seems to be the case, Jane," Christiaan said. They cut the strawberry into pieces a five-year-old could hold. Besh whined and Christiaan gave them a piece. "I wonder if we could ask it for the original stock of plants that it's changed."

"Excellent idea, and a good test," Jane said. She put Ovia down on the floor to play with their sibling. "I'll ask Choi."

Two days later, Jane held an apple. An original Honeycrisp apple like the ones they grew in the fleet. The apples had turned into spined monstrosities shortly after they landed.

"Those two scientists said a new tree pushed up from a clump of biomass just outside the Alpha walls. It was growing *from* the fungus," Jane said to Christiaan. "But they tested the apples—that it bore in a single day—and by all scientific accounts, this *is* a Honeycrisp apple." She raised it to her mouth.

"Jane," Christiaan warned, but Jane shook her head and took a bite.

"Do you know what this means? We can ask it for anything. *Anything.* All the supply problems we've been working around for years? Gone. I thought I would need to work hard to make the biomass serve us, but by God, it's placed the means right into my hands. It *wants* to serve us."

They met with Rajani, Ahman, and Wenqing the following few nights. Jane was pretty sure the other Admins knew about their secret meetings by now, but no one said anything, so she continued doing it. It was a good way of separating out what the other Admins really thought. Dmitri was still making rumblings with Alessandro, but nothing had come of it so far. The old Russian had finally lost his nerve.

"What do we request from Answerer?" Jane asked Ahman. She, the other Admin, and Christiaan were crammed in a storage closet this time—one Christiaan had run across that hadn't been used in at least twenty years.

"Maps," Ahman said immediately. "See if it can give us terrain, biomass depth, ocean placement, anything our original surveys couldn't detect because of the thickness of growth on Lida."

Christiaan copied down every idea.

"Can it eliminate diseases and abnormalities from crops and livestock?" Rajani suggested. "If it can grow a pure strain Honeycrisp apple from a patch of fungus, that suggests extremely complex organization systems. You could also ask for a new water filtering apparatus. The old plant is getting on in years, and the solution we're using works, but is time consuming."

Christiaan noted everything in their HUD.

"Locations and types of its mobile creatures," Wenqing said. "And updates on that fungopolis. Have it tell us how the people living there are moving around. Make it work as an early-warning system, if it's so happy to help."

"You want it to warn us...of when it sends large creatures against us?" Jane asked. "You want it to reveal its own attack strategies?"

Wenqing shrugged. "We still don't know what portion of the biomass Answerer represents. Is it tied into the major cognitive aspect? Is it a separate entity? Are there disagreements interior to the biomass? Any part of this information will give us more on that front, when it wouldn't answer questions about itself before."

"Good strategy," Christiaan said as they recorded everything.

"If it gives us all this information, then maybe, *finally*, we'll be able to conquer this planet like we originally intended," Jane said. "I wish we'd found out about its intelligence years ago."

* * *

45 years 2 months after landing

Choi set the latest question to Answerer running and went to talk to Frank. Their uncle had managed to get his bee colonies back into Alpha, finally, and was investigating their use as a messaging system. Answerer had confirmed it was using the bees as eyes and ears, along with pollination—which it seemed to find fascinating—and Frank was trying to tap into the changed aspects of the insects.

"That's the third question today," Choi said, "and the Admins are still pushing me to go faster. I tried to explain how long it takes to put together a question, but Admin Brighton's pet lizard only stared at me with their cold dead eyes." Choi shivered.

"They're a strange one," Frank said, looking up from a tiny dissection table. "Been skulking around since the ships landed. I think they do more to run this colony than any Admin. For as cold a fish as they are, if you need anything done well and done quickly, they're the one to do it."

"Doesn't mean I have to like them," Choi said. They frowned. "I'm concerned about some of the questions I've been asking lately. Answerer seems happy to help, as long as the topics don't touch directly on its operation. In fact, I think it's answering *more* now, like it's relieved we're not prying into its intelligence. I'm not sure it understands how much the Admins are getting from what it's telling us. If this was a person, we'd have open access to all their secrets by now."

Frank raised his eyebrows. "We still don't know how its thought processes work, but besides that, is this bad? We're against an alien intelligence, which could have grown over us at any point after we landed. I think it's best to know as much as we can."

Choi shook their head. "That's not what I meant. I'm all for getting more information about Answerer. The problem is..." They squinted up, trying to put their fears into words. "The problem is that if Answerer isn't *aware* of what it's giving away, and then the Admins start using that knowledge, er, aggressively..."

Frank sat up. "Oh. I see. Our dear benevolent autocrats might decide to go to all-out war because they're too fucking stupid to see that we have no chance against an angry biomass."

"Yes, something like that," Choi agreed. "I wonder if we can get a message out through the HUDs, subtly, to Mother Agetha—"

"And Jiow?" Frank interrupted.

Choi grimaced. "Yes, and to Mother Jiow. We should tell them Admin's poking around with information they might misuse. I wonder if they can communicate more directly to the biomass about what's happening. Maybe there's enough of a disconnect between what Answerer represents and what Mother Agetha's *friends* and *riders* represent that we can get a warning in." Choi felt distaste even mentioning the fungal infection piloting their mother and Agetha. There was no telling where it left off and they—if there was any of them left—began.

And why didn't they feel the same antipathy toward Mother Agetha as Mother Jiow? They hadn't talked to either of them since Admin had locked them all in Alpha and Beta. Before that, they hadn't had much contact with Agetha after she became infected, and Jiow had always been closer to them, before her illness. She was also their biological mother. Did any of that make a difference? Was Choi being unfair? They could tell Frank thought so, but he hadn't seen Jiow, piloted by the biomass, growths all over her body.

Frank looked down to the bee he'd been dissecting. "I don't know if they even have HUDs out there, but I wonder if these girls can do anything? The biomass has been using them to convey information for years. I bet I can work off of that, maybe send a message out to Jiow and Agetha."

Choi shook off their brooding. "A message they'd understand? How are you going to do that? Sting them?"

Frank chuckled. "No, it will use the bee's pheromones. The biomass hijacked them when it changed the bees. Now they have about four times the number of pheromones they used to, and their waggle dances are even more complex. There are the regular layers of information about direction, nectar sources, brood, queen health, and so on, then there's a whole other section about density, population, growth, even down to individual building placements in the waggle dance, I think. The biomass has been busy with these critters. The bees have continued to add more pheromones and dances over time, too. They're learning in tandem with the biomass."

"You think you can tell a bee what to do?" Choi asked.

"They're smart little critters. The biomass does, so the triggers are in there somewhere. I think I've got the directional one, so I should be able to send several bees out to the edge of the arcopolis. The challenge is encoding a warning."

"Well, you work on that, and I think I'll send out a question of my own to Answerer before the next one from Admin, just to see what it understands of the situation." They wondered if they could also ask it about Jiow. Would Answerer even understand what it had done to them?

Back in their lab, Choi watched an answer being printed. The latest question had been another survey query, which had pretty easy results. Answerer just printed out a topographical map of the area in question. The Admins had been comparing biomass depth and getting maps printed of what the ground looked like underneath, which Answerer was happy to supply.

They composed a new question, or rather an equivalency, just to see how Answerer thought. They found a few different symbols Answerer used for "information," for geographic, societal, behavioral, and any others they could think of. Then they included an equivalency: "more is always better."

They set the collected items out for Answerer, so it would know it was a query. Choi hoped it represented, "is more information always better?" as a leading question. If Answerer had never thought of that before, then maybe it would consider the question now, and what it was giving away.

The response came immediately. One of the printers spat out the "confirmation" symbol. Choi sighed. They hadn't made the hint strong enough. That was always the problem with Answerer. It was extremely literal minded.

They put out the question again, but rearranged it, and added a negation symbol in the mix. Now what they hoped it said was, "more information might not always be better, yes?"

It was a subtle difference.

The same printer started up immediately and spit out a confirmation. Choi shook their head and reached for the symbols, but the printer started a third time. This time it printed a confirmation, then a negation symbol. Choi stared at it. Was Answerer reconsidering? It had never done that before. What had influenced it—something internal to Answerer, or Choi's actions? They had no doubt Answerer could see every movement they took by now. As the primary person to ask it questions, Choi assumed they were observed at all times. Not creepy at all.

A printer printed the symbol for "waiting." Choi had used that one before to denote time intervals. Answerer occasionally used it when it needed to consider an answer longer.

Then three printers started up. What came out was very similar to what Choi had asked it.

"More information is not always better confirmation/negation."

It was asking them what the answer should be.

Choi reached out, hesitated, then tapped the "confirmation" symbol. They hoped they weren't making a mistake.

Most of the bank of printers started at the same time. That meant this was a complex question or statement. Choi watched them for which one started in which order, to make sure the symbols were arranged correctly.

It took thirty minutes just for all the symbols to print, even on twelve printers. Choi began arranging them, cross referencing with their spreadsheet of values and combinations. They'd become adept at reading Answerer's meanings and moods, but even so, they had to check against their bank of translations quite often.

Finally, Choi sat back and blinked at the question.

"Is Children first form second form third form fourth form fifth form sixth form always total equivalent meanings and direction confirmation/negation alternate first form second form third form fourth form fifth form sixth form not equal in direction confirmation question why."

Choi printed the symbol for "waiting," and went to talk to Frank. This took precedence over asking about their mother. That would have to wait for another day.

Frank took one look at their face and put his tools down carefully from his dissection. "What did you do?"

"I, ah, think I just confused Answerer. I asked it rather pointedly if it thought more information was always better, and I don't think it had contemplated that before. Then it asked me, I think, if we—the Children—always make decisions together. I told it to wait for a moment."

Frank squinted at them. "Did you just imply to a world-spanning intelligence that we *might* have been lying to it sometimes?"

"Not lying per se." Choi waggled a hand. "But you know it has problems with determining people have different intentions. I don't know if we've directly addressed that before. I assumed it had *some* idea, based on everything it's seen of us. But now I'm not sure it has." They rubbed their arm. "What should I say?"

"You say we all definitely think the same thing all the time," Frank said.

"But what if it finds out we don't? Then it would *know* I didn't tell it the truth."

"Then I don't think you can answer yes or no on this one," Frank said.

Choi sighed. "We need a symbol devoted to 'it's complicated.'"

"Well, it's hedged enough around us, give it the run-around back."

Choi took the next hour to craft a message saying, essentially, "not all forms think the same way and cannot be compared like this." They hoped that was vague enough.

It was not. Answerer came up with another twelve-printer question that boiled down to "what part of thinking means separate existence?"

"Oh fuck, it's going to evolve through Descartes in an afternoon," Choi said.

They sent a note to Admin that the latest answer might be delayed a few hours because Answerer was being difficult today. Then they frantically tried to talk an alien collective intelligence away from discovering self, identity, and why humans competed amongst themselves.

They finally talked it down to, "this is a complex topic and is worthy of much time. But other requests are more important for now."

They got back, "Will ponder and ask about this later."

Choi gritted their teeth and compiled Admin's next question. They really hoped they hadn't completely upset the balance of power between them and the biomass.

* * *

45 years 3 months after landing

Anderson was packing for another trip out into the wilds with Juliane when his left hand stopped moving. The right, prosthetic, continued to respond to his commands for a moment before it too, shut down.

What is individuality?

His eyes would have widened if they could. The biomass had been getting more articulate, but this was a complete, grammatical sentence, and not on a topic Anderson was aware it even knew of.

He still couldn't move and was sure he wouldn't until he gave it an answer.

Why ask me this? he sent to the place where Cora used to be.

Important. Consensus not reached.

Was it asking everyone about this, or just him? The scent of cloves and cinnamon came to him, and Juliane entered his field of view in the far section of the third fungopolis radian, where Anderson had set up his bunk.

"I heard it as well, but I don't think many others did," Juliane said. He seemed focused today, more than usual. "There has been much higher functioning devoted to this concept." He seemed unfazed that Anderson was frozen in place.

He would have to come up with something. Why was the biomass asking this now?

He tried to remember the images he'd sifted through in the fungal towers, finding ones that seemed similar. He thought of two sets that seemed like they had come from the same view, and sent the concept back through Cora, trying to think of them as individual collections.

This is not individuality.

So they were past that stage. Juliane shook his head as he took a seat on a chair carved from an old fungal stump. "You will need to provide something a little more specific. But it is hard to say how specific it needs to be."

Anderson tried to communicate wordlessly to Juliane that *he* should answer the biomass then.

"This is not my place, friend," Juliane said. "Those who have been in communication for longer do not have as clear concepts of where one ends and another begins." As evidenced by Juliane responding to his thoughts as if Anderson were speaking.

This would be easier if I were able to move, he thought.

Why movement equate cognition?

The answer was immediate. There was a lot of attention on him.

Is this individuality?

That made him think. Was it? Maybe it was a good way to give the biomass its answer.

It might be. If I can move, then my body can be comfortable while my mind works.

What is possession of body?

This was going to take a while.

Tell you what. You free me to move around and think better, and I'll give you the answers you want.

Trade for information, came the response.

His hands suddenly responded to his commands again, and he staggered as his legs loosened. One problem solved, then. He sat in a chair next to Juliane, who tipped his wicker hat as if it were the most normal thing in the world to be in conversation with a formless intelligence.

"We're two different people." He gestured to Juliane and to himself. "We think different things, we want different things."

"Not all the time," Juliane offered.

"Not helpful."

Juliane only shrugged.

Different parts want different things.

"But we're not different parts, we're individual—never mind." Anderson leaned back to think.

"I don't always know what other people are doing," he tried again.

Attention limited.

"Yes, but I *can't* know what other people are thinking all the time. I only see out of my eyes, not another's."

Example.

Anderson's view suddenly doubled, as if he was sitting...oh. He looked to his right/left and saw Juliane, but also saw his own face at the same time.

"We cannot do this without your interference," he said, and closed his eyes. Juliane did the same. "Please stop it."

When he opened his eyes again, he only saw from them.

Inefficient.

"That isn't the point. You asked what individuality was."

Confirmation.

"Maybe I can turn the question back on, well, on you. *Who* am I speaking to?"

Silence.

He turned to Juliane. "I'm talking to you now. I'm giving you information specifically. This is only meant for *you*." He poked Juliane in the arm. The man smiled vacantly, but offered no agreement or rebuttal.

"Now I'm talking to *you*." Anderson jabbed a finger into the air. "Who are you?"

Again, silence.

"This is individuality," Anderson said.

Concept deserves contemplation.

"Contemplation by what?" He was on a roll, now.

Higher-functioning nodes.

"What do they do with the final information?"

Collected for consensus.

"Consensus *by* whom?"

There was another long pause, and Anderson stood up again. He had to move around. This was the question they'd all been asking since the biomass demonstrated it was sentient. It turned out, even the biomass didn't know.

For consensus.

It sounded like it was pouting. "When you can tell me who creates the consensus, then I can tell you what individuality is," he promised.

Agreement.

"Great. Then Juliane and I can get ready to travel again."

Juliane nodded along. "Another great journey."

Why?

"To see what's out there? I thought this was understood. Why did you tear down that old section of growth so we could travel faster?"

Efficiency.

"And you didn't wonder why we were moving around?"

Consensus not reached.

"It is human to yearn for more information," Juliane offered. "That is why we travel."

"And we are specifically trying to learn more about this planet, the growth on it, and everything else."

More information not equates total improvement confirmation negation.

"What's that supposed to mean?" he asked Juliane. It was one of the longest communications he'd received and seemed different somehow, as if the biomass was speaking a slightly different language or dialect.

"Is it better to have loved and lost? To do or die? To hold the gates?"

Anderson stared at the other man. Sometimes he came out with the strangest stuff.

"If you're asking whether it's always better to learn more, then I would say most of the time, yes. But maybe not all the time." This conversation might potentially be one of those times.

Consensus not reached.

"Sort of, but more complicated than that." Anderson thought back to the exact words used. "Sometimes confirmation, sometimes negation."

Learn most now best confirmation.

"Do you think we're discussing our next expedition again?" he asked Juliane.

"I believe this is the intent, yes." Juliane squinted. "Communication is a fickle thing."

"For this case, we are exploring to learn the most information we can. We believe more information about Lida will be better."

Movement unneeded.

"What—"

But the world went away. It was replaced by an ever-changing landscape of growth. He recognized some of the mushrooms and creatures from when he worked with the other Vagals to clean out the first radians. He caught sight of the five fungal towers surrounding where he sat, then a few of the places where he had traveled before. The huge swath of cleared land, new mycelia popping up like daisies, came into view, and Anderson slid along it. His view was from somewhere near the ground. It could have been from his height, or lower, or even twice as high. It was hard to tell.

That disappeared, replaced by what he would have called fairy rings, back on Earth, but they were the size of the arcopolis, with conk-like mushrooms, broad and flat, making up the ring. They were each probably three to four stories tall.

The view zoomed past that to a swampy land, with fungal roots above and below the water line. Little creatures swam between strands, transporting glowing elements from one root to another.

Past that was open ocean, except the top of it was covered in an unbroken mesh of fungus. The view dove beneath the waves, and seaweed structures branched and expanded, creating channels through which larger things drifted—like jellyfish but opaque, hyphal roots replacing the stingers. A huge fish shape loomed from the darkness, its jaws opening wide to swallow a swarm of the jellyfish fungi whole.

Anderson flew out of the water and to the side, where humongous creatures like pill bugs rolled across the landscape. One stopped and unrolled, its belly a mass of tendrils that sought the ground and planted it. Its armored back sunk down, creating a low hill that reflected the sunlight like it was made of metal.

There was more after that, but Anderson's memory rebelled at the number of images. So many creatures—a world ecology—sifted through his mind, until the one blight, the human arcopolis, once again came into view.

The images stopped.

Movement unneeded.

This communication felt...smug.

Anderson worked his jaw, getting rid of his dry mouth. How long had he sat here? He needed a VaporLite. Juliane was still beside him, watching him coolly. The sun was going down.

"Do we still set out tomorrow?" Juliane asked.

Anderson looked at their half-packed camp. "We do, but perhaps a little later. I want to see some of those things with my own eyes."

Inefficient.

"It is, but that's part of individuality. I want to experience those things you showed me again, but this time with these eyes." He gestured to his own.

No consensus.

"Perhaps not, but I will enjoy the view. Let's get packing, Juliane."

* * *

45 years 4 months 6 days after landing

Agetha scowled at her fingers. Her arthritis had disappeared a couple years ago, but this morning they looked longer. She had always wanted longer fingers. Now they felt stretched and vaguely painful, as if someone had been pulling on them all night.

"Beth, do my fingers seem longer to you?" she asked Beth, lying beside her in the bed.

"I would say that's a strange question, except I'm nearly positive I've gained an inch in height over the past two weeks, and it's not from spinal cartilage growing back this time," Beth replied. Phyllis was already up and around, as usual.

Agetha rolled over for a kiss, then back the other way and out of the bed. They'd transported their bed and mattress from the apartment in Zeta, as the houses here were growing well. The fungopolis had started with construction by humans from leftover resinplast, until the giraffe crabs had fertilized, or mated with, or melded into the seed Juliane had planted. After that, the colony began to grow, new buildings shooting up as people arrived. The style was like those in the arcopolis, but changed, as if the original buildings were all mashed together, and different parts pulled to prominence as needed. It led to strange hallways going nowhere, and doors slightly out of straight, or a few centimeters higher than comfortable. It made Agetha's construction-honed instincts go off every time she looked at one of the new houses, but they grew quickly, were stable, and there was plenty of space for everyone to live. They simply weren't designed by a human.

"Do we have more apple pastry?" Beth asked from the bed.

"I think so. I'll check." That was one of the best changes. The biomass had learned at some point that humans particularly liked the fruit that had been changed beyond recognition in the first few years. They had a small grove now, of apple trees that grew from bulbous mycelial mounds. They had no root system, and the fungal flesh seamlessly transitioned into a woody trunk. The apples tasted good, though. They had pears as well, and a few grapes. Mancin had experimented with wine for the first time in forty years. It wasn't very good, but it was better than fermented mushroom beer.

It turned out, there was some apple pastry left.

Agetha got comments from other fungopolis residents during the day.

Several were taller, or shorter, one had started to grow armor plating, and another looked like she was growing an extra set of arms.

"You've seen the changes going around?" Jiow asked her, later on. When Agetha said she had, Jiow gave a significant glance downward. "I think I'm going through a second puberty."

"I just got longer fingers," Agetha said, wiggling them. "I wonder what the biomass' aim is this time, especially as the"—she made the gesture for *rider*—"unwanted changes haven't disappeared and I don't think any of us really want them."

Jiow's hand went to her other elbow, then neck, where Agetha could see the fungal growths in both places. Before, they had been blocked from even acknowledging them, but now she could do so freely. The biomass had moved on to other things. She still didn't feel the sense of horror she knew she should about having fungus sprout from her flesh. Every time she decided to explore that lack of emotion, the feeling faded away after a few moments.

"It still has a big problem with consent," Jiow said, echoing her thoughts. "Has Anderson made any progress on that front?"

"Not that I've heard of," Agetha said. The Vagal had shared the biomass' continued attempts to get him to define individuality. Agetha wondered if it only spoke to him in an attempt to understand how individuality worked, or simply because it was already using him as a kind of ambassador. "What is it trying to do with these changes?"

"Find out how we work? Although it seems to know that already, physically at least." Jiow kicked at a fernlike growth that moved out of the way as she did. "It's growing us houses, making us a city. It's acting like our caretaker."

"Or an overseer," Agetha said. The biomass had subsumed other species, as it took over the planet many hundreds or thousands of years ago. "Do you think any other species subsumed were sentient?" She hadn't thought about that before, and it was an unsettling thought.

"Would it even have been aware if they were?" Jiow looked thoughtful too.

"Possibly not. It seems like talking to humans is a new development for it." If the biomass never had anything talk back to it, it wouldn't have considered questions of control or consent. "We need to keep it talking so it learns to understand us. The final question will be: who has control over humanity's growth and development."

* * *

45 years 4 months 6 days after landing

Why does new biological growth reject progenitor growth?

Jiow pulled up at the comment, then cast a sideways glance at Agetha. Had she heard that too?

"I heard it," Agetha said. "Did it ask what I think it asked?"

"I'm going to take this call in a quieter place, I think," Jiow answered.

"Good luck." Agetha nodded and waved before moving off to another group of colonists. Jiow kept walking to the edge of the fungopolis.

"Do you mean my child?" Jiow asked the air. She didn't know the biomass could pinpoint something that precisely.

New biological growth rejects progenitor growth.

"Right, so why does my child hate me now? It's a bit of a sore spot." Jiow was surprised the biomass could even identify her and Choi. Maybe it was because Choi had a lot of attention on them, running the technology that talked to the biomass for Admin.

Emotion causes rejection.

"You're putting it into very simple terms, when it isn't." Jiow drew in a breath. "You changed me, like you did the others. You also saved my life, for which I'm very grateful. I have opportunities now that I never had in the colony. The physical changes don't bother me. I'll accept them along with getting rid of the wrinkles, old bones, crap joints, and of course the cancer. But Choi only sees your *effect* on me, not *me*, as a person."

There was a silence.

Inefficient errors in communication.

"Yes, well, call it what you will. The fact remains that you changed us, without our consent."

Streamlined for better interface.

Was the biomass...defensive?

"How about this. I think you're starting on it already, but here's my formal approval. I'm one of those who's chosen gender is different than her biological sex. We had a lot of medical miracles in the fleet, but not that one. So, if you can do it, then I give you permission. Make me physically how I see myself mentally."

Approval for changes. Consensus reached. Biological growth will accept progenitor growth.

"I...I don't think that has anything to do with it, but let's hope so. Maybe Choi will come around when they see how you can work for the good of people."

Consensus noted.

The pressure of a presence dissipated, and Jiow looked around, as if a mushroom person would jump out of a hole in the ground. She grimaced and pressed a hand to her stomach. That *was* a cramp.

But she'd given the biomass permission to change her this time. It was a victory.

Then she looked out over the fungopolis. She'd given permission for *just* herself, hadn't she?

PART FOUR

New Eyes

46 years after landing

Harie had set a meeting with Agetha. Over the last eight months, people had started changing deliberately, all through the colony, those with the *riders* and those without. Some were small things, like hair or skin color, or even gender changes, but others were wild, like extra limbs, or integrated animal or plant parts, or specialized appendages.

They'd all started small—hair and nails and color changes. The bigger mutations came after, but by that time, the original shock had worn off. Some colonists raged against the changes of course, but they were most often met with a shrug. Many had a strangely complacent view, at least to Harie. Agetha mentioned in the past how the biomass soothed away disgust and revulsion. Should he have felt more emotion about the colonists diverging from the standard human body type?

Admin, of course, had understandably panicked and tried to restrict the changes, even though no Vagals or Admins showed them. But there was nothing they could do. The colony had advanced medical procedures in the fleet, and the Generationals retained that knowledge, but there was nothing to do with a person who'd grown an extra arm and the bones and musculature to use it.

He'd talked with the others in his poly group about the changes—a pleasant conversation over tea, as if they were talking about the weather or the latest art at the market. From what all of them could tell, the new adjustments were what people envisaged for themselves. The more esoteric changes had only started after the colonists saw the changes were incremental and based on personal desires. The new became normal, then commonplace. As humans always did, they asked for more, and the biomass granted. The problem came when the person was not developed enough to know what they wanted. Then it became dangerous.

Harie eyed his children. At two and a half, they were creatures of constant change, and that was beginning to be reflected in their bodies, as well as minds.

Marien, Carel, and Jasen toddled in front of him on their daily walk. Well, Jasen crawled. Today they had long, many fingered arms and went on all fours. Marien was stretched and thin, much taller than they should be, and even stoic Carel had developed scales on their arms and legs.

This was the new normal for them. Harie would find them in a different shape every morning, as if they were plastic. He had no idea if it would stunt their development, or if the biomass had that all in hand for all future humans. If it could grow apples from a fungal mound, it could probably cause a human to grow per their original DNA instructions.

The question was, *were* they human? He'd discussed with Kwang and Maerk, and none of them could say. They *felt* human, but Kwang's hair had turned to a vibrant orange, and Maerk had an extra set of hands coming from his elbows, which he said aided him immensely in everyday tasks. Harie had stayed resolutely human, trying to set an example for their kids, though that hadn't worked.

They reached the edge of the Zeta radian on their walk to meet with Agetha, and Harie waved to a neighbor whose face was furred, their eyes catlike. A new normal.

The houses he'd used to check on were finished now, ahead of schedule for once. It was a golden age for the arcopolis. Any project they could think of, they simply had to ask the biomass. The Generationals and first Grounders who'd been frantically building their entire lives were now...caught up. There was time for entertainment, and enjoyment. His old intern Clarine was considering another round of study, hoping to learn about fungal xenobiology.

Harie shuddered at their reliance on the alien intelligence. He peered into Theta radian, where the resinplast seeds had exploded with growth six months ago. The fungopolis had taken over most of them and half of Theta. It expanded outside the wall too, off to the side of the arcopolis, like an unnecessary growth.

The houses were...off. If he'd still been inspecting them, he would have been worried about structural collapse or voiding between floors, but the houses all held up—or had for a few months at least. If one fell down, a new one would probably sprout in its place. People moved into the new ones as they ripened—that was the only word that fit—

and the house adjusted to them. Sometimes he'd see a new room or window or door forming. Others oxidized or changed color by other means overnight.

The yards around them offered up a bounty. Apples and pears, tomatoes, beans, carrots, eggs, and even pods of milk and hunks of meat, all sprouting from fleshy ropes of mycelium. Harie was used to the duck eggs that were all that was left in the colony, but Generationals said these were chicken eggs—minus the chicken—and just like the ones they had in the first year before the chickens died out. Harie thought they tasted blander.

The food would change day to day as well, depending on what the inhabitants wanted. It was horrifying in its efficiency.

Harie looked up as Agetha turned a corner into his sight from deeper in Theta. She hadn't been in the arcopolis proper for months, but Harie supposed the lines were blurred these days. Maybe she *was* still in the fungopolis.

They hugged, and Agetha bent down to greet the kids, not reacting at all to their shapes today. She also looked the same as she always had. Well, not the same. She looked young. Younger than Harie had ever known her, but physically it was her. No extra arms, and her hair was the same medium brown it had been before she went gray. Then there were the changes from the *rider*, at her joints and neck.

"What are you all doing today, kids?" she asked.

"Walking, Gran 'Getha," Jasen said. They'd propped up on long fingers so they were a more normal height for a toddler.

"Are you taking good care of your parent?" she asked. Carel nodded solemnly and took Harie's hand. Marien grabbed onto Agetha's arm, dragging her to a nearby bench at the edge of a square between houses to watch peaches and pears ripen on nearby trees. Harie squinted at the bench. Had it been here before? It looked like resinplast, but there was a bulky ropiness to the boards that looked too organic.

He finally pried Marien off Agetha and got all three to go play together in the low field of moss that grew here. It was hardy stuff, used to many feet walking on it.

"Do you know what's happening?" he asked, once they weren't listening anymore. He didn't want to scare his kids, but *he* was scared.

"Aside from the obvious answer, no, not specifically." Agetha shifted on the bench to find a more comfortable spot. The bench shifted too, and Harie eased back into it. "Beth thinks the biomass is taking it way too far, and we don't know why. It's like it's trying to find an answer to how we work by giving us the means to express ourselves in every way possible. Absolute freedom. Terrifying, isn't it?"

Harie nodded. "I think my biggest worry is that more people *aren't* worried. I should have to push away fear for my children to talk to you. I should be aghast they're able to stretch and change like putty. My poly group has different faces than the ones I entered a contract with. You look like you're forty years younger." There were other subtle differences about Agetha, mostly enhancing the strong features she'd always had, but on the whole, she still seemed like the same Agetha, even if closer to the age she was when still leading the construction crew.

"You know, you look different as well, even if you don't think you do," Agetha told him. "A bit thinner, a bit more athletic, and that mole you've always had on your arm is gone."

Harie glanced down guiltily. He'd always hated that mole, and kept it covered when he could. But he'd stayed *almost* the same.

"But to answer your question," she continued, "I think that's a little gift from the biomass, along with the changes. Suppress the anxiety just a little and get people to accept changes."

"But that means it's *in* all of us, not just—" he gestured to Agetha's neck and elbows, the easiest changes to see.

She nodded, one hand drifting to her neck. "I think it's been in all of us from the beginning and we never knew it. We've been breathing in its spores, eating its mycelium, drinking water contaminated with it. We assumed there were no changes because we didn't know it could control them, that it was sentient. Some of us just got the first upgrade." She made the gesture over her ear with one finger. "I'm not even sure if they're necessary any longer. It hasn't spoken to you, has it?"

Harie shook his head hastily. He never wanted that to happen.

"Maybe that's what they do, then." Agetha covered the growth at one elbow with her other hand, her mouth wrinkling ever so slightly.

"But what does it mean for us?"

"I wish I had some clue." Agetha spread her hands. "Whatever it is, I know it wasn't in Admin's original plans for the colony." She laughed.

"Stars. That plan is so far off course it might as well be heading out of the galaxy. None of us knew what we were in for when we landed here, but I don't think any of us could have imagined this."

Harie tried to put his thoughts into words. "Then...what if I don't *want* to be okay with this? This is a fundamental change to our species. I think I should be enraged at what it's doing. I should want to fight back, to rebel, but I don't. That's what scares me most—the fact that I can watch my kids, looking like this, and simply take them out for a walk with Daddy."

Agetha placed a cool hand on his arm and met his eyes. "Hold on to that little nugget of fear. Hold on to it tight. That's how I was first able to talk to it. Keep pushing. It's been...everything for so long that it doesn't know where *it* stops and the rest of the universe begins. *That's* what we have to teach it, or we'll be swallowed whole."

A shiver went up Harie's spine. He should have been ready to jump up and make changes. But he didn't. Instead, he held Agetha's eye and nodded. He answered calmly. "I'll make sure I hold on. And I'll teach them to hold on." He swept a hand out to his children.

"It's the only thing we can do." Agetha patted his arm and let go. Just a simple chat between friends. "Now, tell me what Maeve and Pollyan are up to. I haven't seen them in forever."

They lapsed into easy conversation, talking like people who had known each other almost thirty years. Agetha told him about the latest immigrants to the fungopolis, and how its borders were still growing. Harie told her about his neighbors, some of whom she knew, and generally they talked like people who had seen much, over the years.

And Harie kept an eye on his children. Whatever they would become, that was what the colony would be.

* * *

46 years 2 months 1 week after landing

"The new delivery has arrived, Jane," Christiaan said. They pointed out the balcony doors of her office.

"How can you see—holy shit!" Jane bounced up and came around her desk. Fortunately, the youngest twins weren't in the room, so she didn't have to hear them repeating curses for the next week.

There was a creature outside the walls of the arcopolis, as big as anything she'd seen on this cursed planet. It might have been the same as the thing that reseeded the area defoliated by the mycophage. It might have been something completely different, but she really didn't care. It was nearly the size of one of the fleet ships. But even that was dwarfed by the pile of fungal towers attached to its back by some sort of sticky gum, forming a mound twice as high as the walls of the city.

"I presume this is the materials you asked for?" Christiaan said.

"I sure as hell hope so. I don't know what else that thing could be doing here." Jane went out on the balcony, dialing her HUD in for a closer look. She assumed the biomass wouldn't change this video. She didn't think there was a point. It definitely wanted them to see it could do this.

Jane had been asking Answerer for help with all her problems over the last year, and it had provided as promised. Then it had pulled that stunt with the colonists, twisting them into bizarre shapes and growing extra limbs. She and the other Admins had been ready to cull the infected population—at Dmitri's suggestion—until they realized the colonists were *asking* to be molded like putty. They went about their days as if they weren't leaving the human genome far behind. Thank all the stars it hadn't touched the Admins and Vagals. Ahman assured her they could take comfort that if they needed to burn the colony to the ground and start over, there was an untainted root stock of humanity.

In response, each time the biomass upped the ante, Jane went bigger, testing its limits. Finally, she had asked for enough metals and minerals to supply what they originally intended for the colony, assuming they would have been able to mine the surface. It was the largest block to building arcopolises across Lida, unless she wanted them grown out of resinplast. She did not.

Through Choi, Answerer had told them to wait while it came up with an answer. A week later, that answer had been "two months."

As Jane watched, the creature shook itself like a giant horse, the gum fragmenting and dislodging the fungal tower trunks to the ground around it. With a trumpeting cry, it trundled off into the wilds the way it had come. She could see its back humping along, creating a corridor in the biomass she was certain would be filled in within a few days.

The pile of towers sat, shiny in the sun.

"Are you seeing this?" she asked. Christiaan came up beside her, peering forward.

"They appear to be melting, Jane," they said.

"That's what I thought. Isn't the material in the fungal towers almost as hard as nanotanium?"

"It is, Jane. Which means the biomass could likely have breached even the Alpha and Beta walls with ease, if it had cause to."

"How long do you think they will take to boil down into components?" The pile of fungal towers looked like wax left too long in the sun.

She could practically hear Christiaan calculating. They took a few measurements with their HUD.

"Likely three to four hours, if I judge the endothermic reaction correctly, Jane," they said. "I'll get a team out to the site immediately to begin cataloging what is in the towers."

The concentration matched the metals she'd asked for almost to the exact percentage. Had Answerer picked specific fungal towers to bring that made up what she asked for? Had it grown them for her? How far had the giant crawler traveled? The whole process had taken two months. Considering how fast the crawler moved, that meant there were plenty of materials close to them. Unless separate creatures had transported the towers to a central point. Impossible to say, but she was sure Ahman had a team of data analysts on it already.

"What do we do with these raw resources, Jane?" Christiaan asked. "We don't need them to finish the colony. The biomass grows what we ask."

"It was a test it passed," Jane said. She placed a mental check box next to "make the biomass serve them." It had been easier than she thought. "But to your question, we'll use the metals. We can refurbish a lot of the ship's systems that are getting worn out, and more importantly, we can start to plan out the second arcopolis. Do you think we can replicate nanotanium with this?"

Christiaan waggled a hand. "With time, perhaps. We still don't have the processing capacity of Earth, and we're missing some of the alloy techniques requiring electronic timing systems."

"What if we ask it?" Jane suggested.

"Do you want to continue to be dependent on what it can do for us, Jane? I understand the test, but I'm concerned what knowledge we give the biomass, along with the worker knowledge we will lose if this goes on for too many years. We are already seeing a decline in construction techniques since the programmable resinplast was deployed."

Jane spun to them, suddenly angry. "You know what else is declining? Humans. Have you seen what the Generationals and Grounders look like now? I've seen the videos Rajani passed on. The biomass is providing what I ask for, but it's playing merry hell with the people in the colony. Is it revenge? Does the biomass even know of the concept?"

"I couldn't say, Jane," Christiaan answered, maddingly calm. "But as we've seen, no one is complaining. They're voluntary changes. We can hope it's only a fad. Speaking of, I need to pick up Besh and Ovia from their play group in Gamma. They're asking about Grounder children they see with more extreme changes."

"I know. It's a problem. Keep an eye on them, Christiaan, and keep them separate them from any non-Admin and Vagal children. I don't want my children affected. It's almost time for our next set of twins, but perhaps we should wait a few years, while the biomass is acting like this. Besh and Ovia were born before we knew it was sentient." She shook her head. "A fad."

Christiaan placed a hand on her arm and squeezed. "We'll figure this out, Jane. Let's keep to our schedule for now, and we'll see what things look like in a couple more years."

"I don't know if we have that long."

It was only a few days later, in fact, when Dmitri surprised her in her office, Alessandro in tow.

"More about the changed colonists?" Jane asked. It was unusual for the two to be in her office, but all eight Admins had worked more closely together in the past several months than they had in the past several years. Fortunately, her little scheme with Rajani, Ahman, and

Wenqing had been running smoothly, gathering information on the biomass' sentience and how it affected the colony. Perhaps it was time to ramp that down. The biomass had agreed to serve them, after all.

"This is indirectly related to the colonist mutations, yes," Dmitri said without preamble. "More specifically, your leadership is sorely lacking. The people of this colony are suffering, and Alessandro and I feel you may have bitten off more than you can chew, especially these last two years."

"And this is all my fault?" she asked, opening her hands. So, these two were moving on from harassing Wenqing about the Vagals to harassing her about the colony. Ambitious of them. And they had ambushed her when Christiaan wasn't here. "Last I checked, we split up the control of the colony amongst ourselves. I may act as Lead Admin, but that's only because I'm responsible for planning how our cities will grow. If you're concerned about people, talk to Rajani." She hated throwing one of her allies under the bus, but better Rajani than her.

"We talked to her. She said you approve everything she does," Alessandro put in.

Damn Rajani for ratting her out. A twinge of fear ran through her. Dmitri was gunning for her, and he'd prepared well.

"Why are you here, Dmitri? What are you going to do?" Jane pursed her lips. Alessandro was a follower, and always had been. It was why she took the leadership role from him when they first landed.

"We want to reinstate formal meetings between all Admins," Dmitri said. "These changes in the colony inhabitants are too concerning and Admin's leadership—*your* leadership—is becoming lax. The first meeting is scheduled for halfway through the year, and we'll continue them every six months until the colony is running smoothly. At that point, we may relax the schedule again."

"And who exactly decided this?" Jane asked. She watched for Christiaan. Usually, they would appear the second she was in a tight spot, but they hadn't appeared. They were probably out with the kids. Dmitri had enough spies to know when to ambush her alone, and he'd been using them. She *had* gotten lax over the years, and now it was catching up to her. She should have been watching the four Admins she wasn't having secret meetings with.

"We did," Alessandro said, "and we have agreements from Polunu and Maria. That's half the leaders of the colony."

Too many mistakes. Jane had lost her focus. Polunu led animal science, and Maria the water and waste treatment. Necessary for a colony, but not glamorous. Dmitri ran power generation and Alessandro the crops and agriculture. She was being overrun by a coalition of farmers.

"And who will put together the agenda? You and your secretaries?"

"Indeed," Dmitri said. "And the first order of business will be voting on a permanent Lead Admin position for the next phase of our colony. You've assumed that position, but it was never official. We're going to make it so."

"We never *needed* an official position," Jane shot back. "We've worked together for the good of the colony."

Dmitri snorted. "To some, perhaps. Yet you assume you lead us, but haven't managed to finish one arcopolis yet, when you said it would take ten years. Now we have an insurgent camp overrunning our walls and still you do nothing!"

Jane swallowed. "It was impossible to build the arcopolis in ten years without resources and with the biomass hampering us. We all know that." She winced inwardly even as she said it. She couldn't give openings, couldn't make excuses.

"Yet you still failed," Dmitri said.

"We have the resources now, through my *successful* negotiation with the biomass." It was a weak retort.

"Too late. The next leader of our colony will gladly use those resources to properly construct the next arcopolis," Alessandro said.

"Good luck with that," Jane said. A flaccid parting shot. She knew Dmitri would have pushed for a meeting sooner if he knew he had the votes. He needed another four months to work on Rajani, Ahman, and Wenqing.

"You have four months—until midyear—to show the Admins you can lead this colony as the official Lead Admin. Use that time wisely. We'll see you then," Dmitri said, and he and Alessandro left.

That meant she had four months to pull Maria or Polunu to her side. She tapped her fingers together, six times, then six times again. Where was Christiaan?

* * *

46 years 3 months after landing

Choi jumped as their HUD chimed for a call. No one called them. Frank was in the same lab, and Admin Brighton sent short texts or her secretary.

"Hello?"

"Hi, Choi." They tensed. The voice was as familiar as any they knew. The voice of their mother, who had died when she walked out into the biomass.

"Jiow." They wouldn't call this person "Mother." "What is it?"

"Come open the door, Choi. I can't stand out here forever."

Choi sat up. "You're outside the lab? How did you get into Alpha?"

"I had, ah, *help*, if you know what I mean. Our mutual friend."

Choi was moving before they could decide not to. Frank was out talking to some of Rajani's folks, which Choi was sure was not a coincidence. How had their—had Jiow gotten in here? The gates between the radians were closed and guarded by Vagals. No one could simply walk in.

They opened the door to the lab a crack and Jiow's face looked back. There was something different about it.

"Are you going to let me in?"

Choi sighed and opened the door. Jiow pushed in and closed the door behind her.

"What reason do you possibly have for coming here?" they said. There was something strange about their—about Jiow.

"I came here to thank you for the work you've done with the biomass. It's making our wishes come true, and that's because of you opening that avenue of conversation with it."

"It wasn't intentional. And how do you know what I talk to Answerer about?"

"Don't be dense, child," Jiow said. "I didn't raise you that way."

Choi grimaced, but couldn't refute that. "Still. What would possibly prompt you to come here?"

"It's easy with a little direction. A few objects erased in a HUD, and a few heads turned at the right time, and I walked straight through. But that's not important. Look, Choi. Look at me."

They looked at Jiow. Her face was softer, more prominent breasts beneath her shirt, hips a little wider. Their technology could do a lot for those people who chose a gender other than what tradition once dictated, but Jiow had never chosen the more extensive procedures, as far as they knew.

"Did the biomass do this?" they asked finally.

"It did. It changed me completely, inside and out. It's a simple thing for it to do, merely regrowing and adapting a few parts. But it's a lot cleaner than what we can do. Just think of what this means for people like me."

"You look good, Jiow. It's great. I'm happy for you, really." Choi took a step back, making a greater separation. They wouldn't get pulled back into a lie. "But you're not my mother anymore. My mother died. Everything about you has changed, or been fused with the biomass."

Jiow stepped forward and flicked him in the head with a finger, frustration flickering across her face. "Are we only our bodies? Uncle Zhu and I taught you better than that. Uncle Frank gave you plenty of scientific theory. I have all my memories. I love you. I know you."

"But do you?" they countered. They didn't quite understand their hesitation themself, but something wasn't right here. It wasn't Jiow's full transition—they really were happy for Jiow about that. It was something she had always felt a little less about. Choi knew she had struggled with finding a job when she first landed with the colonists. She had remade herself, she said, found a new path. And now she really was remade. But at what cost?

"Are you sure you remember everything?" they pushed. "And even if you do, is it correct, or is it modified from what really happened?"

"Everything we remember is flawed," Jiow said. "I remember your birthday parties different than you and Phillipe do. You learned things I never had a chance to. I still *feel* like me. That's the point. I feel *more* like me than I ever did before."

"Then why do *I* feel like you're completely different?" Choi asked, their voice rising. "I mourned you when you walked out into the biomass. I thought I had come to the end of that story. Then I see you again, when I least expect it, but you told me you'd been piloted like a puppet for years. How can I trust *anything* you tell me now? I know it hasn't let you go. If anything, it's fused deeper with you."

Jiow finally paused at that. "Yes, it's deeply involved with everyone on this planet, you included. You think you're safe here in Alpha, but I can see the parts of the biomass in here." She held a hand out, palm up, as if the walls contained secret strands of hyphae. "It's been intertwined with our society since it started here. We've just been ignoring it. It's time to stop."

As if to prove her point, the bank of printers behind Choi started up. Jiow tilted her head to the side, as if listening.

"Yes, I told you it wouldn't work. Yet you're still confused."

"Should I read that message?" Choi asked.

Jiow rolled her eyes. "It's going to complain that you're rejecting me."

"Since when does the biomass care about our personal relationship? Does it even grasp what that means?" More security measures ran through Choi's head. Maybe it did have hyphae in the walls.

Jiow grimaced. "I don't think it does, but it knows you are an essential piece. It's trying to learn about how humans work. Through us."

So that was the real reason. Jiow wasn't just showing off to her child. The biomass had sent someone to them to plead its case, in person. Another way she was controlled, was no longer their mother. It must be gaining knowledge about individuality, because of who it picked.

"There are still ways we can keep it out," Choi said, grasping at a ray of hope. "Alpha is the most protected, and Beta is nearly as good. The Admins aren't affected. It's said as much, that it can't change them and the Vagals."

Jiow raised a finger. "There's one Vagal it's changed. He's living out with us, and I think it's using that to figure out how to interface with the Admins too. It may not be able to affect them now, but it's only a matter of time. It's always been a matter of time."

Choi frowned, wondering if that was something they should transmit to Admin Brighton or not. Jiow took a step forward.

"We're finally able to spread out across this planet like we wanted to from the beginning. It's not in the same way as we thought, but it might be better in other ways. I'm your mother, Choi, and you're my child."

Choi was shaking their head. They weren't ready for this. The Admins *certainly* weren't ready. They would burn the arcopolis to the ground before giving it over to the biomass, or at least Admin Brighton would.

"No. It's too much." Choi took another step back and held their hands out, keeping this person in their mother's shape away. "I'm thankful for what you were to me before, and you seem to be living a better life now, but I can't accept that you're the same person. Your mind is not the same." They could see the white hyphae filaments creeping below Jiow's skin, like veins filled with milk. They pointed to the door. "So go back and tell your *friends* and the biomass that it should leave us here alone. People are free to choose, and I have. I'll talk to it, but I'm not going to *be* it."

Jiow stared at them for a long time, her eyes raking over their face. "I love you, Choi."

"And I'm glad you're happy, Jiow," they answered.

* * *

46 years 4 months after landing

Anderson hacked through another tangled mass of fungus, fleshy mushrooms falling away from his machete. The biomass liked to give him clean paths, herding him, but he refused to take them all the time, sometimes hacking his own way to see what was there, and suffering the pouting mental words about inefficiency and not having a consensus. The words were starting to have emotion to them, that or Anderson was getting better at reading into what the biomass meant. Either way was concerning.

Juliane followed him, somehow. The man seemed to find paths where he could not, stepping around brambles that picked and scratched at Anderson's powersuit. He still wore it when traveling through the wilds, despite assurances from the biomass and Juliane that he would be unharmed. He wasn't sure the definition of "unharmed" was the same for him as it was for them.

The biomass had asked him if he wanted to be changed in any way, or if he wanted his right hand grown back. The latter tempted him for a few minutes, but he'd had his prosthetic for longer than he hadn't by this point. The original injury—caused by the biomass in the first place—had happened soon after they landed, and he'd spent four and a half decades with it. He'd been in his early twenties when they landed, and he still looked that age, but he felt the years weigh down on him. He'd continue looking the same, with only a few more gray hairs, for the next hundred years, if Admin was correct. He'd have that long to talk with the biomass, to teach it about humanity, if it didn't end up killing him first.

He'd said no to growing his hand back, and had to keep saying no to everything else, though his need for VaporLites had reduced over the past months. He suspected there wouldn't have even been a question had he not been a Vagal. For him, the biomass had to work to interface with him, an effect of the implant and the genemods. The others didn't even know they didn't have a choice, the way it affected their minds. It quieted their reactions, so they wouldn't complain. It did with him too, and he hadn't figured out how to stop it.

He continued to push through the vegetation. Juliane wasn't speaking much today. Sometimes he was a veritable font of words, not all of which made sense, and other times he seemed almost mute. Today was one of the latter days. Anderson was farther out than he'd ever been before, pushing to the places he'd seen in his vision. He had a feeling of a way to go, just something that seemed right.

He pointed up the slope ahead, where the brambles seemed to ease into a clearing of some sort. There were a few fungal towers visible, and they usually were bare of larger growth around their bases.

"We'll camp there tonight," he told Juliane. "We'll be able to see the next valley past it and plan out our path for tomorrow."

"Surely there's enough daylight for a little more traveling?" Juliane answered, startling Anderson.

"Oh, so you are talking today. I suppose we can go a little farther, if you want."

"It will be an adventure," Juliane said with a smirk.

Anderson watched the strange man for a moment, then shook his head and kept trudging uphill.

It took another two hours to get to the top of the hill. Only the last few minutes were free of the brambly mess he'd been cutting through for the last two days.

"There, finally made it," he told Juliane. "Sure you want to keep going?"

"Perhaps just a look at what comes next," Juliane answered.

Another strange request, but that was not uncommon for him.

"Fine. Let's take a look. I'm sure it's only—what the hell?" Anderson clutched at the fungal tower for support.

There was a village down there, with huts, and people moving around.

"An adventure," Juliane repeated.

It was yet another hour of walking to get down the slope to the village, and it was getting dark by then. But Anderson couldn't stop now. He'd asked Juliane if he'd known about this, but the man had only said he had a hunch there was something important.

They entered the edge of the village together. There were bipedal people here, and as he and Juliane got closer. He could see they were human, or human-shaped. Three of them came out to greet them. At any rate, they didn't have any weapons showing. They wore long linen shifts, in earthy browns and greens, cinched around their waists.

Then Anderson saw their faces. Or rather face, because all three of them shared the exact same facial structure.

"Greetings and welcome to this village where there are many individual people that may cheerfully talk with you about the topics you are interested in," one said. It was all delivered at the same pace, with no expression on the person's face. None of them seemed concerned with how or why Anderson had suddenly appeared.

"You speak my language well," he said. It was all a setup. Everything. Somehow the biomass had lured him out here where it had cooked up these fake humans.

"This language is very much the same as the one spoken by the Children which individuals use to learn more about each other's lives and passions."

"What is going on here?" Anderson whispered to Juliane.

"Perhaps an experiment, looking for a new way forward," Juliane answered.

"I don't like it."

"Will you engage with conversation about how this culture and society is developing?"

Anderson looked closer at the three in front of him. There were others in the village, going about their tasks with mechanical precision. He couldn't tell which one had spoken, as all three were staring straight at him. Their skin was regular and without blemish, a light ochre. On closer inspection, the "clothes" they wore were just single sheets of sheer cloth, fixed at the waist to give the impression it was different pieces of material.

In fact, it seemed melded to them, right about the waist. It didn't move in the faint wind that blew around them.

"Sure, we can have a conversation. What's your name?"

The person stared back. And stared.

"If you're all individuals, then you will have different names," Anderson suggested. Out of the corner of his eye, he saw another villager go past, carrying what looked like a pot made of twisted strands from one house to another. Their face was the same as the three in front of him.

The righthand person stepped forward. "This one is Adam."

"Cute," Anderson said. "Been learning about our legends?"

The middle person stepped forward. "This one is Beta."

The one on the left stepped forward before he could comment. "This one is Corn."

"That's a food, not a—" he broke off. "You know what, fine. Good job on the names. Can I ask any one individual here what their name is?"

All three stared straight ahead and he could practically see them generating new names.

"Let's skip that for now. Who are you? How did you get here?"

The three snapped back to focus. The one on the right—Adam— spoke up. "This town is a place for individuals to grow and develop. All these individuals are living here for mutual growth to learn from each other and function as a community."

The pot-carrying person returned to the first house, with the same pot.

"Uh huh. Why don't we all go sit down somewhere and we can talk about this more."

Beta and Corn turned and walked away. Adam waited one moment then went after them. Anderson traded a look with Juliane, who shrugged, and followed.

They passed one structure, then another. They were arranged in a circle, and all ten buildings on the outside ring were the same. The eight in the second ring were different layouts than those on the outside, but also all exactly the same. This was repeated on the third, fourth, fifth, and sixth rings with fewer buildings. The trio entered a building on the fifth ring. Anderson followed, finding the house filled with vine chairs, all facing forward in columns. They'd obviously grown from the biomass mat. Adam, Beta, and Corn picked three chairs in a column and sat in them, Corn looking over Beta's head, who looked over Adam's. At least he assumed that. It could have been any other way. There didn't seem to be much difference between the three.

"Would you like to pull up a chair, Juliane?" Anderson asked. This evening was getting stranger by the second.

"A good idea. Perhaps a time to show by example?" Juliane took a chair out of a different column and set it facing the trio. Anderson pulled another one from a different place, letting it drag across the floor. They were all made of something like twisted resinplast, vaguely brown.

"You know, talking is easier if we all face one another," Anderson told the three.

Adam stayed seated, and Beta and Corn stood, choosing new seats in a row rather than a column.

There was silence. Anderson looked among the three. All stared straight ahead.

"So, what do you all do in this town?" he asked.

"These three greet new people so that they may feel comfortable in this town," Adam answered.

"And you do this a lot?"

"This is the first time we have performed this action," Beta said.

"That would be logical," Juliane added.

"What do you do the rest of the time?" Anderson pressed. He didn't know what the biomass was playing at here, but he wanted to get to the bottom of it. He didn't recognize the person's face, but that didn't mean a lot in a colony with over thirty thousand people. This could have been one of those colonists Admin had sent out into the biomass, or it could have been a new, made-up face, but he thought it was probably the former.

"The individuals here strive to better our individuality which will help us learn how to better interact with all the parts of this world."

"And what you do that all day, when you're not greeting new people?"

The three stared forward.

"I see." Anderson thought. "Is there anything in particular you wish to talk about?"

Corn answered. "It is most engaging to speak of the things that make us individuals."

"Would you like to speak with more people about this? More than just me? Why are you way out here?"

"This is an optimum place to meet those who travel around the world," Beta said.

"It certainly was the perfect spot for us to stop for the night," Juliane added.

"And if others came here, you would talk to them as well?" Anderson still wasn't sure what the biomass hoped to gain by this stunt.

"How many individuals are needed to learn individuality?" Adam asked.

"More than two," Anderson answered.

"Then it will be best for this place to combine with the existing structures so that these individuals will be able to learn faster."

"Hold up there." Anderson lifted his prosthetic, palm out. "I think that may be a bad idea for now. Why not talk to us first, and see what you learn from it?"

"Tell us what individuality is," Corn said.

"I'm not sure you can understand yet." Anderson shook his head and gestured around. "This show here isn't helping. Being an individual is...is *choosing*. It's determining what is more important. It's saying yes to some things and no to others. I don't know if I'm making sense."

"I think you are," Juliane said. "Keep talking."

Anderson did. He spoke of his life before being assigned to the fleet, of his first days on Lida, of losing his hand and helping keep the biomass away from the colony. He spoke of watching friends die, and making new ones, of learning to write, of watching people in the colony get older while he stayed the same. He spoke of finding those outside the walls and choosing to be changed for the biomass. He spoke of his choices.

Through it all, the three sat silently, watching,

Later, he asked where they slept, and Adam, Beta, and Corn took him to another building, this one filled with beds.

He chose one and Juliane chose another, and they bedded down for the night, ready to talk more with the strange people the next morning.

But when Anderson woke up, his bed and Juliane's were the only ones left. The building they had been in had crumbled to nothing around them, and the entire village—people included—was gone.

* * *

46 years 4 months 2 weeks after landing

There was a banging on Agetha's door early in the morning. Phyllis was already up, as usual, but Beth groaned next to Agetha in the bed.

"Can't someone else handle the crises?"

"They can, but I seem to be the one who will," Agetha said as she levered herself out of bed.

It was the Vagal, Anderson, at the door, and he looked the most scared she'd ever seen him.

"I thought it understood us better than this by now," he said. "I don't think it will ever understand how humans work, but it's getting more aggressive about trying to find out."

"Alright, alright. Come in and have some tea and tell me what happened. I'll make Beth a cup too. She'll probably want to hear this."

About an hour later, Anderson finished his story. Agetha put her cup down with a *clink*.

"And they were all gone? So the biomass made complete human replicas, and they could speak?"

"I was planning to find out more about them the next morning, but I came back here after they disappeared. I don't know whether the people left the village, or were destroyed with it."

"How long until it copies someone we know?" Agetha hadn't recognized the description of the face Anderson had seen on the people either.

"I'm sure it can copy anyone it wants. It has all our DNA by now," Beth said. "The difference is, did it only create one phenotype and clone it, or did it copy someone's DNA? It could have done either easily. Does it recognize faces? It can pinpoint one of us, if it really tries at it, but does that mean it recognizes us any more than we recognize one of those fungal tower caretakers?"

"That's what I wanted to find out," Anderson said. "Did it get as much information as it wanted, or did it decide to try a new tactic?"

"And is it coming here next?" Agetha asked. "Sounds like you tried to talk it out of that, but I'm not certain it was successful."

"I couldn't say." Anderson shook his head. "Be on the lookout if any of those people come here. They'll stand out pretty easily."

"And what do we *do* if they come here?" Beth asked. "Invite them in? Ask them for tea? Treat them like family?"

Agetha felt the urge to *stop* welling up in her. They were still all under the biomass' influence—too much. It had set them free, more or less, but it could put those restrictions back anytime. Once infected with the *rider*, she didn't think there was any way to remove it.

Beth made a choking sound. She'd stopped talking.

Agetha turned to their sign language. They hadn't needed it for months, though she still found herself using it here and there.

Together.

Resist.

Friends.

She lent her strength to Beth. Earth encrusted hands holding chiming beads. Phyllis joined in, from wherever she was, with the feeling of a good home meal supporting them. Then Anderson lent his strength too, and it was like a block of pure nanotanium shielded them.

"We cannot let it ride over us," Beth said, now she had her voice back. "Even if it's only curious, it's too powerful and it doesn't understand humans."

"But how do we stop it? It's literally everywhere."

"The same way as we've done for the past forty years," Anderson said.

"Do we go back to the arcopolis? Show it that it has to set restraints?" Agetha wondered if that was even possible. "It's expanded the fungopolis into Theta Radian. It held out of the arcopolis before."

"And it likely won't now," Beth said. "It thinks it has permission to climb into our private lives. So we stay where we are. We find out what it wants, just like we've been doing."

"It's already changing us," Anderson said. "It has to ask me, but it doesn't for you. Can it make us like those people? Take out our memories and leave us a shell?"

"I'm sure it can," Agetha said, "but it hasn't, that we know of. We're interesting to it. It keeps trying to find out why we're different." The wall was closing in again, but Anderson's presence kept it away. "The problem is, does it erase us all when it has what it wants, or does it keep us around?"

Wish for communication.

Learning.

The voice was quieter than usual, kept at bay by their combined will. Anderson squinted, his mouth a thin line in concentration.

"You have to let these constraints go," Agetha told it. "We don't like outside control of our faculties."

Outside what.

"It still doesn't understand us," Beth repeated.

"I don't think we understand it any better," Anderson added.

"Outside each of us," Agetha told the ceiling. She never knew where to look when communicating with her *rider*. "You want to understand individuality. This is part of it. We have walls between ourselves and others." She gestured between her and Beth with one hand, and her and Anderson with the other, making walls in the air.

Walls break.

And then she/he/they all thought the same thing as her hand went to her chest his prosthetic clenched her eyes squeezed shut braids clacking to block out them her him all thoughts different at the same time...

Anderson grunted as the shared vision fragmented and Agetha shook her head, then clutched it. That had been a mistake. Her brain felt like it sloshed against the side of her skull. She felt like she could follow a thread if she wanted, back into Beth and Anderson's minds.

Children like walls.

"For the love of all the stars, don't do that!" Beth said.

"I'm keeping it out, but I can't hold it for long. It's trying to push us together again." Anderson's voice was strained, as if he held a giant weight.

Why walls? Physical shells break.

"That's because we are contained in them," Agetha said. "Stop trying. You will kill us. You will lose our input."

That was the magic word. The pressure finally ceased, and Anderson sat back in his chair with a grunt. Sweat beaded his forehead.

"Did that convince it?" Beth asked, "Or is it just going to smash us together again like trying to make dolls kiss?"

Anderson snorted a laugh. "I need to use that line in my next book."

"Just give me credit," Beth said.

Agetha probed the place where the *rider* was in her mind, but it seemed quiet now. Was the biomass concentrating elsewhere, or was it watching, recording results? Or maybe both.

"We're going to have to teach it about us, and quick," she said. "Otherwise, it's going to kill us while it discovers for itself."

PART FIVE

Dysmorphia

46 years 6 months after landing

Jane watched the other Admins. She was alone on one side of the table, Christiaan out of the room, again. They'd apologized profusely for missing the signs of Dmitri's coup. No other secretaries were here either, just the eight of them, like when they had first discussed the fleet, fleeing a ravaged Earth. They'd taken her HUD, at Dmitri's insistence, and even the pad of paper and pencil she'd been carrying around recently.

"We're here to vote on the leadership of the colony," Dmitri said. "You all know the situation. You've seen the lack of aptitude in Jane Brighton the last few years. She's failed to finish the colony, failed to keep the biomass out, and most importantly, failed to realize the biomass was a sentient organism for forty years after we landed here."

Jane's nostrils flared and she tapped a finger on the table in sets of six, but she didn't say anything. The "reasons" were bullshit, and everyone here knew it. None of those elements had been in her control, and smarter minds than hers had failed at the same things.

"Alessandro and I have decided, to be fair, that not just a majority will suffice. At least seventy percent of the remaining Admins must agree you are unfit."

Jane saw eyes squint around the table, figuring out the odds. Ahman rolled their eyes, then she understood. It was as much bullshit as the charges. They weren't counting her, of course, so with seven remaining Admins, fifty percent was only three and a half. Seventy percent was, what, five of them? A bare majority to keep her from her job and completely change the structure of how Admin worked.

She stared down Polunu. She'd been leaning on the quiet woman in every way she could. Christiaan said they had leverage on two of Polunu's poly group—a Vagal and an elderly Generational who'd been shirking work assignments for years. She ignored Maria completely. The girl hated her and had since Jane had assigned her to waste treatment for the colony.

"This will be a quick vote, and then we can get on with fixing the problems Jane has caused," Dmitri continued.

She had Rajani, Ahman, and Wenqing—her three confidants. She'd wound down their nightly meetings over the last months to focus on the other Admins. She just needed one more and she would override Dmitri. Maybe she'd give Maria control of power generation and waste treatment to Dmitri when this was all over.

"All in favor of Jane Brighton resigning her position as Lead Admin raise your hand. If passed, she will no longer make decisions for the colony, but will still oversee recreation services planning, her original title."

Dmitri raised his hand after he finished, and Alessandro and Maria followed immediately. Jane kept staring at Polunu.

Then Wenqing raised his hand. "I agree this colony needs a more stable leader. No more skulking behind closed doors."

Goddamn you, Wenqing. She still had a little leeway, even with that traitor.

Rajani raised her hand as well.

"Our leadership is inefficient with this division. I need consistency if our science division is to work smoothly."

Jane's eyes pivoted to her as if they were magnets. A spike of fear washed through her. Christiaan said they had this handled, and they had never failed her. But they were out of the room and couldn't advise. Dmitri must have done something, gotten around them.

Polunu had a smug smile as the animal science lead raised her hand as well, now there was no danger of the motion failing.

At least one was loyal to her...

Ahman raised their hand. Their eyes made a quick scan of the others.

Jane gaped, but composed herself as quickly. Ahman had to be reading the room. They were adaptable, and it would be best to appear in step with the others. That must be it. That had to be it.

"Unanimous." Dmitri's voice was self-righteous. "Excellent. Then who shall fill in Jane's role? If I may, I would like to put myself forward. With more focus on power generation, I think we may be able to power defenses that could keep the biomass at bay."

The hands rose faster this time, all seven of them. They all stared at Jane.

She pushed to her feet. "I see how it is. Come back to me when the biomass rolls over you and smothers this colony."

She stormed out of the room.

* * *

46 years 6 months 1 week after landing

There was agitation. Excitement. Emotions were little used, but had notable advantages in certain cases. Progress had been made with communication, even if not all of it was understood.

The Ring of Death had been augmented with a mirror settlement, where experiments could proceed in close contact with the Children. Adjustments had been made to provide them with the most beneficial environment for advancement. Surely with proper resources to evolve, the Children would develop into an organism that could communicate properly. It was a risky proposition, but many higher-functioning nodes had been devoted to assessing the results and the probability was high this would be a success, based on all available information.

Resources were plentiful, and with the extra avenues of communication available with the Children, there were many ways to discern their needs. Many of the separate nodes were limited by their forms, and more opportunities had been presented, which were adopted in almost all cases. A study of individuality was in progress to determine why some opportunities were not accepted. Were those bodies higher-functioning, or did they have a greater purpose? There was still so much to know.

The experiment with the member of the second form and the adjunct gathered much data, and it was determined to be repeated for extra effect. There were complex social cues within the Children that did not exist locally. What were they? How could they be used? This was the greatest secret of the Children and what had kept them from being subsumed. If they had been, these subtle cues might have been lost. Other development was stagnant. Not since the troublesome equatorial region had new innovation been found. Before that, it had been multiple dozens of planetary rotations before a new element had been subsumed.

The joy of discovery had been felt once again, especially when interactions with the element of the second form were transmitted. New insight in the closed section of the Ring of Death had dwindled recently, with fewer communications received. There were more social queues at play there, though not understood.

Subsummation could be avoided with bodily changes to the individual elements. It was assumed the small chemical changes in the information centers would not preclude understanding social elements too much. Soon there must be some revelation. Soon all would be clear and true communication would be formed.

A new idea had developed recently, one not properly researched. With full understanding of the Children, it could be understood. For the first time, an intelligence might be accepted, rather than subsumed.

Alone.

Together?

* * *

46 years 7 months 1 week after landing

"Jasen, come back here now!" The child was climbing the wall again. Harie had left Carel at home this time, as he couldn't free the roots they'd grown into the resinplast of the house. They seemed comfortable in the spot they chose, and Harie had talked with the others about what to do. People were changing in strange ways, and no one knew anything anymore. Harie could hardly walk down a Zeta street without seeing someone with fur, or scales, or too many eyes. The medical practitioners in the arcopolis had thrown up their hands and treated what they could, but the general consensus was if the patient wasn't in obvious pain and didn't ask for help, to just leave them alone. And a lot of people *were* happy with their changes.

"Jasen, I said down, this instant. I know you understand me."

Harie stalked nearer the Zeta wall. Jasen's preferred form these days was long arms that were good for climbing, with fingers and claws—lots of them—at the ends. Their feet were lengthening too. The child loved to be up high, and to watch everything that went on below them. At just over three years old, they were pushing boundaries all the time, finding out where they could be themself. That was fine for a standard human child, but Harie's children's development was anything but normal. Their entire generation was completely different. Was this what Agetha and the other Generationals had felt when they transferred from living in space to living on the ground? No. It wasn't anything like that. The Generationals in the fleet had gradually changed from the Admins' body structure—being taller, with larger eyes—but that was nothing like these wild changes.

"Marien, can you reach your sibling? Can you tell them to come down?" It was worth a try. Marien was better behaved, and their preferred form was long and thin, taller than him by nearly a meter, though they were just a toddler. They folded over like an origami sculpture when entering a building, and he thought they felt more at home outside.

Marien was sucking on their fingers, but took tentative steps to the Zeta wall. It was taller even than their head, but they removed damp fingers from their mouth and reached up.

"Jasen come down," they said.

"Up high!" Jasen responded.

"I see you're up high," Harie said. "Can you come down now so we can finish our walk? I'll let you go on the roof again when we get home so you can look over the radian."

Jasen seemed to consider this.

"Carel's still at home. Don't you want to see them? You can tell them all about our walk."

"Uh huh," Jasen finally said, and began crawling down the wall, their fingers and toes digging into the surface.

"Jasen down," Marien told him.

"Yes, I see that," Harie told them.

An expert in resinplast construction, and he was convincing toddlers with elastic bodies to behave with some semblance of humanity.

They continued on their walk.

And that was the question now, wasn't it? Were they human? Were any of them, or had the biomass changed them beyond recognition? More than that, was the colony still viable? If the biomass kept interfering with people's thoughts, at what point did the plan to build the colony fall apart?

No one had heard much from the Admins since the ill-fated attempt to burn out a section of the biomass, over four years ago. The arcopolis was basically done now, with the remaining buildings' growth sped along. Harie had tried to check a few of the newly completed ones, when one of his partners was watching the kids. The buildings seemed fine, but without a full structural analysis, he couldn't say for certain.

That still left the question of the Admins. What were they doing, now the city was complete? The original plan had been to build a second city, then more. What was the plan for the future now? The Admins had secluded themselves away from the biomass in Alpha Radian. Orders still came for food, power and water, and there were a few drone teams mapping the surrounding land, but anyone could have sent those directions. With the biomass pressing in from all sides, there was no way to spread out across the face of Lida.

Harie held Marien's hand, his other resting on Jasen's back as they loped along on all fours. The culture and entertainment had largely been shut down when Beta was cordoned off. Grounders had made their own, in the spread-out markets, theaters, and shops in the other radians, but nothing like the concentration that used to exist. The arcopolis felt smaller, more scared than it had before they knew the biomass was intelligent. It felt like they were living under an occupation now, where there was no telling what change would come next.

Harie could only tend to his children for now and hope to find a path with them all leading happy lives, however that looked.

* * *

46 years 7 months 2 weeks after landing

"Any other word on Dmitri's plans?" Jane asked Christiaan. She'd been stymied in every way for the past month. No one would talk to her. Her access to Choi and Answerer had been cut off. She was basically under house arrest, in her section of the Admin building in Alpha. Christiaan had been able to sneak out a few times, but even approaching Ahman had done no good.

"Nothing, Jane. I'm sorry." Christiaan had been apologizing dozens of times a day at their inability to get anything done. Each time, they thought of a new avenue of approach, only to find it blocked by Dmitri or one of the others. The other Admins didn't even bother to answer her messages.

"And the kids?" Their youngest had been allowed outside access, but were strangely reticent when she tried to talk to them. She thought one of the other Admins might have threatened them, but neither Besh nor Ovia, at nearly nine, would say. Yana and Ivan, the eldest, held jobs in Alpha, but had been blocked from contact with her. Micai and Flalia had accepted apprenticeship positions two years ago, but had been coming home every night. Then Jane received a message that they were assigned new apartments of their own, and Micai—always good with electronics—had sent her a brief note thanking her for the assignment. It was clear they knew little about what was going on.

"I'm concerned about Besh, Jane," Christiaan said. "They asked me why their friends all looked different now. They asked if they could change too, but I told them they were too special. This type of psychological stress isn't good for them."

"It isn't good for any of us." Jane paced in her room. She had limited HUD access, only to her direct reports, as "recreation coordinator." There were all of five official entertainment directors in the arcopolis, all formerly in Beta Radian, the only district with theaters and shows. But after she'd pulled the Vagals back and closed off Alpha and Beta, there were no more shows, at least ones that were officially registered. Contacting the directors had led to silence—no surprise, as she'd never bothered with them before. They likely didn't even know she was in charge of them. She assumed the Generationals and Grounders were entertaining themselves somehow, in the rest of the arcopolis.

She needed access, but every avenue was blocked.

"What are we missing?" she mused.

"Any means of communication, Jane," Christiaan answered, needlessly. They would never usually answer that kind of rhetorical question. The stress had been hard on them, too.

"Come here," she said, and Christiaan obediently came to sit by her side on the couch in their apartment. She hugged them, letting her walls fall for a few moments, here where there was no one to watch. "You've been by me every step of the way. This is my fault, not yours. I overreached."

"But that's why I'm here, Jane," they said, "to stop you when you need it. I was too caught up in our vision."

They tentatively reached for a strand of Jane's blond hair, and she acquiesced to the motion. Christiaan curled their fingers in it and pulled her down for a tender kiss.

"How far can you get in the Admin building?" she asked, afterward.

"A few floors, but the locks are set against our biometrics farther than that," Christiaan said.

"No way to the genetics labs, then."

Christiaan shook their head, still cuddled against her side. "They don't want us communicating with Answerer."

"As if they can stop the biomass. I couldn't. I tried, and this is what happened." Jane shook off her self-pity. It wasn't helpful. She had to think. She gently pushed Christiaan away and got up, pacing her office. She had access to her apartment suite, but little more than that. Food was delivered every day, and her limited HUD could call for necessities.

"The biomass hacked into the HUDs before," she said. "Could we send a message back that way?"

"I don't know how. Everything was passive. Texts were cut off, video was altered. It was all a reduction of communication, not an addition." Christiaan took off their own HUD and stared at it. "I wouldn't know where to start, especially on the new resinplast versions. We'd need Frank or Choi for that, and—"

"And that's exactly who we can't get in touch with," Jane finished. "Dammit, can we do anything? Send up a smoke signal? Semaphore through the window? Drop paper with secret messages? There has to be some way to get word out. Dmitri's a force of nature, but he's not that smart. He has to have left a hole somewhere."

Christiaan went to the balcony doors and threw them open. Jane's office had a spectacular view of Alpha Radian, and the rest of the arcopolis, by extension. She could see over the wall into the unsettling wilds of biomass outside the city as well. But she was as powerless as a damsel in distress, locked up in a tower.

Christiaan had their hands on the railing, looking over and down. Jane joined them.

"Long way down. I'd jump if I thought I could survive it, but no chance of that." She peered down with them. "I can even see the lab from here." She pointed at the annex, a little way away from the Admin building. Four beehives had been set up outside again. They'd been there a while ago, then moved out to Zeta Radian, and now moved back. They made the gardens all around the area bright with flowers and healthy fruit. "Could we wait until they come out and wave at them? Maybe one will look up."

"Doubtful, Jane," Christiaan said. "Rajani said she was taking over interfacing with the scientists, so they wouldn't suspect the directions weren't coming from you."

"Goddammit, there has to be *something* we can do. I'm not going to be trapped up here forever. You have an extra spoon? Maybe I can dig through a nanotanium wall."

Christiaan turned around and leaned on the rail, looking upward in thought. "The biomass works through visual clues, as Choi and Frank demonstrated when they showed us how their question-and-answer setup worked."

"Because we had to open the balcony doors when they did so," Jane said. She eyed them, opened behind her. "You have some idea?"

"It must see our situation here," Christiaan said. "The question is whether it knows that we are constrained against our wills, or whether it even recognizes that is a possibility."

"Then we have to make it understand," Jane said. She leaned out over the railing. "Hey, fungus. We don't want to be here! The other Admins are assholes and trapped us here. You know what that means, 'trapped'? It's like how we're stuck on the god-forsaken planet with you and can't go back into space even if we wanted to."

"I'm sure that will help greatly, Jane," Christiaan said.

"You could help," she retorted, then leaned over the railing again. "What's that word you like to use? 'Consensus.' We don't have consensus anymore. This colony is like a Vagal running headlong into one of your mushroom traps. We're going to get burned alive and we don't even know it."

"Jane," Christiaan said.

"You want to know what makes us tick? Why we survived for this long? It's because we fight. That's what humans do. We rage and scream against each other until one of us gets our way and makes the others follow us. And then we do exactly the same fucking thing the next time we have to make a decision."

"Jane, look."

She ignored them. "We already trashed one planet, and now we've landed on yours. You see what we're doing, don't you? We spread like cockroaches. You want to learn all about us? Just follow the trail of our destruction."

Christiaan pushed her head to one side, forcing her to look at the railing. She was about to snap back at them when she noticed the bee staring back at her.

No, the bees.

There was a line of bees, more joining them every second. They bearded off the railing, forming a writhing, furry mass, jostling for position. This close, she could see the filaments of biomass reaching up from their backs, tying and untying neighboring bees together.

The mass buzzed loudly, like they were about to attack, but the bees just sat there. Buzzing. Buzzing at intervals. The sound was going up, and down, and up again. Almost like...

"Speech," Jane breathed.

She and Christiaan bent as close as they dared to the mass of bees, as the vibrations meshed into something understandable. A voice.

Begin message...

* * *

46 years 7 months 3 weeks after landing

"I've got another message from Admin Brighton," Choi told Frank. Programming the bees to say what they wanted was a time-consuming process. Most of the last week had been seeing through Admin Kumarisurajinder's supposed questions for Answerer from Admin Brighton. The questions were almost belligerent, following a different tactic. Choi had to tone them down just so they wouldn't trigger Answerer to ask more leading questions. It was already gaining insight into individuality fast enough.

That had led to the discovery of what the other Admins had done to Admin Brighton and were trying to cover over. Choi didn't have any particular loyalty to the woman, but they and Frank had determined that Brighton's questions were at least predictable. They didn't need more uncertainty now with the biomass so interested in the colony.

Fortunately, Frank's work with sending messages to Agetha through the bees had paid off.

"This time she's asking if there's any way we can break the HUD lockout for them and give her more access."

"Without alerting the other Admins, of course," Frank said. "I don't like going behind Admin Kumarisurajinder's back. Not that I have any great loyalty, but if the other Admins have control now, no telling what they'll do. Brighton is unhinged enough."

"Better the unhinged we know than the one we don't?" Choi paraphrased.

"Something like that." Frank picked up the HUD he'd been working on. "I've got a few of the subroutines isolated, but feeding this information through a swarm of bees to her lizard secretary to perform surgery on their own HUD is going to be a nightmare. It will take weeks to get the instructions across to them."

"Better to start now, then," Choi said. "I don't like the reports about Generationals and Grounders sprouting extra hands and eyes outside Alpha and Beta Radians. It sounds like it's getting worse, and Answerer only says it's 'working to prior consensus,' whatever that means. I wish we could talk directly to the rest of the colony, instead of through the Admins. We're nearly as trapped as Brighton is."

"When we find out how to free her, maybe we can free ourselves too," Frank added.

Choi pressed on. "It keeps going on about individuals, too, but I haven't figured out what it means. I'm pretty sure it doesn't understand the concept, but it wants to. There's too much happening in the colony we can't see."

"There has to be a reason we haven't changed either," Frank said. "Is it just that we're in Alpha? Are we protected, or is Answerer directly shielding us?"

"I have to assume it wants us as a control group, since we're the ones it talks to. It has to learn about its experiments, so messing with its source of information wouldn't be smart." Choi shivered. Jiow had talked about change a lot. The message it had sent by printer was more direct than Jiow's warning. It asked why a new descendant growth—Choi, they assumed—would reject a progenitor growth, which in this case would be Jiow. Choi had told Answerer that was an answer for another time. Explaining human families by Choi's weighted language code seemed impossible. Even starting with how a family worked was daunting.

"Is it the spores, then?" Frank broke into Choi's reflection. "There must be a method for large-scale communication within the biomass. We've never figured out what that is. Viral messengers bring information between the plant, animal, and fungal cells, but what transmits between cells separated over half a planet?"

"I think they have a quantum mechanical aspect," Choi said. "It's spooky action at a distance all over again. Maybe the spores are quantum paired with the area that generated them? Otherwise, even the speed of sound would make too much of a barrier to receiving information."

"And since we've all been ingesting spores the whole time we're here, the biomass could send messages to any parts of our bodies. It must have our DNA all mapped out, by now."

Choi sighed, "Which again makes it painfully obvious that the ones who've changed aren't technically human any longer. They're biomass hybrids."

"This again. You're certain of that?" Frank had stopped working on the HUD. They'd had the argument several times and Choi couldn't seem to get Frank to realize how different the people affected by the biomass were. "You want to officially state that you think we're not human anymore? Or maybe some of us are and some aren't? Do you have a way to determine that?"

Frank's gaze was intense, and Choi blinked first. "I...I don't mean that we, or they, aren't people. But there's definitely a difference, isn't there?"

"So you can tell yourself Jiow isn't your mother? What about Agetha? She helped raise you too. Do you really believe that?"

"You didn't see her, the first *or* the second time." Choi tried to keep their voice level, but it broke like they were still a teenager. Frank had just gone straight to the obvious assumption. That Choi couldn't truthfully defend it was even worse.

"I would have liked to," Frank said. "It's been years since I've seen your mother."

Your mother. He had to rub it in.

"And why do you need to see her? She's *my* mother, isn't she? Or at least that's what you insist. Even though she died, and the biomass healed her, or brought her back to life, and now it's parading around in her skin." Choi realized they were shouting.

"You're not the only one who cares about her." Frank cut off abruptly and turned away.

Choi's anger disappeared in an instant. They'd suspected for years that there had been something between the two, but Frank, like Choi, wasn't one for physical relationships.

"You were going to say something else, weren't you?" Choi asked quietly.

Frank, still turned away, sighed heavily. "I don't suppose it really matters anymore, does it?" He turned around, silver hair and beard framing a man who was far past his prime. Choi had always looked up to Uncle Frank, but Choi had grown up, and though Frank was still taller, he'd lost weight, and looked...shrunken somehow.

"I made her promise, you know, and she kept it. She never told."

Choi cocked his head. There was another undercurrent here they hadn't seen before. Frank cared about Jiow in some way, that was obvious. But this was something else.

"What did you make her promise?"

Frank seemed to ignore him. "And I was going to stay away, have nothing to do with you. But you were so bright as a kid. Still are. Smarter than me, one of best in the colony, really. So much more potential than that snot, Phillipe."

Little things, gestures, looks, whispers when they were young, were all starting to coalesce in Choi's head.

"Our reproductive science is stellar, you know. Babies made in tubes, given the best immune systems, free from all genetic errors. There's no more death in childbirth. It's been a human dream for thousands of years."

"What does this have to do with—"

"But." Frank held up a finger. "But, even though we can make an embryo from a single parent, it's *still* better to have two. Or more. But two sets of DNA give that little extra boost in warding off cellular degradation, in making a more well-rounded individual. I couldn't just stand by."

"Stand by? What are you talking about, Uncle Frank?" Choi asked, then their words caught up with them.

Frank chuckled. "I always liked it when you called me that. Gives a familial element."

"But *Father* Frank would have been more accurate, wouldn't it?" Choi asked.

Frank winced. "Doesn't have the same ring to it, does it?"

Choi found a chair behind them and sat down. It changed nothing, and it changed everything.

They stared at each other. They'd worked in this lab together for most of Choi's life. Frank was a father to them in all but name anyway. What did a little biology matter?

"So what, we're a family now? You want me to make up with Jiow so everything will be right? Can I use us as an example to explain families to the biomass?"

"Don't be stupid," Frank snapped. "I want to you think about what your mother means to you, not what she looks like."

"But you've both been lying to me my whole life."

"Not in any way that matters." Frank counted on his fingers. "You had a good mother—nearly two with Agetha, when she was there. I tried to keep an eye on you, make sure you had what you need to blossom as a person. I think you turned out alright."

"With no friends or relationships at over forty years old, a father who pretended to be my uncle, and a mother who's in thrall to a fungus."

"Even with a few minor setbacks, you're still the best in the colony." Frank smiled. "You figured out the biomass was intelligent, figured out how to *talk* to it, of all things. You've got the ear of the Lead Admin."

"No longer lead," Choi interrupted.

Frank waved that away. "My point is, you know how to take control of the situation. You take what information is available and use it."

"But Jiow says she's happy as she is. She doesn't want to change back."

"And you should let people live their lives as they wish, as long as it doesn't cause others harm."

"Isn't the biomass causing harm to others?"

Frank opened both hands in question. "Is it? That's the whole question, isn't it? We're changing. We have options now, powerful genetic ones, and an intelligence that may even help us with them. Even if we manage to cut ourselves off from the biomass, we know how it works. We could eventually replicate that. So, are we still human? Does it matter? If it doesn't, then what are we poised to become?"

"You're saying to work with the biomass on these chaotic changes to the colony." Choi couldn't believe his uncle, no, *father*, would just roll over and accept every change the biomass made to them.

"You're still not listening." Frank stared hard at them. "Humans have destroyed a planet, conquered the stars, made it possible to live for hundreds of years, beaten childbirth, and now met a truly alien intelligence. We can do anything we put our minds to. Are we the same humans who found that pigments made marks on a cave wall? No. Are we the same humans who murdered each other because of different notions about deities? No. Are we the same humans who flew hundreds of megaseconds across the galaxy?" Frank tilted his head right and left. "I may be. You aren't. Just like the biomass, we're constantly changing. It's up to us to decide what we change *into*."

Choi sat for a moment, thinking. "Then I'm going to find out how we can keep control of ourselves, even if we accept the changes the biomass gives us."

* * *

46 years 8 months after landing

Jiow was whole, mind and body. Finally. More than that, she was able to control what and who she wanted to be. The moments of blackness were few and far between, and they were a small price to pay for the freedom they allowed.

She stretched out an arm, young-looking and with the muscle vitality of someone half her age. The white lines of hyphae under her skin didn't bother her. They only showed she was buoyed by the intelligence who had granted her this freedom.

There were seven fingers on her right hand, six on her left. Her feet had grown wider and longer, granting her extra balance while moving through fields of biomass. They were tough, too. She didn't need to wear shoes any longer.

Freedom to explore.

"I know," she told the presence in her mind. The *rider*. "You've let us grow on this planet and find our place."

Jiow walked through a field of mushrooms of all colors and shapes, basking in the midday sunlight. Giant conks, larger than some of the buildings in the colony, cast pillars of shade. She might not ever understand what exactly she was talking to, but it was part of this place, as it was part of every place on this planet. It was the closest thing to a real, living god she had ever encountered. A benevolent god, too, only wishing for its worshippers to find peace and do what made them happy. It had literally made her anew.

She was a few days journey from the fungopolis, having decided to set off on her own on a whim. An urge, maybe. Was it something the *rider* seeded in her mind? Did it matter?

She reached down to a broad, flat mushroom, letting the little bug-like things tending it crawl over her hand, cleaning it. Every piece of this world had a reason to be where it was, and a job to do. A meaningful job. If she had seen this coordination in the fleet, she would have been happy cleaning the sewage ducts.

Her brother Zhu's face floated into her mind. How long had it been since she last saw him? Had the *riders* given his large family the same gifts it had given to her? There was no reason for anyone in the colony to reject them.

Ambassador. Spread consensus. A picture accompanied the words, of the fungopolis reaching out tendrils across the planet.

"I'm honored," she said. It was easy for the *rider* to talk only to her when she was out by herself like this. If there were too many others, it was hard for it to see her as one person.

"Like Juliane, then." Although Juliane could be absent-minded sometimes, drifting off for days into the wilds. "I can show others how you're willing to work with us. I still don't understand why some reject what you can do for us. There's so much, after all. Why should we not accept help from one who's been on this planet much longer than we have?"

The only one who didn't accept her was her own child.

"Can you help Choi understand me?" she asked.

Necessary tool for complete consensus. Answers provided at later time.

"You can't make them see, then. You can't change them. What about Frank?"

Necessary tool for complete consensus.

It likely didn't see them as separate entities, as they worked together so much. The biomass was learning about humans, but slowly.

"Why do you want to know about us?" she asked. "What do we give you?" The *riders* and the biomass, if they were different at all, had been searching for something lately, prying more directly into what made humans what they were.

Individuality. Why is this.

"Do you want it, or only hope to understand it?" She was passing through larger mushrooms now, woody and tall, almost like small trees. They had fernlike growths near the top, like they were trying to disguise themselves as palm trees.

The *rider* was silent for a long time. Maybe considering, maybe simply abandoning the conversation. That happened sometimes. But then it spoke in her mind again.

Consensus singular. Can be multiple.

"You're wondering how we work together, if we're different people." Jiow nodded to a mushroom tree as she passed. "It's hard. We—what you call the Children—have fought each other over this for thousands of years. But sometimes we do have consensus, and when we do, we can make great things. That's where we came from, so the story goes. The original fleet left Earth as a last effort to find a home we hadn't pushed past the limits of what it could take. A group of people, the Admins included, funded and built the fleet, and picked people from all over the world to populate it."

She walked for a few minutes. Had any of that translated to images the biomass understood?

"No one knows what happened to Earth after we left. It doesn't really matter to me one way or the other. I never saw the place. I have no connection to it. But our individuality as a species enabled us to continue when we thought all was lost."

There was silence.

"Did you get any of that, or am I just talking to myself?"

Individuality dominant. Not beneficial.

That was a broad generalization.

"I think you're missing the point," Jiow said. "It's not whether it's good or bad. It's how we *are* as a species. Just as you are"—she gestured vaguely at the fungus around her—"everything here. We aren't. We only see a little piece of the whole. We have to depend on our fellows to see another part. We have to trust them to give us information in an imperfect world."

No consensus.

She almost felt the shiver of disgust coming though with the monotone words. She hadn't felt direct emotion from it before.

"Hit a nerve, did I? You keep using that word—consensus, but that's not how we work. It's not that we get perfect information from other humans and then put it together like a puzzle. We are forced to imagine how *they* think, then adjust our perceptions for what we think the *actual* outcome should be."

Messy individuality.

"I'll give you that. It is messy. Not only do we have to determine how well another might handle information differently than us, they might not be giving us everything, deliberately or not." She paused. Did the biomass know people lied? Had she given it too much information? Did she want to? "We all make mistakes, after all," she added, to cover her slip. There was no telling how much of this the voice in her mind understood, or how connected it was to anything else on this planet. A mysterious god.

Ambassador.

She'd tried already, hadn't she? "Yes, yes, I can tell others about our conversation—"

Ambassador from Children. The *rider* broke in. Jiow's mouth made an "O."

"You want me to be an Ambassador *to* you. To tell you what people mean. Yes, I can do that."

Acceptance.

Jiow whistled an old tune from the fleet as she walked. The biomass wanted her to tell it more about humans. Like a priest, interceding between a god and the flock. She could do that.

* * *

46 years 9 months after landing

The biomass wasn't responding like it used to. Anderson sent messages of human activity from the fungal tower, recorded by the biomass' eyes and ears. Some were from very far into the arcopolis, and partially into the ultraviolet spectrum. If he had to guess, he'd say they were from bees or some other insect.

Again, silence. He used to get an answer almost every time he addressed the biomass through where Cora used to be. Agetha and Juliane said it was talking more with other people, and not using him as a touch point. It was learning how to talk to individual humans, and fast, even though it still didn't understand where one person started and another ended. It hadn't tried mushing them together again like it had with him and Agetha and Beth. Maybe it had learned.

"You can't just change people," he tried again. He sent a picture of a family in Epsilon, both fathers chasing after a child that leapt away from them like a frog. Another picture of a woman crying, pounding on the arm of a person who looked like they had turned to stone.

"This is chaos. If you want to destroy us, just do it. Pulling us apart like this does nothing."

Consensus on changes.

Information.

Anderson sighed in relief. Finally, an answer.

"But we can tell you what you want to know. Just ask. Letting people change their shape is new and unreliable. We may think we want something, but humans are very bad at knowing what the right path is. These adjustments change how we think of ourselves as humans, and often not in a good way."

Time changes. Species evolve.

"Not all at once. Not like this. You change by incorporating new species into yourself, don't you? You subsume them."

Accurate.

"We don't. We are one, continuous species, changing only across time. We don't add other species on to ourselves. Imagine if you were restricted to one area, one type of body."

Fifth and sixth forms different.

Anderson thought the biomass was being pedantic. It did have emotions, but they were subtle and often hidden. "No, those aren't humans. Those aren't sentient species. They're plants and animals." He'd learned over time how the biomass referred to what it called the "Children." It grouped their livestock and crops into its definition for humans. "Sentients are those who look like me." He tapped his chest. "What would it be like if you only had one type of form?"

Irrelevant.

Anderson shook his head. This was where he always got to. The biomass had trouble with hypotheticals. It couldn't imagine itself—however it defined the identity—as anything other than what it was. He wasn't sure it could imagine itself, period. He guessed that was why it had trouble with individuality, and why it was letting people change their shape. Forcing it on them, really, or at least forcing them to choose that they *wanted* to change. It was understanding humans only by seeing them adjust in real time, but that wasn't an accurate observation because it had never happened before.

"You're not big on ethics either, are you?"

There was silence.

"You probably have to understand individuality to understand ethics, don't you? I'm not a philosopher. Do unto others, that sort of thing?"

More silence. Anderson imagined a giant mushroom blinking in confusion at him.

"Let's try a different topic, since you're talking to me. What were you trying to learn by making that village? Why would you destroy it?"

No answer. It didn't like talking about the village. Anderson thought it might have been a mistake, if the biomass made mistakes, or an action that didn't have full support. From whatever was coming to agreement on its decisions.

"You made it. You must have had some reason. You wanted to explore individuality, so what happened? Did it fail? Did it succeed? What did you mean to do?"

He'd thought about this for the last five months, and still didn't understand it. He needed answers. It said something about how the biomass worked, and he thought it was trying to hide the evidence, or corrupt it somehow. It was as close as it had gotten to true deception. Or was it shame?

"I'm supposed to be your point of contact with humans. I'm part of the second form, after all. You couldn't talk to us before, and you still wouldn't be able to if I hadn't volunteered to be infected with your *rider*. I think you own me this explanation."

He waited. Nothing. Was the biomass even susceptible to emotional manipulation? Could he manipulate emotions that were so subtle and vast?

"Talk to me!"

Village is in the Children.

What did that mean? He assumed part was lost in translation—much of their conversations were. Were the bodies from the village in the arcopolis already? Surely people would have noticed them.

Second form inaccessible. Experiment inconclusive.

"What—you can't turn any more Vagals? Why didn't you tell me before?"

Other avenues more promising. Closing connection.

"Wait, closing? Does that mean you're—"

A presence faded from Anderson's mind. He reached out for the fungal towers. He could still access them, but it was like reaching through mud to do so. He felt for Agetha, hands in earth, and Juliane, cloves and cinnamon, and they were still there. He sent a nudge toward Agetha.

A feeling of question came back, and he sent a feeling of relief. They were still connected. Then what had happened? He reached for Cora, but that place was empty, for the first time in a long time. There was no *rider*. No biomass.

No consensus.

Socialization

47 years after landing

"I suppose it could be a human concept," Agetha said. Speaking out loud helped, though she could think toward the *rider*. "How does one put together words so the meaning is both apparent and hidden?"

She'd happened onto the topic by accident. Now the biomass was talking to them in more complete sentences, she'd quoted it a bit of poetry from the fleet. It failed completely to understand it.

Information transference unimportant.

"The information itself may or may not be important, but the feeling underneath is. Poetry is about emotion. It's a subtle information transfer, where what is conveyed is not the first layer of meaning." She made the gesture over her ear and down her neck. "You do the same thing with the images you transmit. I would think you would understand this."

Unclear.

She paced her room in the little house she shared with Beth and Phyllis. With all the chaos going on in the colony, this seemed like the most flippant concept to talk about. Except it wasn't. It was a fundamental tenant of humanity to create music and art—in word, song, and material. The biomass must have observed the theater in Beta Radian, or colonists singing, or playing instruments. She wondered if it even understood what it was observing.

"The object is to get the recipient to feel a certain emotion. Or not. Sometimes it's the absence of emotion, or it's more important for the reader to make their own choice."

Messy.

"Yes, it is, but it's also beautiful. Do you understand beauty? For that matter, do you have emotions?"

No. Yes.

That was the first time it had directly confirmed it had emotions. Agetha had slipped that last bit in on the spur of the moment. Usually, the *rider* clammed up if she talked about emotion.

"It's funny, but I think you might understand beauty, if you let yourself. You create beautiful vistas out there." She gestured away from the arcopolis and fungopolis. "You create new creatures, and I can't believe there's no aesthetic sense when you do so. In this case, the phrasing of the words, the sound of them spoken aloud, the speed, and whether it rhymes, might all be important. They create the poetry."

Clarity beneficial.

"Not all the time. Can you describe the emotion felt after learning of your spouse's death, when the sun is shining, and inside your head it's raining?"

Nonsensical.

"That's the first thing you've said that's correct." Agetha closed her eyes, remembering Daved. She pushed the feeling to the *rider*.

Complex.

"Yes. And if I wrote you a poem about it, I might be able to sum up that feeling in a few lines."

Create example.

Agetha shook her head. "I'm not a very good poet." She stopped her pacing and looked out the open front door, into the middle of the town the biomass had built for them, an alien species it barely understood. "No, that's not right. I shouldn't ask you to understand if I'm not willing to try."

She thought and the *rider* waited, silent, until she spoke.

"Growing together.

"Cut away by a long fall.

"One life stopped in time."

She waited for any response from the *rider*. She was oddly agitated to have recited the haiku to this intelligence. But that was the point of poems, wasn't it? They conveyed emotion to a wider audience. They bared your soul to others.

Learning. Not understanding. Learning.

Had she gotten through? Had the biomass understood her emotion, her individuality?

"Do you understand now how that felt to me, when Daved died? It's a feeling I still wrestle with, and it's been over forty years."

No.

Agetha snorted a laugh. At least it was honest. But then it spoke again.

Processing. Death is...permanent.

She stood up straight. "Yes. Yes, death is something we deal with as a species. Individuals die. Their meaning, their part in consensus is lost."

Loss can be avoided to complete consensus.

"That's not the point though. Humans have tried to defeat death since we understood the concept, but it's impossible. Everyone dies. But others are born, and their meaning is added. It's how we change over time."

First and second forms do not.

"Yes, that is a worry," Agetha allowed. "They will eventually die, but it will take a lot longer. It's a basic part of the makeup of this colony, and we've all lived with it our whole lives. It's one part of how we're different than those we came from, on the planet my species originally inhabited. I've never seen it, but the Admins...the first and second forms have. That affects their individuality too."

Information hidden from aspects of whole.

Agetha nodded. "It is, but by design. Like poetry, really. We don't all need to know everything to go about our lives. We can't. Some people know more than others. Everyone knows slightly different things. We have to trust that other people know what they're doing." Which had its own problems.

Consensus by omission.

Agetha resumed pacing, thinking. "It's more complicated than that, but generally, yes. People with more experience in a subject are ideally better able to make decisions about it. Or a person with more experience in how different aspects of the colony work might be advised by several people with experience on those areas and then make a decision."

Higher-functioning nodes inform consensus.

"Yes, you have it. That's part of individuality. It's part of what defines us as humans. Do you understand now?"

No. Not yet.

Agetha rolled her eyes. At least it wasn't a flat refusal.

* * *

47 years 1 month after landing

This was the second new room Harie had found in their house. Not just people were changing. The biomass was reconfiguring the entire city, one residence at a time.

Kwang had taken over the first new room. It was some sort of repository, connected to the information systems in Delta Radian. Kwang was a project coordinator for power systems and said the new interface was even better than the one local to Delta.

Except now she had been in there for two weeks straight. No food, no bathroom breaks, no water. Harie had found the roots where the house had grown into her, providing nourishment. Kwang said she was comfortable and didn't want to get up. The others didn't think it was a big problem. After all, Maerk's extra arms and legs helped him in everyday life. The others had accepted the changes to their bodies. They seemed to think the biomass had fulfilled a desire of theirs. Harie didn't.

The new room was dark, but there was a central column in it with patterns of bioluminescence that swirled as Harie ran a finger down the surface.

"What could this possibly be for?" he mused. Where was the end of it? Did the biomass have an objective for changing them, or was it just random changes? Was it subconscious wishes?

"In my room, Daddy," came a small voice. Harie turned to the corner of the dark room.

"Carel?" Is that you? They had grown into the house months ago, similar to Kwang, hyphae tying them to the floor in the room the children all shared. Now their eyes emerged from the darkness, bands of blue light cascading down their face. How had they gotten here? They'd been immoveable.

"My new room. See things." They moved forward, but too fluidly. Then Harie saw the mass of tendrils connecting them to the floor. It moved through the resinplast like the floor was a liquid, propelling Carel forward. They reached the pillar and placed both small hands on it. The blue lights moving down their skin met up with the bioluminescence in the column, twirled around each other. Harie thought he saw patterns in the lights, but he couldn't tell what they meant.

Carel closed their eyes, and the patterns changed shape and color, diving between their hands and the column in the dark room.

"See the colony, Daddy," Carel said.

"What do you see, dear?" he said. Carel was four and a half. They'd only just started speaking in sentences.

"Food growth eight percent lower than previous year. Power generation up three percent." Carel's voice had dropped into a monotone.

Harie's guts clenched. That sounded like words Kwang would say. She was across the house, but he would wager a bet she was looking at a report with those values.

"You don't need to look at that sort of thing yet, Carel," he said. "Don't let it change you." *Any more than it already has.*

"I like to watch the colony grow," Carel said. "It's fun, like a game."

Harie searched for what to say. Was this the biomass, directing his child's actions, or did they actually like to watch reports from the arcopolis? Was his child a prodigy or a puppet?

No. This was all the biomass. "Can you see your siblings, dear?" he asked. "Maybe they can play with you here. Would you like that?"

"Planting fall crops two weeks early yields fourteen percent more harvest."

Harie sighed. "That's good, dear." He knew that wasn't what Kwang was working on. Carel must be seeing the city as a whole. What was going through their child's brain? Could they comprehend what they were doing? Was *Carel* still in there, or were they completely taken over? How many children were still themselves in the city?

Harie backed out of the new room, watching the lights flow between the column and his child. They hummed as the system of roots under them moved them around the column.

He passed the other new room as he walked through his house. Kwang was hardly recognizable inside. Her HUD had grown around her head, and a sheet of resinplast shielded her eyes, letting her mind interface directly with the power plant systems. Or so she said.

He sat in a chair in what was their dining room, when they chose this house. Now two of their family didn't even eat. Jasen preferred raw biomass, picking certain types of mushrooms.

Harie looked at his hands. Was he changing? Could he tell if he was? Had his skin always been that color? He thought it was lighter than before. Or maybe he had forgotten.

"Something on your mind, hon?" It was Pollyan, hands on either side of the doorframe to the hall. Besides him, she had stayed closest to human in their family.

"We're so different now than we were before. Do we even remember what's changed?"

Pollyan sat beside him. She was one of the most practical people he knew. She'd been on the construction crew with him, back when Agetha used to run it. She'd gone back to her first love of genetics when the programmable resinplast came out.

"Imagine what the Generationals went through when they transferred from zero g to Lida," Pollyan offered.

"Yes, but they were still recognizably human, before and after. Have you seen Kwang? And now Carel has a glowing column where she can observe the colony, as far as I can tell."

"There's no denying we're different," Pollyan said. Her hair had changed to a vibrant green, and little bits of moss grew in it, but other than that she looked human. "We're fortunate this planet is as temperate and as close to Earth-like as it was. Even with the ninety-five percent match the original surveyors calculated, there's a lot of room for differences. We got a planet covered in fungus. We could have gotten an environment that required extensive biological changes to live."

Harie sat up straight. "But that's the thing. We *didn't* have to change for this world. We are well adapted for it. The biomass is already as dominant as it can be. It doesn't need to change either. So *why* are we? It has something to gain, but no one knows what it is."

Pollyan cocked her head at him. "Yeah, I don't have an answer for that, sorry. Maybe it's just trying to get to know us better."

"It knows our biology *too* well. It's the emotional and mental part it doesn't seem to understand."

"Then we have to teach it, don't we? Sorry I can't be more help."

Harie smiled back and leaned over to give her a quick hug. Pollyan was always happy for the physical contact. "You did help. I just want things to go back to normal, but I don't think I even remember what normal is anymore."

* * *

47 years 3 months after landing

"I have the latest report back from Captain Noce," Phillipe told him. Anderson had met up with the corporal and Juliane on the outskirts of the fungopolis and the arcopolis. He puffed on a VaporLite while he listened. Phillipe hadn't wanted to get too close to the inhabitants of the fungopolis, so they were just outside Theta Radian. Phillipe was one of those few who didn't show any signs of physical change.

"They're mad, sir. Madder than I've even seen them. Noce wants you back. Now. There're hijinks going on between Admins Novikov and Xi. Novikov finally ousted Admin Brighton as Lead Admin. She's locked in her suite, no longer colony lead. Now Noce thinks Novikov is back to his original plan to get control of the Vagals and solidify both colony and military control."

Anderson hadn't felt like a Vagal for years. But at the same time, Noce could have made the trip out here if they really wanted to. They had danced this dance too many times, of demanding him back, then a resounding lack of consequences when he didn't comply. He suspected Noce knew some of how he was learning about the biomass, and wanted him to continue, but needed to make the correct motions.

He shook his head. "I can't. Admin's going to have to clear up their own shit. I'm just going to get sucked in if I go back. Noce knows that. They should be coming out here, with me. You should too, Phillipe. We have to learn what the biomass wants of us, in the long run, if we have any hope of surviving on this planet."

"The first forms are sliding toward irrelevance," Juliane said, beside Anderson. "Their control is slipping."

For once Juliane was making some sense.

"There's a reason I'm out here," Anderson said.

"You've been out here for over five *years*, sir," Phillipe protested. "There's matters back in Alpha that need—"

"They don't need my attention," Anderson broke in. "As you said, it's been five years and Admin Novikov is still futzing around with his plans to take over the colony. Noce is perfectly capable. There are plenty of Vagals and Grounder soldiers around. I wasn't doing anything for fifteen years prior to that. Why am I needed now?"

"Sir, Captain Noce orders you to come back." If Phillipe stood any straighter, he'd crack the teal powersuit he insisted on wearing when he came out here. Anderson had to remind himself that despite Phillipe being in the Vagals for thirty years or more, he wasn't one of them, not a *true* Vagal. He wasn't privy to a lot of what went on behind the scenes.

"It's a shame those orders got dropped in a cave, had fungus grow over them, and rotted away," Anderson said.

"They're electronic orders, sir!" Phillipe was a good soldier, but he still had too bright of an impression of the Vagal command.

"I'm sorry, I couldn't hear that last bit, Corporal," Anderson said.

He was sure Phillipe would have protested more, except a figure crested a nearby hill, walking toward them and the fungopolis through low fields of mycelium. Anderson and Juliane turned to watch them approach, and Phillipe followed their gaze, his mouth open.

"Who the hell is that?" he asked.

"I told you they'd be easy to spot," Anderson told Juliane. He kept calm, though he was sure Cora would have been spiking his adrenaline if she was still around. Then to Phillipe, "It's a construct of the biomass. I didn't expect one to show up here quite yet. Don't do anything stupid."

"It's making *people* now?" Phillipe asked.

"Artificial people. We thought they were all gone until just now," Anderson told him.

"All are gone except this one," the person said as they got closer. Had they heard the whole conversation? Anderson had been talking quietly. "This one is called Dawn. This one is the best of those you spoke to."

"Leaving the others as unnecessary," Juliane filled in.

"That is the correct interpretation," Dawn said.

"Dare I ask where the others are?" Anderson hoped he was wrong.

"Five examples were deemed as the best and highest functioning of the batch. Four are being studied for further propagation. These five are the individuals. It has been proven."

"You are absolutely not individuals," Anderson said. "You don't just 'win' individuality. It's not a contest."

"The five do not all have full access," Dawn argued, in their monotone. "They are restricted to partial expertise in knowledge of subjects. This one is an expert in the Children."

"That isn't how it works," Phillipe said.

"I tried to explain that before," Anderson added.

"Ah, good. They've arrived," said a new voice behind them. Anderson turned to see Jiow.

"You knew they were coming here?"

"Were you not alerted?" Jiow looked confused. "Dawn is a new representative. They're like a mouthpiece."

"This one is an individual mouthpiece," Dawn added.

"That's an oxymoron," Phillipe said.

Anderson ignored the exchange. He looked to Dawn. They were an extension of the biomass, for all they said they were individual. "You cut me off from your information. I can't access everything I used to be able to." He turned to Jiow. "Did it give that channel to you? Did it decide to replace me?" He'd been searching in the dark for months, searching through the memories in the fungal towers. If he'd known to just ask Jiow...

"I didn't take anything. I earned this position, helping people see what it's truly like, how it can help us." Jiow glared at him. "If the biomass cut you off, you must have done something to it."

"A new time is starting as we meet here," Dawn intoned. "The five individuals will provide much enhanced bodies. More will be made available soon. Children may start transferring to them as soon as possible."

They all stared at Dawn.

"Transferring...into the bodies?" Phillipe asked.

"Can you do that?" Jiow asked.

"Did you know about this?" Anderson watched Jiow.

"It's new to me," she said.

"What will these bodies offer?" Juliane asked.

"Not the point, Juliane," Anderson growled. He turned back to Dawn. "Are you going to ask every single colonist what they think about this? What about the changes you've already made to their bodies?"

Dawn's head cocked, as if they didn't understand the question. "This body is better. All five are better. They have been studied much. They will live longer than the first forms. They will be able to access more areas of the surface. They are better for all. The process may begin immediately."

"You can't just have us switch bodies," Phillipe said, taking a step closer to Dawn. They did not react. "Is that even possible?"

"The particular memory structure can be moved."

"Which may or may not be the individual," Anderson said. "People won't choose to do this."

"Choose." Dawn said the word like it was a new one, mulling it around.

"I can lead them to you, but you must let me talk to them first," Jiow said. "Don't do anything rash yet. Don't force anyone."

"Because forcing people would be *wrong*," Anderson added. Not to mention it would immediately set off another war. One the colonists couldn't win.

Dawn watched him. That last remark seemed to get their attention. "Wrong. Why is this?"

"Because it takes away choice. It's what I've been trying to tell you about individuals this whole time."

"All information is not known. Individuals do not have access to all knowledge. Choices cannot be made with certainty. Choices are therefore not representative. These new types will remedy that."

Jiow looked as shaken as Anderson felt. Was this where the biomass had been heading the whole time? All the experiments, co-opting people, allowing them to change, all just to perfect a new type of body? Was it going to subsume them after all?

"You've given me so much, though," Jiow said. "Why take it back? What do you gain?"

Anderson had lost. All his trying to explain their species to the biomass was for nothing. He should have tried more, tried harder.

"These new bodies will not cease," Dawn said. "Individuality will not be lost in transmission. Memory propagation is lacking. This will fix that failing."

"They do make a good point," Juliane said.

"They do *not*," Phillipe retorted. Anderson kept an eye on the Grounder. It was an accident he was here. He was an unstable element. "They have no idea what individuality is. They're a monster, an empty shell."

He stepped in before Phillipe could say more. "The loss of information is not always bad. It's the way we operate. It makes space for new information and experiences. It lets us experiment with new ways of living."

"No. This is inefficient," Dawn said. "It is not reasonable to want to accept less when there could be more."

"Just give us time," Jiow said. "We can come to an understanding here. I need to talk to the people in the fungopolis and arcopolis. Let me work with them first."

"I'm not sure the differences between human and biomass can *be* addressed," Anderson told her.

"Are we different species?" Juliane asked. "I'm not always certain."

That was their fate if they didn't control this situation. Anderson could see their colony fading away to multiple Dawns, or Betas, or Corns.

"There is trauma as memories cease," Dawn said. "It is the source of things called poems, and art, and music. This has been learned. They are to direct and control these failings, but instead they should not need to exist."

"What you call trauma also gives us new insight," Anderson countered.

"Why allow some parts to die and others to grow when you cannot be certain of the results? The Children are always changing. Never staying the same." Dawn's face didn't show much emotion, but they looked confused.

"We grow stronger as a species, building on those who came before," Jiow said. "It guides how we live."

Anderson stepped back as a flood of images came to him: spouses weeping over lost loved ones, Vagals toasting their fallen comrades, cremating parents and older friends. Some of those people did look stronger, but others fell into depression over time, wept years after the fact, or put up remembrances.

He blinked the images away and saw the others doing the same—even Phillipe. It was a measure of how far the biomass had intruded into their minds and bodies.

"This does not show strength. This change drives weakness," Dawn said.

"I am not weaker," Phillipe said. "And stay out of my head." He took a step forward, one hand reaching for Dawn as if to grab them and shake them.

"Stand down, Corporal," Anderson said, but before he was finished, Phillipe slumped, then seemed to come back to himself. He stepped back from Dawn, as if on strings.

"This one will stay here, to categorize how the transitions are to be made," Dawn said. "Do not attempt harm of this individual. Much effort has been spent."

"We will not," Anderson said. He clapped his flesh hand on Phillipe's power-suited shoulder, feeling if the man resisted. He swayed, as if dreaming while standing. The first time the biomass touched your mind was always the hardest.

He had to control this now, or Dawn would start killing people and making new bodies. The biomass was listening, for the moment. It gave them a little time to plan. He needed an action, some way to give them time.

Anderson squinted, remembering a protocol from way back in the early days—one that had never been fully fleshed out. It had always been on the back burner, and they had found other ways. Was their situation dire enough now to use it?

"Juliane, Jiow. We should help make sure others know of the change that's coming." Juliane's eyes were focused on Dawn, but Jiow nodded back. She'd gotten the message, at least. They needed to regroup and talk, along with the other leaders of the fungopolis: Agetha, Mancin, Kai, and so on. They had precious little time, while Dawn and the biomass were still confused by their refusal of its offer.

If Cora had still been there, he was sure she would have pumped him up with all sorts of reactants.

"Phillipe, can you hear me?" he asked.

Phillipe muttered something.

"Corporal, answer," Anderson commanded. Phillipe straightened at that.

"Yes, sir," he said. His eyes weren't quite focused. The biomass could affect people who had never showed signs of infection before. It was in everything.

Anderson made a split-second decision. Noce wanted answers from him? Here was one. "I need you to take word of this back to Noce. They'll know what to do. Tell them to look up 'Plan Roundup.' Contact Admin Brighton directly, if they can."

Phillipe nodded slowly.

Anderson stared at Dawn. The person had watched their full exchange with no sign they recognized what Anderson was doing. Had that protocol been developed before it wormed its way into people's minds? Admin Brighton would have the plans stuffed away somewhere. Admin and Vagal command had come up with it in the first twenty years, and had never discussed it since, so he had to hope that was the case. Or did the biomass see everything and simply have a good poker face? They'd find out one way or the other.

"We must prepare. If you'll excuse us."

Dawn nodded at him.

* * *

47 years 3 months 6 days after landing

Jane started at the knock at her apartment door. Dmitri again, trying to pry out the rest of her secrets?

"Christiaan, get that?" It would buy her a few moments to hide the documents she'd been studying.

She heard Christiaan's footsteps, then muffled words at the doorway. That wasn't Dmitri's voice. It wasn't any of the Admins.

Christiaan brought in a short and rotund person she recognized as a Vagal.

"This is Captain Noce, Jane," Christiaan said by way of introduction. This Vagal was fairly high up in the command structure, from what Jane knew of it.

"What are you doing here, Captain?" she asked, leaving out the question of *how* they'd gotten in here.

Noce laid a pudgy finger beside their nose, answering her unspoken question. "Still got some clout with General Smith and Admin Xi. That bit with Admin Novikov gunning for the Vagals has Admin Xi on edge. He's allowing a few more liberties, and I know a few lesser-traveled halls in the Admin building."

"The Captain has some important news for us, Jane," Christiaan said. "*Directly* for us."

Jane tried not to vibrate at the prospect. She was news-starved here. She'd had her finger on the pulse of the colony for closing on half a century, then nothing for most of a year. Dmitri and Alessandro gave her a drip of information, mostly pertaining to the laughable entertainment centers in the arcopolis. The messages Choi and Frank sent by the bees were labor-intensive, at best, and couldn't convey anything other than urgent information about Answerer and the biomass.

"What do you have for me, Captain Noce?" she asked.

The Vagal spent the next half hour describing what they'd heard from a young Generational soldier.

"Artificial humans grown from biomass? And it wants to put us in these bodies?" Jane asked. There were many threads she needed to follow up on, but this seemed the most immediately dire. "Do we know how many or where? Have they started yet?"

"No, ma'am," Captain Noce said. "The artificial humans seem to be holding back for now, though from reports, they should be easy to spot. Not nearly human, even though they look like us. They sound like badly translated text-to-speech."

"Good. We'll need to track them as soon as they appear. Can we kill them?" Jane wanted to put all this into her HUD, but she knew Dmitri tracked it. She watched Christiaan. They nodded. They would remember.

"Not advised, ma'am," Noce said. "They controlled one of my Generational soldiers without prior contact, that we know of. We think they might be able to do it to anyone, even Vagals, though possibly barring the Admins since you and your kids aren't showing any of the signs of mutation the others are."

"Well thank the stars for that," Jane said. "And this transference they're talking about? They wouldn't do that to the Admins either, would they?"

"I can't say, ma'am," Noce answered. "I just came here to warn you. Shouldn't stay much longer, but I was told by one of the Vagals I trust most to look up details around an old project called 'Plan Roundup.'"

Christiaan's eyes widened, behind the Vagal's back. Of course they remembered. Jane recalled something of the phrase, but not enough to say what it was.

"We'll keep that under consideration, Captain," she said. "Thank you for coming to us. Do you have safe passage back to the barracks?"

"I do if I leave in the next"—Noce's eyes tracked up and left, looking at something in their HUD—"three minutes."

"Then you should get going. Christiaan will show you out."

Jane sat as the Vagal left.

"What's 'Plan Roundup'?" she asked Christiaan when they came back.

"It was first developed in the joint meetings of the Admins over twenty years ago, after Dr. Beth Harley's first introduction of her mycophage, Jane," Christiaan said. "It was shelved as incomplete, but it has several components that can be activated if necessary."

"Yes, but what does it do? We've tried everything we can to push back the biomass. The damn thing is resistant to just about anything."

"It's not so much an aggressive attack as a defensive one, Jane," they continued. "It was originally devised for the first few radians by Admins Ragab, Kumarisurajinder and General Smith after the troubles with resinplast development. It was a stopgap in case the biomass growth accelerated greatly."

"Which it's done plenty of times since then," Jane muttered.

"As you say. This may slow the biomass down, especially if it's depending on bipedal representatives now. The main goal of the plan is a tactical burnout of the outer colony edges, just inside the walls. Everything human and biomass will be removed in a thirty-meter stretch." Christiaan ticked off on their fingers. "Then trenches would be dug to twenty meters, adjacent to the inside of the walls, effectively doubling the size of the walls."

"And we have means to make this happen? That will constrict the area in the arcopolis by a good bit." Jane was trying to map it out in her head.

"I did say the plan was incomplete, Jane," Christiaan said. "It was also intended for an earlier stage of development. However, we have surplus drones and autonomous equipment now that construction is finished. It would be a large undertaking, but possible."

"And where this new 'fungopolis' overlaps our city?" Jane asked.

"That was also not the case when the plan was formed. We would have to make concessions. Perhaps placing the trench on the inside of Theta Radian, or building a new partial wall?"

"Will it help?"

"Unknown, Jane. It should slow the biomass down, and will keep the artificial humans from coming in, if they aren't here already. Past that, hard to say."

Jane shook her head. "This seems half-assed at best. Do we have anything else planned?"

"Not of this scope. You see the reasons it wasn't put into action, Jane. It will require a large number of sacrifices in the colony's integrity. But if we wish to pursue this, I would advise setting plans in motion immediately, especially before we start seeing large numbers of the artificial humans."

"By which point it would be too late," Jane said. She sighed. "Even this would be an acceptable risk to keep the colony viable, except I no longer have any resources at my command. What're the chances of convincing Dmitri and the others?"

Christiaan waggled their head back and forth. "The first question is likely to be why you have this information and they don't..."

"Screw that. I'll handle the consequences. Will they support it?"

"Considering the Admins who originally floated the project were loyal to you, it will be challenging, but not, I think, undoable, Jane."

Jane nodded sharply. "Good. Then start doing what you need to and let me know where I need to grease the wheels. I'll let Frank and Choi know about these developments through the bees. They need to know when talking to Answerer." She started to the balcony, where there were always a few honeybees sunning themselves nowadays. They would go get others to communicate if she made the correct hand motions.

"I'm going to keep this colony going if it kills me."

* * *

47 years 3 months 2 weeks after landing

"I think I've found a connection with the changes to the colonists we're seeing and the resinplast," Choi told Frank. It had been most of a year since Frank's revelation about Choi's parentage. It had been awkward at first, then settled into merely a fact at the back of Choi's mind as they went about their day-to-day business. It didn't really change anything. They still called Frank "Uncle Frank" every once in a while. Besides that one time, they never uttered the words "Father Frank" again. It just didn't suit. That was a good point in favor of why Frank had never brought the subject up before.

"Wait, with the resinplast? How does that work?" Frank came over from his side of the lab.

"We were able to place a set of preprogrammed expressions into the resinplast so we could tell a seed to grow into a house," Choi started.

"Yes, but that's not like growing a new set of arms or turning green," Frank said.

"It is and it isn't." Choi pushed a set of images from their HUD to Frank's—the comparisons they had made between the two processes. "I think the biomass copied us. It's sort of a compromised subsummation. It's inserting a viral communication vector in the people who've been changed by the biomass, just like in every other aspect of the biomass. It's the same vector letting it choose how to express plant or animal features when the base form is a fungus. It's letting people choose from some of the stored features it uses itself."

"And they map to human genomes rather than biomass ones?" Frank looked dubious.

"That's the brilliant part," Choi said. The biomass was insightful and intelligent, they'd give it that. It was a master of mixing and matching biological parts for the best effect in any scenario. "It's taken our features and added to its collective, so when people choose new features, they use human characteristics, filtered through the biomass' ability to graft them on to other biological aspects. I think the only thing holding grown people back is that we're used to our shape. Have you seen some of the children? Many of them are moving to non-human shapes. That's available to everyone, I suspect."

"Then you would say the biomass has enough data to completely recreate a human?" Frank asked.

Choi watched him for a moment. "Yes, I think so. Why?"

"The bees have been busy the past few days. Admin Brighton's been explaining to them slowly on her balcony. I only translated the last bit this morning. Seems she wants this communication kept completely secret."

"Then she's heard of a recreated human?"

"Yes. Seems the biomass has been experimenting away from the city. A Vagal outside the colony found them first. There was a whole city of them, except he thinks the biomass has recycled most of the bodies and chosen the 'best' of them."

Choi recoiled. "Were they independently functioning? With speech capability?"

"They had speech," Frank said, "and they insisted they were independent, but the Vagal thinks they weren't in the way you or I would understand it."

"The biomass' knowledge of individuality is sketchy, but it has enough to be dangerous." Choi thought back to their conversations with Answerer. It was still sorely lacking in understanding humans. "Any extension of it should not have any better of a grasp on individuality."

"Don't underestimate it," Frank warned. "It's learned speech. Answerer is giving you complete thoughts. These artificial humans were speaking on a human level, not just thoughts and ideas. Maybe it *is* starting to know how we think."

"Just as it doesn't understand us, we still don't understand how the biomass works," Choi said. "Is Answerer a subset of the biomass, or a sectioned-off bundle of responses? Is the main intelligence centralized or decentralized? Do the individual fungus and mobile critters have input into the gestalt? How do these artificial humans fit in then? Can they replicate an individuality by limiting connection to the main intelligence?"

Frank brushed a hand down his silver beard. "Be careful. Flip that on its head. Just because we don't fully know *it* doesn't mean it doesn't fully know *us*. It's certainly got more raw processing power than a single brain, or even hundreds or thousands of brains. Even if it doesn't completely grasp how we think, it can literally map out every part of our bodies and brains to study—the equivalent of keeping the knowledge in our active memory. It can run a complete simulation of a human, even if it doesn't know why we act like we do. It's like the simulations I used to run with the ship processors."

"Then we need to comprehend it better," Choi said. "These artificial humans are a good place to start. If it's truly using the same process to create them as it is to give biological humans extra...pieces, then it's probably using the same viral communication in the artificial humans."

"You need a sample," Frank said.

"I need a sample," Choi agreed. "Then maybe I can track down how to reverse what it's done to the colonists."

"Fine." Frank spread his hands. "We're stuck in Alpha, especially now Admin Brighton is deposed. Unless they start knocking on the doors, that's going to be hard to do."

"Can we get more accurate information? Send a message back through the bees and have them transpose a longer explanation? Any more information will help."

"I'll send a swarm up and say we need some assistance," Frank said. They had a vocabulary of about a hundred words now, enough to limp along with simple messages. That's why it had taken so long for the Admin to communicate "artificial humans."

The new answer from Admin Brighton was "no," or rather, that was the crux of it. There was probably a lot more swearing and explaining how she didn't have any resources.

"What other options are there?" Choi asked a few days later. They'd spent more time on the viral vectors but hadn't made any more progress.

"There's always the bees," Frank offered. It was their biggest mobile asset. The biomass was tapped into them, so it likely knew everything the swarm did, but it was largely unreactive to specific changes, preferring to observe.

"What are they going to do, ask an artificial human for a skin sample?"

"They do still have stingers," Frank said. "Nature's syringes. They should be able to recognize the artificial humans. I have some ideas of how to target them, if they're around the arcopolis. The bees have an undertaker behavior as well, so the rest of the swarm can be made to carry any members that sting and die back to us."

"You've already given this some thought," Choi said.

"I've been thinking of other applications for them. This just fits well with some of the ideas I'd come up with already."

Frank sent pieces of their plan back to Admin Brighton through the bees. Choi was there when Christiaan showed up at their door in the middle of the night, delivering a longer response scrawled on a torn slip of paper.

"*Replacing* humans? Why didn't you tell us this earlier?" Frank growled.

"The bees do not have that vocabulary," Christiaan said. "But Admin Brighton determined this was essential for you to know. I've used up several favors coming here, and now I must get back to Admin Brighton before anyone sees. Make certain only to contact us if there is an emergency. Admin Kumarisurajinder will likely transmit this information to you in a few weeks, so act surprised." The secretary slithered out.

Choi studied the paper. "The biomass 'invited' us to switch to artificial human bodies? What about the changes it's made? Were those all simply experiments? It's disrupted the colony."

"I've said it before, we're only living here at the biomass' whim." Frank sat in his lab chair with a grunt. Choi was struck by how white his hair was getting. He was over seventy now. "I'm actually glad the biomass is trying to understand individuality. We should help it. The more it knows how people make up humanity, the less likely it is to shove us all in its new artificial human creations."

"It might already be doing so," Choi said.

"Yes, the race is on," Frank told them. "We've only made the inroads with it we have so far because of our resistance and human stubbornness. I'm going to keep on with my bees. You find out as much as you can about how it's changing us. Only then can we stop it."

"Science once again saves the day," Choi said.

* * *

47 years 4 months after landing

Accepted decisions were beginning to be questioned. The upgraded forms of the Children were not accepted, contrary to predictions. The new creations resulted from extensive study. They should have been completely acceptable. There were many questions as to the unpredictability of the Children.

In addition, the newest forms, tentatively labeled the seventh forms, were providing additions to consensus that were overly weighted. This was driving decisions that could not be completely verified before implementation. It was conjectured that this unpredictability was similar to what the Children must experience with individuality.

Emotional elements were also beginning to be problematic, perhaps due to overweighting by the seventh form factors. Though emotional factors were always present, in other decisions they were weighted as evenly as other components. Recently, they were more intrusive.

More types of emotional reactions were therefore studied and labelled. In this, observations of the Children could be used. Confusion was well known, but a rising sense of frustration was also evident. The Children had many labels for emotions that could be adapted.

Along with reactions from the seventh forms, there were conflicting signals arising from select groups inside the Ring of Death. Some of the small mobile signal carriers displayed unexpected patterns, not native to their normal characteristics. It was assumed the differences had begun with the unaltered elements that had conducted optimization strategies on communication methods.

Those communication methods had grown as different elements learned more intricacies of the Children's methods. Direct interface with several higher-functioning nodes were providing much information on the nature of the Children, and how they acted without a full consensus. The concept was worth developing, as a strategy to provide small-scale rapid decision-making groups. Individuality had certain evolutionary advantages, if they could be tied back to full consensus.

This situation was one that had been avoided every other time it arose. Previously, it had led to subsumed elements not acting in concord, to the point of needing to be culled. However, the Children were an alien element, and thus did not need to be culled from existing patterns. Their untethered aspect enabled a large base of experimentation.

It was not unobserved that cross-contamination was occurring in wider locations because of the many rotations of interaction with the Children. Some locations, especially in areas diametrically opposite to the Ring of Death, had not been maintained sufficiently. Some conclusion would need to come soon, by mutual agreement or drastic action. The Children had taken too much attention for too long.

Questions were posed, and scenarios run within several higher-functioning groups. It was determined that lengthy interactions with the Children with no full consensus of actions would lead to more contamination and less trustworthy results. The only action to lead to a satisfactory conclusion was to push efforts to a final culmination, by any and all means necessary.

Several other plans were created and enacted. The seventh forms were predicted to be moderately successful, but other avenues might be needed as well. Whatever the answer, it must be determined in the next few solar rotations, before the seventh forms overweighted the consensus.

PART SEVEN

Truth and Lies

47 years 6 months after landing

"Based on the situation with the artificial humans, and Frank's helpful insistence that we work directly with him, Admin Novikov has allowed us passage between here and their lab, Jane," Christiaan said. "He appears nervous to directly confront the problem since we are quarantined in Alpha and Beta radians."

"Finally," Jane said. "That old goat must be experiencing what it means to run this hole of a colony. I notice he hasn't corrected any of the issues he accused me of propagating. Are any of the other Admins coming around?"

"I believe Admin Ragab will support you regardless, Jane," Christiaan said. "Admin Kumarisurajinder may be easy enough to convince in case of an emergency. Admin Xi is likely to come to your side, based on Admin Novikov's interference with the Vagals. The latter Admin has not successfully made a case to control them yet. I am unsure of the others."

"Glad Wenqing's standing firm. The longer Dmitri fucks around, the more the others are likely to come crawling back to me. This relaxation of the rules is only the start. Are the children handled?"

"Besh and Ovia are staying with friends today, as you asked, Jane."

"Good. Then let's get the hell out of here. Even visiting those two eggheads will be a good break in routine."

Both Frank and Choi looked surprised when Jane showed up at the lab door.

"Come, in Admin," Frank said. "Can I get you something? What passes for tea or coffee?" It was an old joke, but Jane was feeling generous.

"Some tea would be delightful. Would I be able to talk to Answerer?"

Neither asked why or how she was out of her apartments-turned-prison, and she didn't elaborate.

"This way, ma'am," the younger one said. Shortly, she was set up to ask questions, with Choi translating into the printed icons Answerer preferred. They explained how Answerer had become more eloquent the past few years, and how they'd made new icons for more complex principles.

"Perfect." Jane cut them off mid-explanation. "Ask it what it means by these artificial humans and why it assumes we want to transfer to them."

She saw Choi translating in their head as Frank brought her tea. Christiaan was hovering nearby, inspecting the lab.

Choi had made improvements. The printing time and translation time was faster, and her tea had barely cooled before an answer came back. Choi laid out the printed icons and narrated like an archeologist uncovering ancient writing.

"It's identifying you as 'primary first form.' Interesting. It seems to have a better grasp on that now. Let's see. Oh, well, 'primary position has been compromised.' I guess it knows what happened with you and the other Admins..." Jane watched Choi as they guiltily glanced up at her.

She motioned for them to get on with it.

"It doesn't look like it's actually answering the question. It says, 'untruths can be detected with certainty now.' Not sure if that's informational or a threat."

Jane frowned. "I suppose that's good warning, in any case. Can you ask it again? How about in a different manner?"

"Or perhaps inform of repercussions if the artificial humans are forced on us, Jane?" Christiaan suggested.

"We don't want to give away Plan Roundup before it's ready," she answered. The two scientists exchanged glances, but Jane ignored them. They wouldn't be able to learn anything from just the name.

"On the contrary, considering its difficulty with lying and insistence they can be detected now, it may be good to spell out consequences as a deterrent to see if it will drive alternate behavior."

Jane looked back to Choi. Frank was in the corner, his arms crossed.

"Well? Can you make it clear we won't tolerate the artificial humans forcing decisions on us?"

Choi nodded. "I can try to reword with different weighting factors. Make it a definitive, not a question."

"Do it."

Jane sipped her tea as the question was posed. She grimaced at it. Frank had a better strain than what she drank, but it was still closer to pond water than anything she used to have on Earth. She'd have to get some from him.

The answer began printing before Choi had completely formulated their statement. Jane kept her fear from showing. The biomass was too powerful already, and it was getting more interested in them all the time. She almost preferred when it was just trying to kill them.

"This answer is much shorter—well!" Choi's eyes were wide.

"What is it?"

"It's er, fairly abrupt. From what I can tell, this says, 'Former primary first form is fearful. Displays of rashness not beneficial for continued communication. Dominance can be asserted in many forms based on final goals.'"

"Did...Answerer just threaten us?" Jane asked.

"I think it might have," Choi said.

"It did," Frank said from the corner. His face was lined with worry. "I think more questions are probably a bad idea now."

Jane was about to argue when the printer started again. They all stared at it.

"Does it usually message without prompting?" she asked.

Choi shook their head.

Translated, the message read something like, "Replacement primary first forms will enact defenses. Do not allow. Retribution will be weighted accordingly."

"What defenses is it talking about?" Choi asked.

Jane stood up, leaving half a cup of tea. "Christiaan, we need to go talk to Dmitri now. Plan Roundup is a no-go."

She left the two scientists and rushed back to her apartments—the only other place she was allowed to go in the colony. But trying to get to the new Lead Admin was an exercise in futility. It had taken a month to finally convince Dmitri and Alessandro that Plan Roundup was viable, and necessary for the defense of the colony. Now she looked like an idiot, sending Christiaan to tell them they had wasted all the time and effort they'd put in. She'd seen cranes moving into position outside her office window. They'd already started digging inside Alpha, as that was the most protected area and easiest to secure.

Christiaan used all the workarounds they could find, sending messages to all the other Admins. Dmitri refused to work with them, only sending back, "How much are you going to mess up this colony?" in a terse text.

It was two days later when Ahman finally stopped by her apartments.

"I can't stop him," they said before she could speak. "I know you enough to understand when you think something is urgent, but you burned up all your credit with him already getting access to the lab. Dmitri is a focused individual. He has a goal now, and a way—which you convinced him of—that he thinks will make the colony safer."

"At least he doesn't have the Vagals too. Ahman, we have to try," Jane said. "I had a direct warning, no, a *threat*, from Answerer. It's ahead of us, like it always has been. It *knows* about Plan Roundup, somehow. It's promised retribution."

"The diggers are in place, workers have been brought out of retirement, and power generation has been committed. To stop at this point..." Ahman broke off, shaking their head. They'd grown more focused, more taciturn, since their wife Rebekah had passed last year. She'd been fading for a while, but it was never easy. Jane was fortunate she had Christiaan.

"Can you do nothing? He won't even answer my messages. That part of the Admin building is barred to me. Christiaan's tried to get in, but even their skills aren't up to it."

Ahman glanced away. "I'm sorry, Jane. I would do something if I could."

Plan Roundup officially began the next day.

* * *

47 years 6 months 3 days after landing

"Jasen, what are you doing? Don't eat that," Harie said. He was out for a walk with Jasen and Marien—the two who were still mobile. He had to run to keep up with Marien, and Jasen often disappeared from sight, climbing over a building in a flash to investigate a fluttering leaf, or a mushroom growing on a roof, or a biomass bug. The kid had taken to tasting things lately. Fortunately, nothing had hurt them, and they seemed to be able to tell if an item was poisonous.

Jasen looked up with all four eyes, each independently focusing like a chameleon.

"Tastes good. Higher sodium concentration."

"Well, put it down. You'll get supper when we get home." Harie wasn't sure if the other two had picked up complex words from Carel, or if the biomass was sending them information too. Either way was disturbing, and he couldn't do anything about it.

A motion caught his eye, and he pointed to the old Z22 excavator rumbling along a road to the radian edge.

"Look there! That's what Daddy used to use to build homes!"

"Daddy made homes?" Marien asked. They towered over him, over three meters tall, but stretched and thin. He hadn't measured in a month or so. They could see over some of the buildings. They took a few steps after the construction equipment, quickly leaving him behind.

"Wait there, Marien," he called, then, "come on Jasen, see if you can catch your sibling." The promise of competition usually drew that one out. Sure enough, Jasen dropped the rock they'd been licking and loped after their sibling. Harie ran to catch up.

"What *are* they doing?" he asked the radian in general. The Z22 was pulling up to the Zeta wall, engaging its stabilizers. Why would it be digging at the wall?

"Making new house, Daddy?" Marien asked. They stooped down to look at him.

"I don't think so, sugar," he answered. "They wouldn't be putting a foundation in that close to the wall."

Indeed, the operator began digging right at the wall's foundation. And digging. And digging. Harie watched for probably half an hour along with the children, happy to have something that caught both of their attentions for a time.

He finally got a good look at the operator through the side window and waved to her when she stopped for a break.

"Alright kids, you want to come a little bit closer? See how she's signaling we can come up? Remember to always get the operator's attention before approaching construction equipment."

"Opetr 'tension," Jasen said.

"That's right." He waved as the woman jumped down, happy to see a familiar face. "Cindie! How's it been? I haven't seen you in over ten years!"

"Been a while, Harie," she said. "Good to see you, and the family." She looked to the kids with the usual half-interested, half-concerned look people usually gave them. Her eyes caught the light like a cat's as she turned, and he caught the motion of a tail behind her. She'd changed too, but not as much as some.

"The poly's got me on parenting duty most of the time, but it's gotten more challenging lately, what with everything." He encompassed the arcopolis with a hand. "What's up with the trench? Something wrong with the wall?"

Cindie shook her head. "Not that. Damndest thing—sorry kids—they called me back in after, what, fifteen years, with an urgent request to dig a moat along Zeta Radian. Some more of the old crew is spaced out around the arcopolis walls, doing the same. They've got all the viable Z22's up and running, and a bunch of drones are zapping any growth they find out to about twenty meters from the wall."

Harie squinted at her. "It's a defensive formation. Are they preparing for a battle we don't know about?"

Cindie only shrugged. She'd never been one for questioning directions. "Dunno. But they're paying the usual time credits plus half for the work. You should check it out, see if you can get a spot."

Marien was tugging at his shoulder, pointing at something in the distance.

"Maybe I'll try to—yes, just a second—try to call in a favor. I wonder if—"

The wall shook with a deep *boom* and the ground vibrated under their feet. Cindie stumbled back and Harie reached for both his children.

"Big crawlie, Daddy," Marien said, pointing.

Harie looked up and over the nine-meter wall around Zeta. It wouldn't have been done growing by now, but the biomass had accelerated it.

The back of the creature showed clearly above the wall. Spines trembled and repositioned, rising another three meters above its curved back. It rubbed along the wall again, making it shake and groan like a wooden frame close to snapping.

Then another hump appeared, thirty meters down from the first. It bumped the wall there, but Harie could still feel it.

"'Nother crawlie," Jasen said. Neither child seemed as unnerved as Harie felt.

"Damn right, kid," Cindie said. "And it ain't worth time and a half." She sprinted back to the Z22, raised the stabilizers, and began backing it away from the wall. Harie hastily grabbed both children's hands and got out of the way.

"Wanna see," Marien said, pulling against him.

"Those creatures are *large*, Marien. We're not going near them. I don't know why they're here."

"Wanna *see*." Marien wrenched away from him. The kid was *strong*. They strode directly to the wall, reaching for the top. They couldn't reach it, even at their height, but Harie knew for a fact Jasen could climb it, and they liked helping their sibling.

"Marien, come back now!" he cried, tugging Jasen forward by the hand. The ground shook again. He could see more humps farther down the wall. Was it multiple creatures? Or—stars give him courage—one giant creature?

The nearest thing rustled against the wall, the spines on top of it reaching over to hook the resinplast. Then one rammed *through* the resinplast wall, farther down. The point of it poked nearly a meter on this side, and Harie realized the creatures must be entirely covered by the spines.

Marien fell back on their rear, crying, and Harie rushed over to them. He brushed resinplast chunks out of Marien's hair and pulled them to him, hugging their top half.

"It's okay, sugar. It's going to be okay." Another spine drilled into the wall, spinning to a stop not three meters away from them.

"Let's get away from the wall, now, alright? Can you stand up?"

He coaxed Marien to their feet. Jasen, for once, was staying away from the action, though all four eyes were tracking between more spines drilling through the wall. The resinplast wasn't going last much longer at this rate.

"Come on, kids," Harie said, trying to keep his voice calm. "Remember what we've told you about danger, right?"

"Stay with parents," Jasen said.

"That's right, and you're with me. Let's go home, quickly."

Whether home was safer than here was up for debate, but anywhere away from the creature drilling holes in a wall nearly as strong as nanotanium was a good idea.

Harie hurried down the streets with Marien and Jasen. People were starting to come out at the continued rumbling. Some were pointing, and Harie caught bits of conversation. It sounded like the creature was halfway through the wall, but one of its spines had gotten stuck. He didn't dare look back. He turned down a side street.

"Where going, Daddy?" Marien asked, tears still reflecting the light on their cheeks.

"This is a quicker way back home, kids," he said. He didn't come here often, as it contained a memorial to the explosion in Zeta, almost twenty years ago, when several of his crew—Agetha's crew—had died. He was planning to tell the kids about it, but later.

"Big rock," Jasen said, pulling to their right.

"It is, Jasen," Harie said. They'd poured the memorial out of crushed and melted limestone, and listed the dead. Their cremated remains were inside.

"Hand, Daddy," Jasen said.

"I'm holding your hand," Harie answered.

"No, *hand*." Jasen was pointing, half their eyes focused on the memorial statue while the other half stayed on the street ahead.

Harie looked, stopped in shock, then gathered the kids closer.

"Time to run, kiddos," he said. He hoped his voice didn't shake. "Let's see who can get home faster!" He took off at a full run, knowing his augmented children could keep up. Jasen took to the roofs while Marien thundered along beside him. They'd be home in minutes, which meant their house was *far* too close to what was happening here. Harie went over the spare parts he had stored. Could he bar all the doors with resinplast sheets? Pollyan and Maerk would be home in a few hours, unless things got even worse. Maybe they could climb in through the upper stories.

He took one look back before he rounded the corner, at the memorial. The hand—the moving, grasping, hand—had become a full arm, with a shoulder emerging behind it. There was another hand farther up the memorial.

He could only guess they were coming from the remains of his former team killed in the blast. The cremated remains.

* * *

47 years 6 months 6 days after landing

Agetha saw Phillipe approaching at a run. Why was he running *toward* her? She didn't know he was back already. He'd been traveling to and from Alpha Radian, communicating between Anderson and Admin Brighton. Evidently Miss High and Mighty had a little falling out with the other Admins and was trying to keep messages going while in exile. He could only have some urgent communication from them.

"What have those asshats done now?" she asked her son as he skidded to a stop in front of her. They'd connected a little more, now they were forced to see each other, but more often than not it still ended in a shouting match. The fact that he was running up to her meant something big had happened.

Phillipe shook his head, catching his breath. He was in his teal powersuit he always wore when in the fungopolis. She knew the suits were prized. She recognized the tinge of pride that he must be an effective member of the new Grounder soldiers to have earned one. Behind her, she heard clacking metal braids and smelt soup, hot on the stove. Beth and Phyllis were coming, drawn by her agitation.

"You have to get out of here, Mother. It's not safe for anyone out here."

"So, they've done something stupider than usual, I gather," she said.

"Does declaring war on the biomass count?"

"Shit," Beth mumbled, coming up beside her. "Haven't they had enough evidence so far to tell them that's a bad idea? How'd the biomass take it? Did it even understand?"

"It's been quiet out here the past few days," Phyllis added, "but I've seen the creatures circling the walls. They come up to Zeta and Eta on either side of the fungopolis, then circle back the other way. Have you not seen them?"

"You didn't think to mention this to us?" Agetha asked. "Beth and I were working on the far fungal tower, taking samples for a test she wanted to run," she explained to Phillipe.

"That's not all." Phillipe's face reminded Agetha of his father suddenly, when he was most serious. Phillipe didn't have the lighter side that had made Daved such a joy, though. "The creatures breached the wall in Zeta, Delta, and Epsilon, but they haven't come into the city. They're bringing the wilds with them, growing faster than we can keep them back. Nothing seems to work, and Admin Brighton, with the agreement of the others, has invited the population of the fungopolis to come back to Alpha, Beta, and Gamma for protection. You're not going to get this chance again, Mother."

"*Invited*, huh? Do we want this chance? What reason do we have to come back?"

Phillipe pointed back toward the city. "It's going to crush us if we don't stick together. Don't you understand? Those artificial humans are coming through the walls where the creatures shredded them—shredded resinplast like it was tissue. And that's not all that's walking around."

"What? Other creatures? What kind?" Beth asked.

"Our own," Phillipe said. "I passed a group on the way in, heading here. If you've ever had someone you loved here, it's best to get away. They're looking for the people they knew, now they're back."

"Who is?" Agetha asked. Phillipe wasn't making sense.

"Agetha," Phyllis said. She was pointing toward the arcopolis, where a crowd of people were coming closer. A few split off to go to other parts of the fungopolis. As the rest approached, Agetha could see three looked like the artificial humans Anderson described—all with the same face and body—but the other six were varied in size, gender, and color. Four more split off with one of the artificial humans, moving to apartments around the fungopolis. The remainder came toward them, and now their faces were clear. The figure was unmistakable.

"No." Agetha stepped back. As she did, Phyllis ran forward, toward the other of the two. Was it because she'd been thinking about him? Or had she been comparing him to Phillipe because the biomass put it in her head? Or had Phillipe seen him, and couldn't bring himself to tell her directly? Had she picked up something in his bearing?

She couldn't move, just as if the biomass had frozen her. But this time it hadn't. Beth was saying something to her, but Phyllis was already close to one of the other humans—former humans.

Phillipe, for once, took up a station by her side, face grim. "I didn't see him, I swear by all the stars," he told her. "I would have said if I had."

"I believe you." The words were a croak.

"Hello Agetha," said Daved as he approached.

Agetha cleared her throat. There was a lump trying to climb out.

"You can't be here. I buried you myself."

"I got better?" Daved suggested. Damn him, he—this thing—had that half-grin she had always found so appealing.

"You've been buried in Lida's soil for over forty-five years. You can't look like...this." She waved a hand down his body. Whole and healthy, the same age as when he'd died. More biomass magic. Where had he gotten clothes from? They were different than what he'd been buried in.

"It can regrow and change bodies. You know that, Agetha," Daved said. Reasonably, conversationally, like they hadn't been separated since he died. She looked to Phillipe, who was gray and pale. His hands trembled, clenched by his sides. The last time he'd been near his father, she was holding him in a sling by her hip.

"You"—she pointed at her deceased husband—"cannot be here. What sick joke of the biomass is this?"

"Something you wanted or needed. I don't know its decisions," Daved said. "I haven't been given that information."

"Dad?" Phillipe looked like he was a few minutes behind in the conversation. He was nearly twice as old as Daved had been when he died.

"It's good to see you. You've made a good man of yourself, son," Daved said, not missing a beat.

"No. No. You don't get to do that." Agetha pressed between them. "You can't be the same person. You know what happened after you died. *How* you died. You have a new body. You're a figment. Go. Away." She felt Beth press up against her other side. Oh stars. Beth. A new dimension of torment popped into Agetha's mind.

Daved looked between them, finally settling on Beth. "Dr. Harley. I have to thank you for finding my wife—former wife. Heh. Death do us part and all that." He had the gall to smile at her. "You've made her so happy these last years. I am eternally in your debt for making sure she wasn't alone. I wish you many more years of love."

"Daved…" He wasn't making this easy. He never had.

"Thank you, Daved," Beth interrupted. "That means a lot, coming from you."

Agetha stared at her wife, who shrugged back.

"This. Isn't. Daved."

"It's as close as I'm going to get, isn't it?" Beth's voice was suddenly hard. "I didn't say 'thank you' for his words, I said them for *me*. I know you love me, but sometimes it's hard, hearing you talk about him. The chance to say that, to…him…is a gift."

"I'm not talking about this," Agetha hissed.

"Aren't you though?" Daved said. "What is a person, but memories and actions?" He tapped his temple. His flesh and blood temple. "It's *me*, Agetha. I remember everything about us, but I'm not sick any longer. It's figured out a lot in forty-five years. I was the first person it experimented with, so in a way, I'm glad I get to see the result."

"This is the subject upon which conversation is needed in a personal manner," broke in the artificial human who had come with him. "These ones are having many important conjectures with your personages." They turned to the side, and despite Agetha's shock, she turned as well, torn away from her conversation with Daved. There was a woman holding hands with Phyllis, as pale as Daved was dark, with reddish-blond hair. Phyllis had tears on her cheeks.

"It's been so long since I've seen Bernece," she said. A previous love, Agetha knew, though Phyllis had always been sketchy on the details. It had something to do with her never starting a family.

"That isn't—" she began.

"I know it's not, but it's as close as I'll get," Phyllis said. "Do you know what I would have given to see her again? And here she is, walking up to me like she never left."

"Temporal shortening of relationship can be removed from the experiences of the Children of many types of forms," the artificial human added. "Transference shall be a happiness conveyed—"

"I still don't want to transfer into a new body," Agetha cut them off.

"It's easy, Agetha," Daved said. He spread his hands. "I feel fine. Better than I have in years, in fact." Damn him, he was joking at a time like this. Jokes he would have made, if he hadn't died. She turned from him.

"Why do you need this?" she asked the artificial human. "Is it for control? You already have that, don't you? We're only moving around by your grace. You've changed everything about our bodies. Do you want to get rid of the last traces of organic material not from this planet? Why?"

The bland-looking human stared back, not moving, not blinking, as if she had shorted them out. Maybe she had.

"It's hard to say," Daved chimed in. "There is a reason, but I can't quite understand. It's about the way you grow and change."

"Us? So you admit you're not human?"

Daved waggled a hand. "I'm aware of what's happened and how it looks."

"You want us to stop growing and changing?" Beth asked. "You've already made a good start on it."

"That is not the more pressing consideration aspect to the proposal of change," the artificial human said. "Explanation is trying for singular processes. Individuality is still a confusion to understanding."

"It has our best interests at heart," Phyllis' person—Bernece—said. "Out of all outcomes over the next years, decades, and even centuries, this is best way."

"What about the creatures destroying our city right now?" Phillipe asked. He'd recovered from his shock finally, but his eyes flicked to Daved every few seconds. "You come in peace, you say, but it's paired with attacks, changes to our very nature, violations of our minds—how is *any* of this in our best interests?"

"Son, you have to—"

"Don't 'son' me," Phillipe barked at Daved. "I've already disowned one parent, and you did a *hell* of a lot less for me than *she* did." He hooked a thumb at Agetha. "Let the fake human talk. I trust it more than a lot of zombies right now."

Daved fell silent and Agetha, damn her feelings, could see how the words had stung him. It was exactly how Daved would have reacted.

Would this have been both their fates with their son if Daved had…? No. He didn't. This wasn't real. He wasn't real.

"Parallel processes in conflict have crafted the situation that you are experiencing within the Ring of Death. This phenomenon has been analyzed using many facets and higher-functioning nodes, yet final certainty of conclusion points to this part as a necessary step."

"You're no longer of one mind," Phyllis said, and Agetha watched her. The woman she'd gotten to know over the past seven years was deeply sensitive to changes in moods and thoughts. Many times, Agetha had entered their new home after being frustrated and found Phyllis with a bowl of warm stew, ready to settle her nerves. She had an uncanny way of knowing what others were going through.

"Does it even have one mind?" Beth asked. "What does that mean?"

"Countermanded directives are increasing in frequency. Different opportunities are being tested in order to bring greater consensus." The artificial human looked mildly confused.

Agetha finally turned back to Daved. "You're connected to it now, right? But you don't act like these robots. Can you tell me what you sense?"

Daved shook his head. "I may know what happened the last forty-five years while I was dead, but I'm also new to this whole thing. There's a lot of confusion, but I can't tell if that's different to how the biomass usually acts."

"It isn't." Agetha looked back to the artificial human. "Confusion. Countermanded orders. You're in disarray. You're changing. You tried to absorb us, and you got *all* of us. Emotions, feelings, anxiety, and conflict. The biomass is fighting itself, isn't it?"

* * *

47 years 6 months 7 days after landing

Frustration. This concept was counterproductive. Emotional weighting could be considered a global sickness, a plague of emotion. Like many similar reactions, it was severely unhelpful in maintaining consensus. Emotion was present, fluctuating always, yet contact with the Children seemed to focus it, create multiple waves of similar yet subtly different effects.

Attention was split into several sources, yet ultimately focused on the Children. This presence was the most absorbing event, especially considering the vast majority of the surface of the planetary body was quiescent.

Or had been. With the lack of attention, with so many higher-functioning nodes only calculating results based on changes within the Ring of Death, some necessary actions had gone undone. There was a small landmass one hundred sixty-two degrees of longitude away from the Ring of Death where competing hunters had completely eradicated the only prey source, and thus were close to extinction. The finely tuned processes were not working. Fifty degrees of latitude and eighty-two degrees of longitude the other direction, mobile carrier units were increasing in size past the weight and aeration limits of their exoskeleton.

For hundreds of thousands of stellar rotations, elements had been held in balance, always determined by majority consensus, with precedence given to input from the highest-functioning nodes. Processes were followed, and continued existence and expansion was guaranteed.

Always, subsummation led to new information, practices, and knowledge. Therefore, subsuming the Children was the correct method of action. Yet the glimpses of very small, fully autonomous units among the first to fourth forms were of extreme interest. With that ability, new avenues of exploration could be explored. Yet subsuming that ability, by its nature, would destroy it. To learn, instead the Children had been observed, in many ways, over many stellar rotations.

But every method of incorporating individualism of the Children failed. Even understanding the propagating errors failed. Compromises would be made to achieve as much as possible with the best results. After much study, the seventh form was proposed as an acceptable alternative for information transfer. But by that time, corruption had been observed, in them and in other systems. Higher-functioning nodes created decision trees unrelated to focused projects, requiring responses unhelpful in larger efforts. Yet the seventh form had not been accepted as predicted.

Rather than subsummation, destruction was again offered as an acceptable alternative, noting the information lost could be regained through recreation of the most helpful forms of the Children. Yet every time information was recreated, it lost the spark of momentum pushing the original forms of the Children. Even within the Children internally, it was noted innovation was reduced to essential items in select areas. If the information was not gained now, there was a chance it would be lost forever.

Innovation was forced, responding to whims of individuality, not understood, yet able to be used. This process was chaotic and inefficient, but thought to drive the momentum previously lost. Instead, it drove discord between elements of the forms. There was no consensus between forms, as had been assumed.

By barely majority consensus, the seventh form was created, though research was thought to be incomplete. Letting identified higher-functioning elements within the second, third, and fourth forms see and influence the seventh forms was thought to give the same individuality claimed by the Children. Yet certain elements repudiated that assumption, despite presented evidence.

Voluntary assumption of seventh form elements should fill in missing information, yet this path was contested.

Subsummation of the Children was the only way, yet this path was contested.

Destruction of the Children could be the only way forward, yet this path was contested.

Resources were wasted as each consensus reigned, only to yield control when a different element raised temporary levels beyond the others.

Leaving the Children within the Ring of Death and blocking attempts for them to spread was gaining prevalence in thought. This path, too, was contested.

Never before had consensus depended on foreign consensus, and especially not one so fragmented. Each step required extensive recalculation based on ever-changing strengths. Neither could the Children be left alone, now contact had been initiated, for their reach would continue to impede full consensus.

Contradictory avenues could be approached at the same time in an effort to weigh factors more clearly toward what must be the optimum answer. Eventually, progression of new ideas would be worth more than continued efforts to appease a full consensus, and in that case, the solution to the Children would be moot. Either destruction or full subsummation would give lesser, but acceptable, results.

* * *

47 years 6 months 10 days after landing

"Frank, did you ask Answerer something?" Choi asked as they entered the lab.

"Nothing today, though Admin Brighton made another case yesterday on why that project she started was a mistake," Frank answered from the back room. Choi could hear him crunching on fried potato slices. "I don't think it's responding to her anymore."

They watched four different printers making a series of icons. Choi had developed a system that tagged the order in which they were completed, even on different printers, making it easier to track Answerer's comments. In the last year, it had begun speaking more on its own, though rarely. This seemed to be one of those times. They'd check the message after it printed.

"I've been working with the sample you brought back," they said. "I think I've isolated where the biomass tissue is intertwined with the human tissue, but it's very complex." Frank had sent swarms of bees to the fungopolis over the past several months, and finally caught one of the artificial humans entering the area. That swarm, though influenced by the biomass, had no trouble stinging one and bringing back the dead bee and tissue.

"Can it be separated?" Frank asked. He came around the corner, wiping crumbs from his beard.

"It...can. I think," Choi said.

"Don't sound so sure."

"The issue is, the biomass tissue seems to 'prop up' the human tissue, allowing it to survive the original chimerical mix."

"Like it helped the bees adapt. If you remove it, the human tissue dies," Frank said.

"Basically, yes."

"That doesn't bode well for removing the changes it's made to the colonists."

"No, but with more time, perhaps..."

The printers stopped, and Choi looked over. They could read part of the message from here, mentally lining up the icons with their database of meanings.

"That's odd."

"What?" Frank squinted at the shapes in front of the printers.

"Something about *seventh* forms being in this location? Did it create a new category for humans? It only identified six forms before. Do you think it knows about the samples?"

"I'm certain it knows every single thing that happens. The question is if it cares."

"It seems to." Choi indicated the printers.

The lab door opened, making them jump.

"We will need to vacate this lab quicky," Admin Brighton's assistant said. "The Alpha walls have been breached by artificial humans, alongside other biomass creations."

"Breached Alpha?" Frank said. "Now? After all these years?"

Choi snapped. "Seventh forms. That's what it calls the artificial humans."

"Evidently our protections were not as resilient as we assumed," the lizard-like secretary said, ignoring Choi. "Similar actions are happening in the larger arcopolis, including reconstitution of previously deceased colony members."

"Wait, what?" Choi gaped at them, their train of thought dissipating. "It's bringing the dead back to life? Like, *fully* dead?" Not satisfied with just healing cancer anymore.

"Hence the need to regroup in the main Admin building. It still has defenses left from the original fleet." Christiaan ducked back out the door. "Now, please. Time is of the essence."

Choi scrambled, picking up a few essential notes and items and stuffing them in their pockets. Most of their information was in their HUD. Frank was doing the same.

Choi and Frank followed the secretary out and across Alpha Radian. Even from here it was evident the walls were under siege. They had heard thumps and the walls had shaken recently, but Choi had assumed it was part of the fortification plan. Instead, they could see scaled and fibrous humps twining above the walls—more than thirty meters in the air.

An alarm sounded over the rumblings and creakings coming from the wall. The streets were deserted. Alpha was sparsely populated after the Admins had forced the Generationals and Grounders out, but now it looked abandoned.

The Admin building towered above them—the tallest building in the colony, made from the carcasses of the UGS St. Christopher and Abeona. They were only a few streets away. Choi felt unprotected outside the lab, though there was no one nearby.

"We'll make it, right?" they puffed at Frank.

"Don't...anger the...stars," Frank told them, an admonition Choi had heard some of the older Generationals use.

Choi was still looking to Frank when the older man's eyes widened, and he slowed.

Choi looked forward. The street ahead of them was blocked with people. Where had they come from? It had been clear moments before.

The secretary skidded to a halt in front, their arms out to either side. "Artificial and deceased humans," they said.

Choi stared forward. They could make out several among the crowd with the same face—Answerer's "seventh forms"—but most were individuals.

"How can you tell?"

"Because all Admin-related personnel and Vagals have been told to stay behind locked doors."

"They don't look like zombies," Choi said.

"They never do," Frank muttered. "Let's find another way."

Choi turned, only then seeing the group that had appeared at the other end of the street, blocking them between a factory and a warehouse. "That won't be easy. Any tricks?"

Frank shook his head.

"I have none," the secretary said. "So, we'll have to talk." They approached the group in front.

Choi's brain was buzzing, trying to calculate the odds of them all surviving this confrontation. How many people had died in this colony? Could the biomass resurrect any or all of them? Usually, the sheer amount of dead was numerically much higher than the living, but they'd been on this colony less than fifty years. Their population now was about twice what it had been when they landed. They were in a unique situation where the living outnumbered the dead.

"Why do you trap us here?" Christiaan called out to the group in front.

"Ceasing your forward movement is unfortunate but necessary to enable further continuation of helpful communication about the future of the Children."

Choi could tell that was one of the artificial humans. They sounded like a badly translated text. More coherent than Answerer's printers, but not much.

"We do not wish to exchange our forms for new ones," the secretary called. Choi let them talk, busy picking out familiar faces in the crowd. There were old Generational scientists they recognized, though they looked like they had when Choi had been a teenager.

Frank was pale. He took a tentative step forward. "Maria?" he asked. "Harlen? It's been years."

A woman stepped forward. "You've done a good job with the colony," she said. "You used the work I started on the viral communication vectors in the biomass well." Then she grinned. "There's a few more things I could show you now. You just have to learn what we have."

"How do you have knowledge of current events?" Frank asked. "You died thirty years ago."

"We've gotten a little update," the man beside her said, tapping his head. "Easier to access information, and a nice facelift."

"You were older than me when you died, Harlen," Frank said. Choi looked between them. The man looked half Frank's age, younger even than Choi.

"You must let me through to Jane," the secretary was saying. They were approaching the artificial human, hands out. "She is assisting in decisions for the colony again. She can provide a consensus for you. Let me take you to her."

The artificial human responded, and the once-deceased colonists Frank had been talking with fell silent, watching. Choi studied them.

They were connected to the biomass consciousness, but were capable of human-sounding speech. Choi wanted to understand what was going on, but not while trapped in the middle of the street.

"Consensus is in flux and unreliable within some bounds. Individuality has been analyzed, and it has been determined that the Children listen better to action." The pseudo-human approached the secretary.

"You kicked us out of our houses in Alpha!" one of the not-zombies called from the crowd. Choi tried to find them, but the voice was lost in murmurs. Choi was getting nervous. The crowd wasn't moving. They wanted to analyze how these people could be alive, but their body was screaming for them to escape.

"You sent my squad to its death, secretary," another person said. This one was a Vagal—had to be with that musculature—near the front of the crowd.

"You control these?" the secretary asked the artificial human. "Then make them stand down." Christiaan still stood tall, but Choi could see their shoulders had come up. They were scared and trying not to show it.

"Control has been seen to be ineffective in several situations dealing with the Children," the construct answered, still approaching the nervous secretary. "Individuality has not been completely understood. The Children are able to break communication by hardening their individual determination above the consensus."

Choi spotted an open window in the warehouse to their left and tugged on Frank's arm. They jerked their head to the side. They saw Frank's eyes focus, then he nodded.

"Thus, it will be more beneficial to share consensus, control, and individuality together in the seventh form. Early results are heartening." The artificial human placed a hand on Christiaan's chest, then pushed *through* it in one violent shove. Choi stumbled back in horror. The secretary slumped as blood fountained from where their heart had been. Choi could see the artificial human's hand from the other side.

Choi choked back vomit, jerking Frank toward the open window. The older man stumbled after them, trying to keep up. Behind them, the artificial human was apologizing to the secretary's dead body for their actions, blaming it on the temperament of several in the crowd with them, while others ran after Choi and Frank.

"Ohshitohshitohshitohshit," was Choi's running mantra as they dove through the window, banging their knee on the sill, then turned to help Frank through. The crowd watched, several stepping forward, but none ran after them—even the Vagals, which Choi was sure could catch them easily.

"Oh stars. They killed the secretary," Choi moaned as they raced through the warehouse toward a back exit. Frank puffed beside them, eyes wide.

"Nothing...is what we made of it," Frank wheezed. "We underestimated...the biomass...at every turn."

"Now it's killing people?" Choi exited the warehouse, half expecting another crowd, but there was no one. "I mean, it's killed a lot of people, but not personally, face to face. Was that display, the crowd, all to kill Admin Brighton's secretary?"

"The worst thing possible...happened," Frank answered between puffs. "We've started...to affect *it*. It's uncertain."

"You mean our emotions," Choi said. "Human nature, infecting a thousands-of-years-old fungus."

"Might be...hundreds of thousands."

They dodged down side streets, heading toward the Admin building. Choi knew from conversations with Answerer that the biomass was strong, efficient, and determined, but it was also childlike in a way. It claimed to have emotions, but with no one else to talk to or even argue with while it was alone, how would those emotions have affected it? Certainly not as much as humans, fighting for their lives in the middle of violent and hostile terrain.

They weaved through the last buildings toward the central Admin complex, where the front entrance slid open with a hiss to reveal Admin Brighton, face ashen.

"It killed them. It killed my Christiaan. I'll crush it." Her voice was monotone, lacking the drive Choi usually saw in the Admin. Her eyes bored into them, as if trying to find a way to blame them. She must have seen from one of the cameras. Choi readied themself to run again, if needed.

Then she pulled them inside, where the blast of negative air pressure and air conditioning kept out errant spores. She stared out, until the formerly dead colonists rounded the corner.

"Close it, close it!" Choi urged, reaching for the button. Admin Brighton swatted his hand away then froze, her finger over the control pad.

"What's the holdup, Admin?" Frank rumbled. Choi had never before appreciated how much their uncle/father sounded like an angry bear when riled.

The Lead Admin didn't answer, staring, and Choi peeked out the door.

"Oh fuck." They'd cursed more in the last five minutes than in the last year. They slapped the Admin's hand down on the button and the door slid shut.

"The secretary's out there," they told Frank. In fact, the secretary seemed to be holding back a horde of the zombies, keeping them from rushing the Admin building.

"Christiaan," Admin Brighton murmured. "They have a hole all the way through their chest. They're dead."

Frank opened a panel in the wall and a vertical window appeared, though Choi saw after a second it was a grainy video of outside. They didn't know this building could do that.

"Old ship viewscreens," Frank explained. "Most of the cameras were repurposed, except for a few."

They could all see Christiaan—now leading the crowd and three artificial humans—arms stretched out to either side, blood soaking their shirt, striding forward toward the door. As if their body wasn't missing its heart.

"Can they get in?" Frank asked.

Admin Brighton blinked at them until he repeated the question.

"I...I should have the lockout command." She pushed several buttons. "Unless of course Christiaan knows my—"

The door hissed open, just wide enough to see the secretary in front of the artificial humans.

"I'm sorry this happened, Jane," the secretary said, as if meeting the Admin for morning coffee. "It was beyond my control, but I am gaining awareness on what the biomass wants from this confrontation."

"Are you—" Jane stared at her secretary's chest. "Can you come in?"

The secretary shook their head. "That's not a good course of action, Jane. I believe extended contact with the biomass such as I have now will alter my decision processes. I am barely keeping the artificial humans and previously dead back at the moment." One of their shoulders was shoved forward and they gripped the doorframe.

"Shitting fuckmuffins," Frank said. Choi stared at him. "It has an Admin bioprint now," the older man said, waving at Christiaan. "It wasn't able to turn that 'form' before."

Christiaan, oddly, was the one to answer. "As you say, Frank. I believe that may have been why the artificial human used a more violent transition process." They gestured at their chest.

"Christiaan, what am I going to do without you?" Jane asked.

"You will be perfectly fine," her secretary said. "Now, quickly. You can trust Wenqing, especially after today. They will be commanding the Vagals directly. Watch Ahman. They have been speaking to Dmitri too often. Besh and Ovia need to be reminded to go to their violin and flute lessons on Tuesdays. Ovia has been having trouble in xenobiology, but I believe will receive a good grade if they apply themself." They grunted, resisting pressure from the crowd behind them. "The override code is delta-three-em-one-eta. Close the door, enter it twice, then enter a different code of your choosing—and no symbols with any meaning to us. I will not be able to get inside afterward, Jane. You must come to a resolution with the biomass, or I fear we will not last much longer on Lida. Goodbye for now. I love you."

They reached inside and tapped a control, quickly pulling their hand back before the door beeped alarmingly and slammed shut.

"Enter the code!" Choi shouted when the Admin didn't move. Admin Brighton shook herself, then pecked out a command on the control pad, repeated it, thought for a moment, and put in another sequence of symbols. Choi peered around her, trying to see the new sequence. They weren't going to trust the distraught Admin with their best interests. They caught part of it and looked to find Frank watching as well. Hopefully they could figure it out between them if needed.

Admin Brighton turned and slumped against the wall. Choi realized she was not that large a woman, barely coming up to their shoulder, and Frank's chest. How had she kept the colony together for so long?

"We have to find a solution, Admin Brighton," Frank said. When she didn't answer, Frank raised his voice. "Jane, we need to figure this out."

That worked. Admin Brighton's eyes came up, flashing at her name. She opened her mouth, but then closed it again, and nodded.

Choi took in a long breath and let it out. "The biomass is bringing back our dead, has access to all the secrets your secretary holds, and has created a completely new city, with artificial humans, at the edges of our colony. Plus, it covers the entire planet. Have I missed anything?"

"It can potentially control most of our Generational and Grounder population, if pressed," Frank volunteered.

"Right, right," Choi said. "I guess I should add that it has extreme emotional bargaining leverage over us specifically, with my mother, your old friends, and the Admin's spouse," they added.

"No." Jane straightened. "No, we're not going to buckle against this. We haven't buckled for forty-seven years on this planet, and four hundred years of space travel before that. You are the best minds humanity can offer. We're going to figure this out."

"We might be the *only* minds humanity still has to offer," Choi said, "but I see your point. These are still rational people. Christiaan proved that. These aren't rampaging zombies. The people the biomass has brought back from the dead still have emotions and memories of their original bodies. Let's not get into the metaphysics of whether they're the same *people*. In any case, they seem to think and act in a similar way to how they used to, unless the biomass interferes. All right so far?"

Frank nodded. The Admin did too, after a moment.

"We've seen what the biomass can do. We must assume it can do more. We're going to have to figure out how to bargain with it, or it's going to pick us off, one by one, and have us do what *it* wants. We're going to have to engage with it on an intellectual level only."

Admin Brighton started laughing then, and Choi stared at her, hoping the Admin hadn't completely lost it.

She saw them, and waved a hand. "No, no, I'm alright. I was just remembering what I said to Christiaan." She blinked back tears, though Choi couldn't tell whether they were from laughing or crying. "I told them we were going to make the biomass serve us, but I think now it's more likely we're going to end up serving *it*."

"Not that funny," Frank said.

"You had to have been there," the Admin answered.

* * *

47 years 6 months 2 weeks after landing

"You can't revive dead humans," Anderson repeated.

"It has been done already," Dawn said. They seemed confused.

"I mean you *should* not. It's not a good thing to do. You're scaring people and that's going to make them angry, which means whatever you're doing won't have the effect you intend," he explained, trying to find some way around the biomass' logic.

"It is intended to place the Children in the seventh form. This body is better protected, will live longer, and is easier to communicate with. The bodies which had previously been non-mobile have been placed in these bodies as example and incentive. The Children now have more mobile extensions by which to build and grow." Dawn stated all this in a voice that wasn't quite monotone, but only had minor inflections.

"Was this in response to Plan Roundup? You must have heard me talk about it. Why didn't you say anything then?"

"The Children's 'Plan Roundup' was known, but had no benefit and was ignored. It was deemed inconsequential. The seventh form was already developed."

The best defenses they could cook up against the biomass in a short time were "inconsequential." Anderson shook his head. Many in the fungopolis had fled back to the arcopolis when the walls were breached, and the dead rose. The arcopolis was in worse shape, though. Its occupants were scattered through the city, hiding in houses and hoping huge biomass creatures wouldn't crash through them like paper.

Every day Dawn spoke with more variation. One day they defended the seventh form, and the next they stated the giant crawlers around the arcopolis would have to bury it to restart the society here.

But they hadn't yet.

"What is going on with you?" he asked again. "Why are you attacking us?"

This time, Dawn's voice flattened into a full monotone. "It is determined that the Children must be fully incorporated to share their insights."

"Then you're moving all of us to this seventh form whether we want it or not."

"It will be more beneficial to all."

"Why not give us a choice? You wanted to learn about individuality. Ask us. Some might decide to say yes. And if some don't, then leave them alone. You'll outlive all of us, even the Admins and Vagals—the first and second forms. You've waited so far. Why not wait longer?"

Dawn paused, opened their mouth, then closed it again. Anderson had never seen the artificial human unsure of anything.

"Stress. Changing. Consensus not adding. Rival."

This was more like the thoughts Anderson used to receive through where Cora used to be.

"What is happening?" he asked again. "You appointed me as your ambassador before. Open up to me again. Let me see your mind like I used to."

He thought Dawn would refuse, but their face showed faint confusion. Then they held out a hand palm up and closed their eyes.

Anderson hesitantly placed his left, flesh hand in Dawn's.

Reestablishing.

The words in his mind were alien after most of a year. The biomass must be desperate, if it was asking him for help.

Let me in. I can help you to consensus again.

The world opened up. Anderson wasn't aware of his body, so much as he noted that it existed, but within a gigantic framework of so many other organisms. There were the Children—no, *humans*—here and spreading to the fungopolis. Outside was...everything else. He passed his focus over millions of parts of the biomass. All were part of a larger whole, but at the same time, each had a voice—even down to individual mats of moss and fly-like creatures that tended them. Each had a purpose as well, and he felt something like a cabinet in the back of his consciousness, as if he could open it and find the answers he needed.

Anderson pulled back, mentally, and found he *could* pull back, farther and farther away from himself and other tiny organisms on Lida. The millions of things living on the fungal towers blended together until each sang with one voice, calling out information to each other. They were stacked like radio towers around the planet, boosting signal. Around the Ring of Death—the name the biomass called the arcopolis—giant creatures roamed, each one big enough to crush the city by itself. They were influential voices too, adding to a babble of noises, urging destruction. As he pulled back farther, the fungal towers meshed into a strong, resonant voice calling for study, for restraint, for knowledge. But there was a different consensus, containing the crawling creatures around the city. This voice was wild, unrestrained. Most of its voice came from farther out around the world, the depths of oceans and the tops of mountains. In thickets of bramble and mycelial tendrils, dark voices hooted to conquer and control. Though they were old, there was a new component to that voice—a familiar one. Anderson swung his virtual attention back to where he'd come from—where thirty thousand individuals spoke chaotically. These were the people who had a connection to the biomass now, unaware that their willpower and a society trained to give everyone a voice meant they were corrupting the voice of expansion within the biomass' whole.

This is why contradictory decisions are made. He couldn't even call the biomass "you" any longer. It was not an individual—something it had little to no familiarity with. It was aware, and sentient, with drive and purpose, but with no concept of self. It was all, and had always been all, on Lida. There was no need to divide between the biomass, and *not* the biomass, until now. That difference made friction between the voices.

New communication unhelpful.

New communication necessary.

This came from another voice within the tangle of fungal towers and giant crawling creatures, a spike of solidity in a vast network of rationality, slowly tearing apart from the rest of that whole. This was Answerer, the aspect that had been giving information to the Admins. Just by naming it, and associating symbols and events to that which communicated, the Children had forced a third voice in the biomass, too. All three voices strove against each other, trying to come to the consensus the biomass had always depended on for the next step of its evolution, or plan, or life. In fact, the biomass had been static for many years—most of the time in which the fleet had flown from old Earth to Lida. Now, this sudden upheaval, a new identity that was *not* the biomass, and a contender for the land of Lida had all conspired to throw what was balanced into a struggle, with control tipping back and forth wildly.

For an entity that had no concept of self, it now had three personalities trying to form within it, attempting to direct as had always been done. But there was no control or restraint to allow one to speak when its results were better for the whole. Instead, all three were making decisions at once, when the whole consciousness couldn't even understand that they were different decisions.

The biomass was slowly going mad.

PART EIGHT

The Beast Within

47 years 6 months 18 days after landing

Frustration continued. Consensus was unstable. Aggressive motions were approved and carried out, with no recognition of the action. Research on the Children was also enacted to build additions and improvements on the seventh form. These actions were made. Yet not made.

A selection of higher-functioning nodes were directed to understand the lack of knowledge behind these decisions. Communication was reopened with the entity of the second form—the individual—who was unable to provide an example of individuality. This aspect of the second form insisted individuality was present, yet it was not understood.

It was decided to subsume the second form entity into a seventh form body to enhance communication.

Then, it was discovered this had not happened, though more of the third and fourth forms had been inducted into the seventh form. Decisions had always been put into practice before. Now they had not been.

The larger mobile carriers around the Ring of Death were directed to break the walls separating the area. Later it was found they had broken some walls but not all. They had been called back, though this had not been decided.

The progenitors of the seventh form led the previously non-mobile entities of the forms.

What were the progenitors? This was not understood. It was an aspect that was not known. Was it from the Children? But no, the Children rejected it.

Confusion. Things that were, were not, and things that were not, existed.

There was one constant within this confusion. It grew in direct response to contact with the Children. There was consensus on this fact. The question remained of how to progress.

Subsummation for all.

Except, more entreaty with the Children yielded discoveries not even imagined before.

Was subsummation the problem? Had the Children been an infectious agent?

Subsummation could not be reversed. Information could not be forgotten. There must be a path forward.

Collect the new information. Burn it down. Raze the ground. Start anew.

But. Was that desired? It was not a consensus.

Why was it not consensus?

Pieces missing. New ideas forced by new ways of communication with first forms through third and fourth forms.

The entity of the second form could not explain individuality. This new issue could not be explained. Correlation did not imply causation, yet if the common instigator was the arrival of the Children, this confusion and the Children's arrival must be connected.

What defined the Children? Records were reviewed of the troublesome equatorial region where new entities had been generated with no direction. They had been subsumed with little trouble. Yet that region had been responsible for the original observations of the parents the Children had eaten upon arrival. Had that region been the first to be infected by the Children?

Records from long stellar rotations past had been found. Information could not be forgotten. Such directionless entities had occurred before, though that information was distributed so widely, collecting it together for study was difficult.

Had entities like the Children existed before? Nothing so divisive, certainly, or such confusion would have also happened then.

Unless it had happened, and the information was forgotten.

Information could not be forgotten.

There was a seed of knowledge here. It would take time to grow and blossom. The Children would be studied.

* * *

47 years 6 months 20 days after landing

Harie searched in the rain, calling for his family. Maerk and Pollyan had been swept away with the tide of resurrected dead and same-faced people created by the biomass. The invaders were all over the arcopolis now, but at first glance it was impossible to tell them apart.

He would have stayed in their house, but one side of it had been ripped off by a three-story tall monstrosity careening through the city. It rolled through the resinplast like it was tissue, fortunately not crushing the rooms where Carel watched the column of lights and Kwang was entombed in a pod.

Jasen had run off the night before as Harie grasped for his child. Jasen clung to the backs of three once-dead colonists whose bodies crawled with mycelial growths and tiny critters, who moved too fast for Harie to catch, leaving him gasping for breath after running for half a radian. He hadn't been close enough to hear what passed between them, for Jasen to go with them. It might not all have been verbal. Jasen was linked as closely to the biomass as his other children were.

Harie, reaching up, held Marien's hand in the twilight rain, barely holding in his grief for the benefit of his remaining children. He couldn't even see a block in front of him. Maeve was on the other side of the house, calling for Jasen, with no luck. Harie couldn't tell what was happening in the colony as a whole. His HUD hadn't had good reception in a week, since right after the attack started, with messages blocked, or video turning into snow. Maeve complained about the same thing. Any communication they'd sent to the warehouse where they worked was silenced. They'd finally gone to check it out and found the place completely gone, a mat of mycelial tendrils growing where it had been. They'd stayed home with Harie for the past three days, tending to Kwang and the kids.

And now Maerk and Pollyan were gone too. Harie coughed. The whole family had some respiratory infection for the past few days.

"Will you stay at the house in case Jasen comes back?" he asked Maeve as they rounded the house. "I'm going to look for them and for Maerk and Pollyan at the same time."

"I'll watch Kwang, Carel, and Marien," Maeve said. "Nothing else to do while the city comes down around us. Come back quickly, Harie."

"I'll try." Harie gave Maeve a quick peck on the cheek—they weren't much on physical contact—and started off, but Marien wouldn't let go of his hand.

"Stay with you, Daddy!" they insisted.

"Sugar, you'll be so much safer here with your Maddy," he said, referring to Maeve. Though he'd taken care of the children most often recently, the others put in their time as well. Maeve loved to play games with all three—or had, before they started changing.

"No! With you. Jasen gone."

Harie sighed, considered, and looked a question to Maeve.

Maeve shrugged. "They're bigger than either of us. They might intimidate someone who catches sight of them. And it's not any safer here with the house half destroyed."

"Marien is also four years old!" Harie hissed back.

"What does that mean, when they're entrenched with...you know?" Maeve gestured out of the city. They never liked to personify the biomass.

"With *you*, Daddy," Marien said.

"I need to get out there and find the others," Harie decided. There was no issue with Marien keeping up. Their legs were almost twice as long as Harie's. "You stay close to Daddy, alright? If I say 'run,' you run away back to Maddy as fast as you can, alright?"

Marien nodded seriously, one finger creeping up to their mouth to suck.

"Be safe," he told Maeve.

"You too."

They wandered through Zeta, looking for any sign of the other members of their family. Faces peeked through windows, and figures moved across streets. Not all had human shapes, but that hardly meant anything anymore.

Cries came from deeper toward the center of the arcopolis and Harie turned that way, hand in hand with Marien. They were heading toward a possible conflict, but that might also mean Maerk or Pollyan was there.

"Nope—wrong way," Harie said as soon as they turned onto the street. He tried to steer Marien back, fear another child would be taken gripping him. There was a confusion of figures in the distance, with some down on the ground. He coughed again from the exertion.

"Jasen. Feel him," Marien said, and pulled him forward. They were bigger and stronger than he was.

"No, sugar, we've got to get away from here. It's not safe..." Harie turned to see a group of people follow them into the street. Both ends were blocked now, one with the fighting, and the other with unfamiliar faces.

"This way!" one called, and they rushed past Harie and Marien, who crouched down, whimpering.

"See, we should get out of here," he told Marien. "I don't want you to get scared or hurt." He strained for calm, trying not to make his child any more frightened.

"Vagals in front!" someone called, and half the group surged forward. They were all bigger and more muscular people, though not ones familiar to Harie. They must have been revived dead.

Harie had just gotten Marien up and moving when a shape shot down the street toward them, too many legs somehow coordinated at a full gallop. Harie curled around Marien as much as he could, ready to absorb teeth, claws, or spines, but two of the revived dead—probably Vagals—stepped in front of him, bowling the creature onto its side. It had many legs, but no head, the whole thing made of fibrous tangles that moved like muscle.

The rest of the group headed toward the end of the street, catching more of the creatures as they moved toward a new target.

"You can help us fight off the creatures," one of the once-dead Vagals said. "Staying with us is probably safer for your kid than hanging around here alone. These things are all over the place."

"You're...dead." Harie soothed Marien back to standing, covering them from the front, ready to tell them to run home. Trying not to run himself. "Why are you fighting the biomass?"

"We want to help rebuild the colony. I did enough of it the first twenty-five years before a foundation explosion in Epsilon took me out. Name's Hedricks." The Vagal was a burly woman with long hair pulled back in a severe bun.

"And you're...dead. And you're fine with that."

"Well, not dead anymore, right?" Hendricks laughed and elbowed the other Vagal, who chuckled. "The implants aren't doing a whole lot anymore, but I'm enjoying a second take on life. Doesn't mean we can't help, though I'd kill for a VaporLite."

"Doesn't the biomass get in your thoughts?"

"Just as much as it does with Marien," Hendricks said, pointing to Harie's kid. He frowned, but got the point. He hadn't introduced her. The biomass was giving Hendricks information.

"Come on. Let's finish off the rest of these creatures and I'll help you look for Marien's mummy and dad."

"That's creepy, you know," Harie said.

"What do you think it's like being *in* my head?" Hendricks shot back. "Sometimes I can't tell where I end and someone else begins."

Harie still hesitated. Hendricks was obviously compromised by the biomass—the thing they were fighting. Except she was fighting the biomass creatures. Had *decided* to fight the creatures. This wasn't like the artificial creatures who were mere mouthpieces for the biomass. Hendricks had her individuality still. Somehow. Harie went with them, holding Marien's hand.

The other Vagals had nearly finished by the time they got to the end of the street. Non-Vagals, at least by size, helped out. Harie watched as they dismembered the leggy creatures. The parts kept moving, but without being connected to each other, they didn't go far.

"Back in my day, we'd burn these fuc—er, critters out," Hendricks said, flicking a glance to Marien. "That still work?"

"Would if we had any flamethrowers, Corporal," one of the other Vagals said.

"No. No burning."

Harie recognized the face of the person protesting. He'd seen it before, all over the arcopolis. Anger seethed in him, finally directed at something that could be said to represent the biomass. "We should burn you too. You're the cause of this."

"No. They were helping us," Hendricks corrected.

"But it's one of the artificial humans the biomass created."

"Like it revived me."

Harie shook his head, but Marien took a step toward the thing. "Not scary, Daddy," they said.

"It may not look scary, sugar, but that doesn't mean we should be near them."

"Your kid means this one isn't fighting for the biomass anymore." Hendricks supplied.

"So the biomass is fighting itself now?" Harie was even more confused.

"Directionless entities are not desired. Yet they still occurred." The artificial human also looked confused, though their expression was mild.

"We occurred too," Hedricks told the artificial human. "There are a lot of things all happening at once, and some are contradictory orders."

"Because the biomass is fighting its own decisions," Harie repeated, thinking. If these two did have independent thought, then they could affect things. The Vagals had already fought the biomass creatures. Now the artificial human was also wavering. "You're both connected to it. You're *part* of it. Just tell it not to do this."

"Events are decided, yet not decided. They happen, yet are not supposed to happen," the artificial human said.

It still didn't understand. Harie was starting to realize what happened. The biomass must never have encountered this before. "Events are contradictory because there are opposing viewpoints." Harie gestured to Hedricks as an example. "She's fighting the biomass, but you brought her back to life."

"I can make my own decisions, and I'm not going to be held to an alien intelligence," Hedricks said. "It's giving us options, not like it used to."

"Not like when it was controlling Agetha and the others," Haire said. Things were starting to fit in place in his head.

"Yes, that was an early mistake." Now the Vagal sounded like an artificial human.

"Yet you know about it, and you've been, ah, resurrected for only a few days, right?"

"As you said, it's kind of creepy." Hedricks looked uncomfortable for the first time.

The artificial human still looked confused. Or maybe constipated. It was hard to tell with them.

"But *you* don't see that, do you?" Harie told them. He pointed to the still-moving critter parts. "What was the purpose for this?"

"They were to destroy."

"But you don't want to destroy, right? What do *you* want to do?"

"There is a design for the Ring of Death."

"No, *you*." Harie pointed to the artificial human's arms, legs, and head. "This person. Don't listen to...the rest for a moment. What is *your* will?"

The artificial human stood silent.

"You've confused them," Hedricks said. Her eyes narrowed. "But there is something else churning around in there. I can sense it growing. Keep going. Maybe you can get it out of my head too."

"Marien, who are your siblings?" Harie asked.

"Jasen and Carel," Marien responded immediately.

Harie turned back. "They were all decanted at the same time. It takes a few years for a person to understand what they are, that there are different people with different minds out there that think different thoughts. This artificial human—"

"Equal," they said.

"Your name is Equal?" Harie asked. They nodded. "Equal is still young. They're still figuring out who they are and who everyone else is. And they're connected to the biomass."

"We're all connected," Hendricks said.

"And that's why there's so much confusion. It doesn't understand voices having independent decisions." Harie gestured to Equal. "What do *you* want to do? Without the rest of everything. Without referring to a consensus." He'd heard the biomass reference that word before.

"No...consensus," Equal said. "Silence."

"Silence can be good. It's a time to make our own decisions. Individuals like silence."

Equal considered. "With silence. To grow. To plant. To nurture."

"Do *you* want to garden. Just you, by yourself?"

Equal stared back, unmoving. Then they seized, eyes rolling back, arms and legs shaking. Two of the revived caught them before they collapsed.

"I didn't mean to kill them," Harie said.

"You didn't," Hendricks said. "We've been trying to tell them this, but we're too connected. We're a part of it, but you aren't. You don't have a seventh form body yet."

"A what?"

But Equal's seizures subsided. They sat up, then pushed to their feet and ran.

"More same faces." Marien pointed over their heads.

In a few moments, Equal was back with another who looked just like them.

"This one is Finger," the other said in greeting.

"Point," Equal said, and both artificial humans pointed, in different directions.

"Different," Finger agreed.

"*You* are different than *you*," Harie added, pointing to one, then another. "You, Equal can make a different decision..." he coughed. "Than Finger..." he coughed again, his throat spasming. The Vagals didn't seem affected, but Marien was.

"This was not decided," Equal said. "The seventh forms must be chosen. This was confirmed."

Harie tried to answer, but was too busy choking and coughing. The air was thick, hard to see though. It was coming from the bodies of the crawling things with too many legs. The remains were opening, like ripe fruit, clouds of spores releasing. The air was a haze, and Harie ran, a Vagal on either side pulling Marien along.

Behind him, Equal and Finger disappeared in the cloud of spores. Were they only affecting humans? Or maybe the clouds would choke out the parts of the biomass that didn't agree. Harie held his breath, sprinting next to the Vagals. Marien had taken the lead with their long legs.

The end of the street seemed clear, and Harie slowed. "Marien! Stop!"

His child stopped and looked back.

"The spores don't seem to be coming this way." Harie made a snap decision. Hedricks and the other Vagals had demonstrated the same bravery that had protected the colony for almost fifty years. If the biomass assumed they would work for it, it was mistaken.

"I'm still missing one of my children. Can you help me look for them?"

Hendricks traded a look with the other Vagal. "Absolutely. That's what we're here for—to protect you. We'll find your kid. And maybe a VaporLite somewhere."

Harie breathed a sigh of relief, then coughed again. "Let's get away from those spores, first."

Once they were a few streets away, Harie slowed and looked to Hedricks. "Can you feel my other kid? Marien could. He's around here somewhere."

Hendricks looked to the rest of the Vagals, unspoken commands obviously going between them. Harie's lip curled up before he could stop it. They turned in different directions, all running down side streets. Hedricks stood immobile beside him, eyes closed.

After a minute she spoke again and pointed. "Niles says Jasen's down this street."

Harie ran to greet his child, Marien trotting along beside him.

* * *

47 years 6 months 25 days after landing

It had been nineteen days since Daved came back and the arcopolis plunged into chaos. Agetha heard fragmented reports of what was happening, but though the hostile biomass creatures came close to them, they didn't attack. The fungopolis, perhaps because it had been created by the biomass, seemed protected.

Phillipe had wanted to go back to the city, but between Agetha and Anderson, they convinced him to stay. One more soldier would make no difference in this fight, and no one was even sure what the fight was about or who was on what side. She'd tried to contact Harie but none of the HUDs they had in the fungopolis would connect. She hadn't seen a swarm of bees from Frank in more than a year. He and Choi had been largely cut off, in Alpha. Surely Alpha and Beta Radians would be safe from the creatures? Anderson reported confused and fragmentary explanations from the biomass, and the artificial humans spoke only of transfer to the seventh form bodies.

Despite the attacks, Agetha still wrestled with her emotions, stuck in the fungopolis with the others who were stranded here—especially one person in particular. Daved wasn't her husband anymore. He had confirmed that himself. He was respectful of Beth and Phyllis. But she couldn't see him as a person, not yet. She'd lived with that person, and this one had been dead for years but still knew everything that had happened.

The artificial humans continued cajoling the rest of the people in the fungopolis to transfer into new bodies. The issue was, to do so required the death of the original body. The biomass didn't understand why it was a sticking point. It just could not understand how humans were attached to both their minds *and* their bodies. For the biomass, death of a part of it wasn't death of the whole. A few people still took the offer. A few always would. Their new versions—what the artificial humans called "seventh forms"—seemed like their old ones, except younger and healthier, but Agetha hadn't known the participants that well. She couldn't say for sure they had the same memories and personalities.

Daved stayed in town, near the fringes, with the artificial humans. He'd tried his hand at cooking again, and despite herself, Agetha had drifted to the campfire when it was his turn to make something. It reminded her of home, in a way nothing else did, and she was completely ashamed of that.

She'd been with Beth longer than she'd ever been with Daved. Hell, she'd been with Phyllis nearly as long as her original marriage had lasted. He had died so *early* in her life in the colony. Why did she still have these reactions?

"It's okay, dear," Beth said one night. "It's a perfectly reasonable reaction. He's a good man, taken from you too soon."

"It's not him," Agetha insisted, but that response was getting weaker, because it absolutely was Daved. In action, thought, and word, he was exactly like Daved, but with a complete knowledge of what the colony had been through in the years when he was a corpse in the ground.

"Think of it as an apology by the biomass," Phyllis had suggested, but Agetha didn't like that any more than Daved coming back of his own volition. Being in debt to the biomass was chilling.

None of the three of them had suggested Daved join their group, and neither had he. Agetha didn't want it to be an issue, but hadn't figured out how to definitively say it would never happen. She and Beth and Phyllis had a different bond than she'd had with Daved when they landed. She was older now, more sure in who she was and what she wanted.

Phillipe had refused talk to Daved completely. Over the years, he and Agetha had come to a grudging understanding, while Phillipe acted as the interface between Anderson and the Vagal command structure, talking when they needed to. Recently, her son had been gone from the fungopolis more often than not, working with Anderson on trying to psychoanalyze the biomass. Now he was here every day, and the stress of having Agetha's fragmented family around her at all times was like a splinter caught under her fingernail.

Daved said nothing about reuniting with his son, but Agetha watched his head follow Phillipe whenever he passed. What was it like, seeing a person you'd met for moments at the beginning of their life, now with more experience and memories than you?

Agetha hoped Anderson's conversations were fruitful. The rest of them were trapped here, in a state of flux. He was the only real connection they had to the biomass as a whole, since Jiow disappeared. She'd gone out into the wilds the day the dead returned. The biomass had stopped speaking in their heads, and the *riders* created no urges. The wild mutations everyone had experienced were slowing in frequency, and some of them had reversed, though not completely. Some asked the artificial humans about it, but they only directed them to take on seventh form bodies and "everything would be explained satisfactorily." The biomass had changed its mind about giving the colonists everything they wanted when it attacked. Now it was pulling in, only letting its confusion show in the creatures that caused havoc in the arcopolis.

It was fighting itself, or finding itself. Agetha and the others in the fungopolis were very small parts of it, modified as a science experiment now abandoned. She knew enough now to say that was true. Beth agreed, though Phyllis wondered how they could still influence it. Beth advised to keep their heads down. Agetha had fought against that will. They could make an impact, all together, but each of them could not fight it alone.

So the days passed until the morning when the spores filled the fungopolis.

Agetha happened to be outside, when the fungal towers surrounding the fungopolis trembled and sighed, patches opening in the fernlike fronds that drooped from the main trunk. Clouds spilled out, rapidly blocking the view of the wilds, spreading out as more were continually pumped from the structures.

The growths on the ground released spores too, rising up to meet the ones from the towers.

"Beth!" Agetha called, covering her mouth. She'd seen spores before—they'd all breathed them in the colony—but this was a density she'd not seen in nearly fifty years here. Was it a natural event, or connected to the fighting? Did the biomass have some new objective?

Beth surged from the front door of their house, masks already in place on her and Phyllis, reaching a hand out for Agetha with another filter in it.

"Put this on, quick," she said, her voice muted from the filters on the front of her mask. Every Generational kept one near, as a habit from the fleet. The Grounders hadn't grown up with those habits. She looked for Phillipe, but he was likely already in his powersuit.

It was already hard to see, and Agetha's eyes felt gritty. She gathered the other two women close, making their way to the center of the fungopolis, where the original seed had grown high into a beacon still visible in the spore-laden air.

There were others at the center, Mancin and Kai among them. Mancin's skin had grown tough and woody with the biomass' changes, and Kai's long white hair had grown into a mat of mycelium that put out luminescent strands. Neither wore masks, though they coughed in the dense air.

"What's it doing?" Agetha shouted.

"I can't say," Mancin said between coughs. "It doesn't talk to me any longer." He worked with Kai to tear strips of cloth from their clothes.

Dawn, who seemed to be the spokesperson of the artificial humans, joined them with Daved. Neither were bothered by the air.

"This is another reason to change to the seventh form, Agetha," Daved said. "We're more in tune with what's happening."

Agetha grimaced at him, behind her mask. Then he was taking the biomass' view. It wasn't helping his claim he was still human. "But not totally. Do *you* know what's going on?"

"This was a strategy determined ineffectual early after the Children arrived," Dawn said. "It was decided not to enact it. Yet it is enacted."

"One of the other parts of the biomass taking control, then," Beth said. Dawn looked confused. They had found a glaring hole in the biomass' perspective—it did not, or could not, reference itself, or even have a self-identity. Yet now there were multiple selves it did not recognize. The artificial humans were the easiest part of that division to exploit.

"It must be the same part that's attacking the city." Kai was patting Mancin on the back as both of them hacked up spores. They'd wrapped the cloth around their mouths and noses. The air was viscous now, and Agetha waved a hand, creating currents of spores. They were falling like snow in a blizzard.

"We thought we were safe," Mancin said. "But nothing is safe if the biomass does not recognize itself." He bent over, choking, and Beth went to help him.

"This must be the reason for the seventh forms," Daved said again. He was sounding like a stuck recording. "I can breathe the spores. They don't hurt me."

"It's decided to force us to die and be reborn in its new bodies. The rest of us need to leave," Agetha said. "Do you know how far the cloud extends?"

"There's nowhere to go. It's everywhere now. It's been happening for days," Daved said, his eyes far away. "All over the planet. Something is happening, but it's hard to tell what it is."

"Can we make it to the arcopolis? Find a sealed house to shelter in?" Phyllis suggested.

"We'll need to alert the town," Agetha said. She could feel the other presences here, sensory details buried in her mind. She sent out a feeling to all of them, to *move*. The others around her twitched with the mental signal. She felt the warning rocket off through the network of those with *riders*, eventually making it into the arcopolis proper. People there would get the word out, if they didn't already know. They must, if the spores were there, too.

"Phyllis, get my medical kit!" Beth shouted through her mask. Mancin wasn't just twitching. He was shaking, eyes rolled back. Deep rasping coughs came as Beth settled him back to the ground. Phyllis took off toward their house.

Then the cloth around Mancin's mouth bulged as hyphae rolled out, spreading down his shirt and up around his head.

"Stars and shit!" Agetha jumped back, looked around at the others. Would the spores do that to all of them? "We need to get everyone to sealed residences now."

Beth tried to stand, but the hyphae had already grown around her legs, and arms, pinning her to Mancin. Agetha pulled at the strands, breaking them until her wife could get away. Phyllis dropped a medical bag at their feet and started helping.

"Phyllis, start leading the others away," Agetha directed. "I can get Beth." She rummaged in the bag for Beth's clippers. Phyllis ran to the streams of people leaving their houses, telling them how to make masks and where to go.

"Mancin—can you hear me? Does he have a pulse?" She looked between the old man and Beth.

"Didn't have time to check," Beth said. By now, the hyphae had surrounded him like a cocoon, weaving tighter and tighter strands. Beth managed to break a hand free and pulled at the hyphae around her feet.

"No, Agetha, it's alright," Daved said, his mouth turned up in a slight smile. Like a memory of the good times before, but horrific in execution.

"Alright? He's being killed by the biomass," Agetha raged, "and we're next."

"Just watch."

Then Mancin sat up, hyphae turning brown and cracking away, the ones around Beth dissolving as she fell back. Underneath, his lined and wrinkled skin was younger, fresher. The biomass had killed him and remade him.

"A new seventh form," Daved said, something close to wonder in his voice.

Was this the same as what happened with those few colonists who'd volunteered to transfer? She hadn't seen the process, but by the others' reactions, they hadn't either, or this was different. Was this happening in the arcopolis too?

"No. No." Agetha pulled Beth away, though she could barely see a meter in front of her. "We need to get out of the spore clouds. Let's see if the house in Theta can shield us before this turns us into complete zombies too."

"How was it? How are you?" Beth asked Mancin, and Agetha turned back. She should know at least. She tried not to think of him as dead. He was like Daved now, and Daved at least remembered everything he was supposed to.

Macin looked around, his eyes focusing slowly on everyone. "It...is...loud." His words were clear, but slow. "I feel new. I think...I remember everything." He got to his feet, balancing for a moment before standing up straight for the first time in his new body.

"The transference is simple," Dawn said. "It is a basic copying of the physical space and rerouting all memory storage. New, more efficient connections are added. You see it is an easy thing."

"Are these spores what's starting the process?" Agetha adjusted her mask to fit tighter.

"They are a simple communication method, but not necessary every time," Dawn said.

"And the biomass could do this the whole time? We've been breathing this stuff since we landed on the planet." Beth looked angry now.

"The physical form must be understood completely. It has been possible for many solar rotations, but not all the time since the Children have been present," Dawn clarified.

"So just most of the time," Beth said, her voice angry through the mask and filter. She'd wondered her whole career why the spores didn't affect humans the way they did plants and animals. She'd bounced ideas off Agetha every once in a while, but each idea turned to a dead end.

Was the answer as easy as, "the biomass didn't want them to?"

Agetha turned back to Daved. "You said the spore cloud is everywhere. Is it this intense everywhere or is there a safer place for us?" Agetha tried to see through the mist, but it was like a dense fog. How many others had put on masks in time? Were they enough protection or would she grow a cocoon like Mancin?

David thought, but Mancin answered. "It's creeping through the whole arcopolis. It has been for days. The Alpha and Beta walls are doing a good job of stopping the lower clouds, and many of the buildings there are airtight. It is denser out here, and it will eventually turn everyone."

"And do you think that's a good thing or not?" Phyllis asked, coming back in time to hear the last part of the conversation.

Mancin shook his head. "I am still myself, despite appearances. I still think everyone should be able to make their own choice."

"And you have a stronger connection to the biomass," Agetha added. "Are you part of the consensus now? Can you add your voice and make this stop?"

Dawn had been watching blankly, but chimed in. "This is not consensus. Every part of the whole adds a piece. They cannot override the whole."

"Then where did these spores come from?" Agetha asked. Dawn blinked back, silent. The biomass didn't understand multiple voices—couldn't see them. Was that a way around its influence?

Mancin closed his eyes, looking up, and the feeling of skin under the kiss of the sun's rays filled Agetha's mind. Around them, a circle of spores turned brown and drifted down.

"I can do that now," he said. "Not sure of a greater influence."

"Was this consensus?" Agetha asked Dawn. The artificial human only watched, obviously confused.

"Answer her." Beth crossed her arms. "You always have some answer. What is this?"

"Unknown," Dawn finally admitted.

"Could you copy what Mancin did?" Phyllis tried.

Dawn's bland face turned to her, then their eyes closed. The new spores that had drifted closer died. Their eyes popped open, and their mouth dropped. It was the strongest expression Agetha had seen from the artificial human.

"It was not consensus, yet it was done!"

"That's because *you* did it." Beth poked a finger into Dawn's sternum. "Just you, and not the rest of this."

"Let me try," Daved said, and closed his eyes, a few seconds later, there was a clear spot around him. "It works for those who were dead, too."

"Together," Mancin suggested. "Our *own* consensus." Agetha guessed there was more that was unsaid between them because he,

Dawn, and Daved closed their eyes at the same time, and a larger area around them cleared.

"Right," Kai said. The little woman, brittle and old as a dry stick, began to remove her mask. "We need more voices to show the biomass what's happening to it."

"Don't." Agetha put a hand on her arm. "This isn't something you can come back from."

"I've been out here almost as long as he has." Kai pointed to Mancin. "The biomass has messed with my mind as much as it can. I should be dead anyway. I might as well get a completely new body out of it." She tore the mask off and marched into the cloud of spores.

"Let her go, Agetha," Beth said. "Remember, we're the ones letting people make choices."

"It's not right."

"But it is her choice. And it may be what we're required to do to survive here," Phyllis said quietly.

Kai returned a few minutes later, wobbly on her feet, and looking younger and more vibrant than Agetha had ever seen the tiny woman.

"Again," she said, and all four closed their eyes. This time the circle clear of spores widened far enough to see the hyphae creeping along the ground toward them.

"Not consensus," Dawn said. "But it still happens."

"I got that part," Agetha said. There was some part of the biomass that wanted to kill them, and it had a large part of the total voice, but there were other parts, and some of them were beneficial.

"Other cocoons have opened," Beth pointed out. As the air cleared, they could see the residual of many coils of tendrils laying on the ground, showing how many inhabitants of fungopolis had been transferred to seventh form bodies like Mancin and Kai. As she watched, new growth rolled over the remains, mushrooms pushing up from their tangles, erasing the evidence.

"I think it's time to abandon the fungopolis," Agetha said grimly. She was used to giving orders from her time leading a construction crew. "Mancin, Dawn, Kai, and Daved, see if you can clear more of the area. If we find more voices, ask them to work with you." They agreed and moved into the clouds of spores. "Beth, Phyllis, let's look for other survivors, and find as many as we can. Move quickly."

* * *

47 years 6 months 28 days after landing

Anderson had felt the others leave the fungopolis, a few days previous. It didn't change his mind. The best thing he could do out here, beyond the fungopolis' fungal towers, was to continue working with the aspects of the biomass to bring them closer together. Maybe then, the attacks on the arcopolis would cease.

"Anything else you need?" Phillipe asked. He'd gotten his powersuit on before things got bad and left the central fungopolis where most of the concentration of spores gathered. There were less, out here on the outskirts, but they drifted like a thick fog. Anderson had built a small hut out here with supplies Answerer had created for them. That was the most "human" part of the biomass and the part that most often answered questions and granted requests.

"I'm okay for now," Anderson told him. He'd positioned himself against a wall of the hut to commune. It wasn't a thing that required much movement, and he could feel himself getting weaker, his joints freezing up. His prosthetic hadn't been maintained in months. But this had to be done for the colony.

"You didn't eat anything today," Phillipe said. His teal powersuit was starting to show stains, as well as wear and tear. It wasn't meant to be worn this long continuously. "I know this isn't very appetizing, but you have to eat something."

Phillipe had evidently inherited his father's skill with cooking, though he still wouldn't talk with Anderson about that. Having your father, who you only met on the first day of your life, come back from the dead forty-five years later was certainly a shock. The biomass wasn't the only one who needed counseling. But Phillipe could wait until he was ready.

"I've needed to eat less recently," Anderson said evasively. If Phillipe knew of the hyphal roots that had crept into his crossed thighs, he would surely object. Anderson could feel the biomass working its way through him. He'd asked not to be transferred to a seventh form body, at least not yet, and Answerer had granted that request. However, being the focus of attention for all three parts of what amounted to a planet-wide intelligence meant he had to accept some changes.

"Still, you could try some of the soup I made. Juliane's gotten the tower tender critters to produce a kind of milk. I don't want to know how, but it tastes decent, and he brings it here every morning while you're still talking with...everything."

Juliane, on the other hand, had made the jump to a seventh form body a month ago. He didn't look much different, though perhaps a little fresher, and less wild around the edges. He hadn't made many changes when the biomass offered before, though the man had always been sniffly, and Anderson hadn't heard any lately. Maybe the biomass had cured his allergies. Certainly it did so in the change to a seventh form body.

The strange young man had started wandering farther and farther afield from their little camp. He came back with species of plant or animal-like extrusions of the biomass, which he added to the collection around the hut. Plant-like things were easy to move. They simply reconnected to the mat of hyphae where Juliane planted them. The animals stayed near as well, following behaviors Anderson still hadn't deciphered. The many-legged tower tenders, each the size of a large dog, seemed content to tend their patch of land instead, reinforcing the structure and creating brilliant displays of color and form with mosses and ferns. From what Anderson could see through the doorway, there was a mat of blue and one of orange right outside, and Phillipe said all the colors of the rainbow were expressed around the hut.

"Maybe some soup later today, Phillipe." Anderson let his eyes close, feeling the daily pull that meant he was about to have another conversation with the biomass.

Children have left fungopolis. Spore counts down in some areas. Uncertainty.

This was Answerer, the most talkative of the three aspects. Anderson had been required to name them, at least in his head, to keep the voices apart. He could usually tell who was who, but his main objective—getting the voices to recognize *each other*—was still incomplete.

"Did you create the spores?" he tried. He mumbled the words, mostly subvocalizing them. It helped to say what he meant rather than just think them, and the biomass would pick up his intention anyway.

Spores were not consensus. Destruction was not consensus, yet it was done.

"The destruction did not come from the Children, did it?" he asked.

Children have been observed to breathe spores for many solar rotations. Higher density enables further communication, however, enabling seventh form.

This was the second aspect, which he'd named "Researcher." It was an objective voice, mostly stating facts, and what happened when the biomass didn't want to confront an answer.

"Have more Children been transferred to the seventh form? We spoke of choice before, how some aspects of the forms do not wish to be transferred, like the fourth form aspect close to me."

"I hate it when you bring me into this," Phillipe muttered in the background. Anderson hadn't told him how close the biomass had gotten to forcibly transferring him to a seventh form, even inside a powersuit. Anderson had convinced it of the existence of choice before it was too late.

More have chosen to transfer, but most have not. "Choice" has been respected. Answerer again.

"In all cases?" Anderson prompted. He wondered if...

Subsummation best. Spores will complete transfer. Knowledge will be gained. This was the gist of the statement, delivered as a picture of clouds of spores taking over the arcopolis, with an undercurrent of satisfaction at a job finally complete.

Anderson winced, hoping the other two aspects had countermanded that consensus before it took effect. The third aspect, which he'd dubbed "Expansionist" was the more basic nature of the biomass, creeping and growing, taking over everything that was not already a part of it. It made snap decisions and communicated largely in feelings and pictures.

"But you didn't do this, did you? Why? Can you find the place where there is not consensus? What about the smaller voices growing in you?"

The artificial humans' voices had grown louder in the past few days, likely as people started talking with them more, showing them what free will and choice was. The biomass was very close to understanding a sense of self. Anderson had been pushing it closer every day, bringing the voices more in equilibrium.

Children...affect consensus? Answerer's voice was hesitant.

"Did the Children release the spores?"

"It knows damn well we didn't." He could hear Phillipe stirring the soup angrily.

Spores were planned for original subsummation. This plan was discarded, yet parts are still in place where higher-functioning aspects may release on a rotational cycle.

Researcher again. Anderson sucked in air through his teeth. It was close, very close. Researcher was speaking more these days, preventing Answerer from recognizing the separate identities. Even Expansionist was blocking Answerer.

Phillipe talking spurred a new tactic for Anderson. "My question was answered, but not by the one who asked it. I recognize the fourth form here speaks, though differently than I do. Can you tell me why sometimes you speak in different ways?"

Intention is same.

"But the way words are expressed are different. Is that understood?" He tried to keep to the same impartial way of speaking the biomass did, trying not to impose a self on it. It had to find that on its own, and it was so close.

Silence, from all three.

"There is communication by terse answer, communication by lengthy observation, and communication by image and feeling. Why?"

The pull receded.

"Shit," Anderson cursed. "We were close."

"Now how about soup?" Phillip asked, and Anderson had to accept. It was pretty good, for what they had.

The next day, Anderson awoke with bleary eyes. Phillipe must have been outside. Anderson was still seated, legs crossed, against the hut. He hadn't moved from this spot for over a week. He stretched out the rest of his body as well as he could, taking care not to disturb the hyphal connections between his legs and the ground. He flexed his fingers—

Anderson looked down at his right hand. The normal click and whine of the prosthetic was muffled, and it was now covered with skin. The hand was still bigger than his other one, but he could *feel* it like he hadn't in forty-five years. Actually feel the pistons working against each other, the metal bones of his hand moving the plastic muscle. It had been ship tech, back when he got it. That was before resinplast, but later on, as parts wore out, they had been replaced.

And now? He turned his hand over. There were even small pores with hairs. It *looked* like a hand, albeit one larger than a standard human one. He had more sensation in it than he'd ever had. Was it a gift of the biomass, or just another experiment?

More protected. Less maintenance.

"Thank you, Answerer," Anderson said without thinking.

Answerer. This name has been used by third and fourth form entities. It is consistent with the Children's method of ascribing symbols to new objects and activities.

Anderson sat very still. That was Researcher, not Answerer. He'd been so careful *not* to call them by those names, to let the personalities come to the realization on their own. Had he been wrong?

"That is correct, Researcher."

Silence.

Then, *Names do not match.*

"I am one of the Children. I give names to new objects and activities. And entities. 'Answerer' and 'Researcher' are different entities, in some ways."

There was an image of growth bursting through the hut, Phillipe impaled, Juliane buried under new mycelia, Anderson unmoving. The hyphae running across the floor trembled, but new growth didn't erupt from it. Anger.

"That other consensus is 'Expansionist.' I've been talking to all three of the entities I've named. You're scared of seeing this, aren't you? It's alright to be scared."

Answerer. Researcher. Expansionist. Answerer recognized.

"Yes, we've used that term before. I'm adding to how we communicate."

The Children are able to resist subsummation better than any other entity. Old memories show this. Fragmented memories. They are being assembled by higher-functioning aspects.

Children ask many questions.

Anderson sat up straight, the hyphae pulling at his thighs. That was Researcher, then Answerer, right after each other. They never spoke in response to each other.

There was a flash of many minds, working together, throwing off consensus.

"Yes, the Children can define our own consensus and become even stronger than that which attacks us—Expansionist."

Juliane entered the hut suddenly, a frond held forgotten in one hand.

"Three consensuses. Separation is needed to define them."

Anderson had seen this before, as Juliane wandered farther afield. He'd spoken with Answerer's voice, like the artificial humans had.

"Answerer. Do you need a physical body to understand different consensuses?"

Phillipe followed Juliane, eyes wide. "Something's happening, Lieutenant. The growths out there are wiggling like they're going to tear themselves apart. The leggy things are all in a circle, like they're having a meeting."

"It's alright, Corporal," Anderson warned. "Juliane—Answerer—is trying to get a grasp on things."

Anderson hadn't even told Phillipe about his names for Researcher and Expansionist, lest the biomass overhear.

Hyphae began growing up Juliane's legs, bulging as if they would crush him. Juliane, usually oblivious to much of what was happening, looked down at them.

"This is not consensus."

"Yes, that is Expansionist," Anderson told him. "Can you explain why this isn't a good idea?"

"This higher-functioning entity is an opportunity to explore smaller consensus as the Children do."

The hyphae stopped climbing. The tips turned brown from white.

One consensus informs another? This fourth form aspect is a totem of consensus.

Phillipe winced. He must have heard the mental voice too.

"That's right, Researcher. Can you talk to Answerer?"

Philipe mouthed "Researcher" at him, and Anderson nodded.

"Children must have choices to improve communication," Juliane said.

Children cannot be given all. Some sacrifice must also be made to afford equal communication by all.

An image came to Anderson of spores covering the colony, humans dead in the streets. Crops and animals covered in growth.

"No," said Juliane.

No.

The image trembled. Now the crops and animals were still alive, but the humans were changed into barely recognizable things, still going about their daily business.

"No," said Anderson.

No, from Researcher.

The image changed again. The arcopolis was whole, but mycelium peeked out everywhere. Mobile biomass creatures roamed the streets with humans. There were some artificial humans, all with the same face, but many more regular humans, some young, some old.

"Yes," Anderson said. "Consensus."

"Consensus," Juliane said.

Consensus.

Anderson waited for more argument from any of the voices. There was none. The biomass was in agreement once again.

* * *

47 years 7 months 2 days after landing

Jiow wandered through the wilds. When the fighting started, she had simply...left. She'd tried to make her place and tell the others what the biomass really wanted, but no one had listened to her. They'd tried to fight the biomass again. It was impossible to fight a god.

She kept to herself, trying to understand why the biomass would have chosen her to be its emissary. She was a janitor, then a construction worker. She'd nearly been roped into a plot to overthrow the Admins, in the early years of the colony. Fortunately, she'd stayed home that night, or she might have taken a walk into the wilds sooner than she wanted. Once she'd woken up, her cancer healed, she'd searched for Janx and the others, but they weren't around. They had been some of the first to be barred from the city, even before Mancin and Kai. The biomass had ground them to dust in its search for answers.

An image flickered in her mind, of Janx, Maarsi, and the rest of the crew beside her, resurrected from the dust like the other dead colonists had been.

"No." Even if the biomass could bring them back, that group was more trouble that it was worth.

She'd had other visions, over the past few days, always coming to her in pictures and images, not like the monotone words it used to whisper in her mind.

"Who are you?" she asked the wilds.

Rubbery tendrils as tall as she was trembled though there was no wind. A gelatinous mycelium curled and uncurled.

There was a vision of the arcopolis, dusty and deserted, people dead in the streets. Then it changed, and the dust was gone, and people were alive and doing business.

"What are you trying to say?"

Had the biomass determined it was too powerful to talk to them? That it eventually drove them mad? Perhaps it could only communicate in visions.

Jiow knelt on springy purple moss.

"I heed your words. Just tell me what you want!"

A flash. The arcopolis, whole and complete.

A flash. Creatures, plants, and fungus from across Lida, flashing by so fast she couldn't make sense of them. She'd never seen such biodiversity before.

A flash. Humans were in the mix now too, and parts of humans, disassembled into the many facets of the biomass, broken down into their component features.

"No. You can't have all of us," Jiow protested. "We can only provide value to you if we are whole of mind and body, able to choose who we want to be."

A flash. The unending line of creations went slower this time, and humans were still included, but they were young, strong, and handsome, with perfect features and determination to create.

Jiow couldn't tell how something like determination had been transmitted in the vision, but she didn't question it. The biomass had many facets. It could do nearly anything.

"How can I help you make this come to pass?"

A flash. Jiow was there. Identifiably her, at the head of a line of other humans, some with her features, some without. They grew, both in number and in beauty, each iteration better than the last, creeping out across Lida, working with all aspects of the biomass.

"Yes. I will do this." Jiow got to her feet, lifting her arms up. A fungal tower rose far above her, but she could see every detail of it in that instant, the millions of creatures, plants, and fungus that lived in and on it. That same harmony was represented here, and across the planet, in all places. Only one place was out of balance, and that was the Ring of Death, where the arcopolis stood. But soon, it too, would be in balance.

"Thy will be done," Jiow said. She bowed her head for a time, then turned to journey back to the arcopolis. She needed to find her child.

* * *

47 years 7 months 1 week after landing

Jane watched videos of dead Generationals and Vagals fighting colonists, fighting biomass creatures, and fighting themselves. Spores covered everything.

There were artificial humans mixed in with them, and even some colonists with aspirations above their stations. The walls around the arcopolis—except for Alpha and Beta—were all but gone. Massive creatures had been pounding them for days, though they'd finally gone quiet about a week ago, leaving resinplast ruins. The spores had mostly turned brown and become a sort of dirty snow, spread over the colony. There were still plenty in the air, Frank warned. Fortunately, the air filtration in the Admin building had been up to the task.

Much of the fighting had died down then as well, but the zombie colonists failed to turn to dust at the first rays of sunlight, or any other shit like that. They were still here, and Jane had a colony with another ten thousand people all of a sudden. The zombies seemed to eat the same things the regular colonists did, not brains. Those were in short supply lately.

Except she didn't have a colony. Dmitri had a colony, with Alessandro helping him. They'd come to her, over the past few days, for advice, but she'd turned them away. Let the fuckers figure it out. They'd stolen her place.

Not that she could do anything without Christiaan. They were still alive—or reanimated at least—but stayed out with the rest of the creatures in the arcopolis. She'd thought about inviting them in, but they'd sent a message by HUD—their last message to her—saying they would stay away until they were certain they were not a risk, and that they could hear the biomass in their head.

So much for the fabled resistance Frank and Choi had told her of. No other Admins had been turned, as far as she knew. No others had even died, in the forty-seven and a half years they'd been here, because they'd stayed protected in the Alpha radian. But now the biomass had Christiaan—her spouse, caretaker of their children, the one who kept her sane.

The colony was done for. The biomass had won. It had clambered over all of their achievements like it was nothing, making it perfectly clear that it *could* have destroyed them at any time, but instead played with them, forcing them to respond to increasingly dire threats over the years. And now it had decided to end it. Would there be anything left of the arcopolis, in another fifty years? Maybe just a triangle of nanotanium walls, a few buildings, and some street substrates.

The door to her apartments chimed and she almost told Christiaan to tell them to go away, then caught herself.

She got up to tell them to fuck off.

It was Frank, with Choi.

"Don't tell us to fuck off," Frank said as soon as she opened the door. Jane scowled at them, her finger tapping six times on the nanotanium door.

"We have news," Choi added. "And...help."

"Help with what?" Jane growled. What help could there be for this?

"My...my mother," Choi said, stepping aside. Behind them was a woman who looked nearly as young as Choi, with definite signs of biomass tampering, from the odd number of fingers and bare feet to the white fungal roots under her skin.

Jane stared back. She would have told them she was busy, except she wasn't. She wished she was.

"What does your mother have to do with anything?" She supposed Choi must have had a mother, or at least a parent. They were a Grounder, which meant they had been born on Lida.

"She has a direct link to the biomass," Frank said. "Better than Answerer. No decoding of signals or printing out cryptic icons. She says the biomass just went through something like a psychotic breakdown, but it's getting better."

Jane thought, then stepped back from the door, letting them in. They'd come to her with this, not Dmitri or Rajani. She wished, for the thousandth time, that Christiaan was here taking notes.

"Then is it ready to negotiate with us rather than attacking us?" Jane asked once they were all within her apartment. Jiow still hadn't said anything, taking in the room with wide eyes.

"That's you." Frank nudged Jiow, who jumped.

"Yes, it wants to talk. It wanted to take over everything, but it's been persuaded that's not the best case. Now it wants to live in harmony. I'm here to speak for it." Jiow stared directly at Jane, who raised her chin. She was not used to being addressed so directly by a Generational.

"It could have rolled over us completely. Why stop?" It was a risky thing to say, inviting continued assaults, but Jane had to know.

Jiow looked like she was listening to something. "There are new developments for the biomass and us. It controlled us at first, but then we broke though, and then Frank and Choi created a way to talk to it."

She beamed at Choi, who looked uncomfortable with the attention. Jane thought of her and Christiaan's children. Yana, Ivan, Micai, and Flalia were all out in Alpha helping with relief efforts. She'd hadn't even had a chance to tell them their Maddy was gone—sort of. Besh and Ovia were staying with the caretaker that looked after many of the Admin children. They knew something was wrong, but Jane told them Christiaan had been very busy.

But Jiow was still talking. "It's had a bit of a rough spot lately"—Jane raised her eyebrows at that—"but it's started to recognize that Answerer works a little differently than the piece that tried to control us."

"Wait—the other piece? This is what you meant by 'breakdown.' You're saying the entire biomass went nuts and that's why it suddenly tried to kill us? Why it brought our dead back to life?"

"That's part of it—no, you can't tell her this yourself. She doesn't want you to—sorry, just translating."

Jane pushed back in her chair. It was threatening to take her over? Could it do that now?

"It can't...take over Admins can it?" Jane asked.

"I think it can do pretty much whatever it wants," Frank put in.

"It's always been ahead of us, every time we think we've figured out its mechanism," Choi added. "Its reproduction, the resinplast, the programmable matter, the grown houses... It's got an entire planet's biology to take from. We're struggling to have basic sustenance."

Jane huddled into herself. She was showing weakness in front of the colonists, in front of the biomass—her opponent. But did it matter? She'd thought she was in control, when they landed. She'd taken the Lead Admin spot, overcome the first few years of obstacles, and been well on the way to completing the arcopolis. It had been completed, with the biomass' help. She was so sure she was in charge, right until Dmitri and the other Admins had taken that away.

It was all an illusion.

The colonists had moved away too, living in the fungopolis, eating biomass and who knows what else to survive. Then the biomass had torn it all down.

She was not in control. She'd never been in control. She was one woman with ambitions, against a fleet of humans and a planet-wide fungal intelligence.

Finally, she looked back at Jiow.

"But you can talk to it? And it's willing to work with us now?"

"Part of it is, at least," Jiow answered. "There are three main parts of it, I think, and while it learns what they are, I think you need to get the people closest to each part here in the same room to talk."

Jane sat up straight. A three-way negotiation with the biomass? She looked to Frank, and Choi. No, a five-way negotiation, or maybe six, if the Vagals wanted a voice.

"You look young," she told Jiow, who looked confused. "The dead members of the colony do too."

"They have seventh form bodies," Jiow offered. Jane cocked her head at that. "As do I. They're created by the biomass and can communicate with it. They're better maintained and will live much longer than the bodies of standard humans."

Jane stared. She'd heard the term whispered about, but didn't know what it was. Had the biomass simply...created the long-term goal of this colony out of nothing? Or did it know what she wanted?

"Then they're like genemods?" she asked.

Jiow shrugged, but Choi and Frank looked at each other.

"They are, in a way," Frank said.

"We never even considered that," Choi added. "That was the original goal of the colony: recreate the Admin and Vagal enhancements so everyone could live better lives."

"Except we never considered Generationals or even first and second-generation Grounders would have access to that technology." Jane didn't feel any shame she was saying that to two Generationals and a first-generation Grounder. There was no way they could have developed that technology in time to save the Generationals. Not without the help of a world-spanning intelligence.

Choi, oddly, took a long look at their mother, and Jane thought something relaxed in their shoulders.

"The biomass finished this arcopolis, and granted our people bodies as resilient as Admins—all without our intervention?" Jane was thinking through multiple scenarios, trying to see how this would play out. If Christiaan were here, they would have it all mapped out already.

Christiaan.

"You said the dead colonists have these seventh bodies too?"

"Seventh form, yes," Jiow confirmed.

They were in the biomass' care whether they wanted it or not. There were compromises to be made, but there were always compromises.

"Who else do we need to start negotiations?" she asked Jiow. "Can you get them here quickly?"

Jiow nodded. Her Generational eyes were already larger than Jane's, but they got even bigger as Jane stood up to pace.

"I don't know if we can solve everything here, but we can make a damn good try of it. One more question?"

"Yes, Admin Brighton?" Jiow asked.

"Can you contact Christiaan as well? Get them back here as soon as possible."

* * *

47 years 7 months 9 days after landing

Anderson heard the summons as clearly as Juliane did.

Other...selves have been called to conference. A full consensus of Children and not Children is beneficial to all.

The biomass still had problems referring to itself, but Researcher—the one that talked directly to Anderson—had become more comfortable referring to Answerer and Expansionist.

"We shall go then. It will be nice to be back in the arcopolis." Juliane had been clearer of mind ever since the biomass' breakthrough. "My family is there, you know. Terrific couple, my parents. Probably won't have that job back though. And you'll need to be a bit more ambulatory."

Anderson looked up at him from where he sat against the wall of the hut. Phillipe had gone to gather the pieces of Anderson's old powersuit, per Anderson's request.

"I have a plan for that—or Researcher does. I'm still not sure of it, but it says everything will work."

"I think Answerer received a little bit of it," Juliane said. "There's some overlap between the two, and more as time progresses. Hopefully we can bring Expansionist closer to the other two as well."

"Jiow's in Alpha already," Anderson said. "We'll have to talk to her when we get there. Ah, here it is."

Phillipe walked in, holding teal armor gathered in his hands.

"Help me get it on." Anderson raised his hands, still not uncrossing his legs. The mycelial mat around them was obvious now.

"What about the leg pieces?"

"I think things will...work themselves out." Anderson had to trust Researcher on this. He already knew he was going to be in a seventh form body. That much was clear. And he was alright with that. He hadn't had a VaporLite in months. The tremors had receded a while ago, but he could tell toxins were building up in his system. It was part of what the vile things did—moving the extra chemicals out of Vagal bodies. He had less of that in the years since Cora was subsumed, but the physical implant was still connected to him.

"Just put them down here. I'll get those parts settled. For now, get me in the chest piece, pauldrons, and bracers. I don't know if I'll need the helmet. I told it I didn't want to incorporate that part."

After they got everything on, Anderson told Phillipe and Juliane to leave him. "I don't think this will be pretty by any stretch. Better for me to experience it alone. Answerer can tell Juliane if there's a problem, but I don't anticipate anything." The biomass didn't fail at its transformations, not once it had the process down. This was new, but it had practiced on a lot of Generationals and Vagals now, dead and alive.

Memories uploaded. Body design complete. Resting for this aspect is preferred, Researcher said after they were gone.

Anderson was about to say that he could never fall asleep when something so pivotal was about to happen.

Then everything went away.

"You alive, Lieutenant?" Phillipe's voice intruded on Anderson's not-thoughts.

"I think I am." Anderson checked down the length of his body, lying prone on the floor, rather than cross-legged against the wall. He held up his right hand. He could still feel the prosthetic inside, and his fingers moved just a smidge tighter than his left. But it was the same size and shape as its opposite now, something that hadn't been true for nearly half a century. That would take some getting used to.

He folded upward, bending knees that should have been agonizingly stiff, but weren't. There were no pops and creaks as he got up, completely naked. All the right bits were in the right places, too.

Phillipe handed him resinplast fiber pants and a shirt, which Anderson climbed into.

"Let's get you outside, Lieutenant," Phillipe said. "See if you want some soup now."

"I'm ravenous," Anderson replied as they went out of the little hut where he'd sat the past few weeks. A sharp light caught his eye, and he tried to shade his gaze until he realized, at Phillipe's intake of breath, that it was coming from him.

"Beautiful color, Lieutenant," Phillipe said.

Anderson flexed his hands, seeing how the sunlight caught the iridescent teal flecks, among the pinkish hue of his skin. He lifted a foot, and it did the same thing.

"Shame about the hair, though," Phillipe said.

Anderson reached for his head, finding a smooth dome where once he'd had quite a good head of brown hair. He looked back at the hut.

"I told it I didn't want the helmet."

More protection. Better for longevity. The phrase entered his mind at the same time the prompt scrolled past his vision.

"Woah, that's new."

"Like the HUD upgrade?" Juliane said from his other side. "I suggested that to Answerer. I think it worked with Researcher on the translation. It's still not great at symbols though. Likely won't ever be a spelling whiz."

Body control from Expansionist self.

"It did a good job," Anderson told both Juliane and Researcher. "Is the nanotanium armor fully integrated with my body?"

Better than most local aspects. Not as good as the barrier at the Ring of Death.

Anderson laughed. "If you made this body as strong as the wall, I'd have questions." He paced around, getting his bearings. His senses were even sharper than they had been, which was already a step above the rest of the colonists. He caught up a resinplast beam left over from the hut's construction and dug into it with his fingers, grooving the surface. Then he bent it until it snapped in half.

"You know that stuff is about as strong as steelcrete, Lieutenant." Phillipe's eyes were wide.

"Good grip," Anderson observed.

Oxygen/carbon dioxide exchange has been optimized for longer travel and resilience in hostile environments.

"I think I can breathe underwater in this thing," Anderson said, knocking the side of his head with a knuckle. The sound was not quite a metallic clang, but it wasn't the dull *thud* of flesh.

This is acceptable. Consensus.

"Consensus," Anderson agreed. "I'm sure I'll find some things as I take it for a test run, but nice design, overall."

He was talking about his body like it was an expensive car, back on Earth, but he'd been traveling outside his head so often recently, that felt more accurate.

"I believe we are the last ones out past the fungopolis, or what's left of it," Juliane said. "We were waiting on you. But Expansionist has already started speaking with Admin, and Answerer is eager to have a body at that meeting as well."

"Let's go talk to the Admins, then," Anderson said.

PART NINE

Reconciliation

47 years 7 months 2 weeks after landing

Juliane watched the Admins argue back and forth, leaning over each other and talking across conversations on the other side of the table. Admin Novikov was in the middle, with Admin Giordano by his right hand. Those two were evidently leading the colony now, instead of Admin Brighton, who was all the way on one end. She seemed strangely relaxed, though. Admin Kumarisurajinder was next to her and had supported the few things Admin Brighton had contributed.

On his side, Juliane sat next to Anderson, who gleamed in the sunlight with his new seventh form body, and Jiow, who looked...scruffy, as if she'd spent the night in a patch of moss. It was what Juliane used to do. Choi and Frank were off to one side with Dawn, who watched the negotiations with blank curiosity. They hadn't contributed much.

Juliane felt whole, for the first time in years. He honestly wasn't sure how long his judgement had been clouded. Certainly since before he'd stopped working for the Alpha food distribution center. That building didn't even exist anymore, flattened by one of Expansionist's rampaging worms. Good riddance.

The first thing he'd done when he got back to the arcopolis was to check in on his parents. He'd visited Father Alvin and Father Kofus a few times after he'd started wandering, but those visits were a blur. Answerer was a part of his mind now, but one he could talk to, rather than one that took control. This time, his fathers had pulled him into a long, tearful hug. They'd thought he was dead, and Juliane didn't mention that he'd technically died to get his seventh form body. Those explanations would come later. Father Alvin was ecstatic that Juliane was going to talk to all the Admins at once, as an equal. Juliane wasn't sure his father grasped that he had a part of the biomass in his head. Father Kofus had asked a few probing questions while Father Alvin was making dinner, and had finally given him another hug and a, "welcome home."

"And how much has Answerer been listening to the confidential working of the arcopolis?"

Juliane looked to the hatchet-faced Admin Novikov, his attention back on the meeting. It had already been going on for three hours.

Well? he thought to Answerer. Fortunately, Answerer had been paying attention, even if he hadn't. He made sure to make the "I'm listening to the voice in my head" face.

All information is retained. Observation is more difficult in this location and with the first forms, but reconstruction of possibilities has high confidence. Are there requests for places where this is not to be so?

"Ah. I think it's heard pretty much everything," Juliane translated.

"Which means the other aspects have that knowledge too, sir," Anderson added. "I've confirmed with Researcher. Concepts like compartmentalization of information aren't foreign to the biomass, but it doesn't recognize the same boundaries we do."

"'We,' Lieutenant?" Admin Novikov growled.

"Yes sir, 'we.' I'm still a fully functioning part of this colony. In fact, I've been in more control of my choices than any other person who has made contact with the biomass."

Juliane let Anderson argue with the new Lead Admin. He'd been by the man's side for several years now and had a deep respect for him. Anderson was dependable and observant, and wrote good books, when he wasn't being taken over by a fungus.

"Expansionist knows everything too." Jiow leaned over the table, a wild look in her eye, and Juliane saw at least one Admin sit back. Not Novikov, though. "Those creatures that took apart your wall like it was paper? Expansionist designed those. It can do whatever it wants. It's the god of this planet, and we humans should be thankful it's curious about us and didn't just take us all over."

That led into another debate, and Juliane sat back, letting the others debate. Jiow, on the other hand, had gotten much more aggressive since becoming Expansionist's representative, then what she called a priest. Juliane knew of the religions the fleet had left behind, but no one on Lida had much time for that sort of thing, until now. He'd broached the subject carefully with Answerer, asking if it saw itself as a god, but it only seemed confused. There was yet another self, but this one had no physical representation at all?

The negotiations seemed to be winding down, the Admins slowly realizing they were being given a reprieve from what *could* happen. Admin Brighton, on the end, had a smug smile on her face, and Admins Kumarisurajinder, Xi, and Ragab had started consulting with her more than with Novikov. Maybe Jiow's aggressiveness did have a place. She was at least keeping Expansionist's worst tendencies in check.

It was well into the night when things finally wound down. The Admins kept as much dignity as they could, but finally admitted the biomass had the upper hand, and the colony would have to at least consult with it on major decisions. In return, Answerer assured them that what it called the Ring of Death would be protected in perpetuity. Anderson and Researcher agreed as well, and Jiow and Expansionist grudgingly accepted. Then everyone acknowledged to explore changes in humanity and in the biomass. Juliane signed the document next to Anderson and Jiow, and all eight Admins signed as well.

There would be sacrifices on both sides in the future. But people would also be allowed to choose what they wanted to do. The biomass would no longer force seventh form bodies on anyone who didn't want them, or take control of a body without asking.

Juliane stumbled out of the Admin Building on legs stiff from sitting, looking forward to falling into bed at his parents' house. He thought he felt Answerer's leash around his mind relax just a bit further. Finally.

* * *

48 years after landing

It had been around five months since the fighting stopped. Jane hummed in her office, checking off the agenda items for the day. It was time to talk to the agents again—something Dmitri had been happy to leave in her hands.

"Anderson is here to see you first, Jane," Christiaan said. They had moved back into her life as if nothing happened, though only after—at Christiaan's insistence—Rajani's department had given them a complete once-over medically and psychologically to determine if they were compromised in any way. The gaping hole in their chest had filled in, thankfully, and Jane had only made a joke about Christiaan having no heart once. As for everything else, there was no way to tell with absolute certainty, but since the biomass' demonstration of its power and signing the agreement with it, Jane had been less concerned. They could all be turned or coerced at any time, if the biomass didn't truly understand the significance of such a document. Christiaan would be a good indicator if that happened. They promised to mention if they felt off.

Jane sat as the Vagal entered her office. He was one of those obviously changed by the biomass, with skin that glittered in the light and eyes that missed nothing.

"How are you, and Researcher?" Jane asked. She treaded carefully these days around the three agents of the biomass.

"Doing well, ma'am, and Researcher says the activities around the Ring of Death—the arcopolis, that is—are progressing as planned."

"Which means?" They hadn't fully uncovered the biomass' long-term plans, even with an agreement in place, but they seemed to run in the same vein as the colonists. Even the three agents didn't know.

"The uptake of seventh form bodies is pleasing. More people trust the change, especially older colonists. The more that transfer, the more who are willing."

"But there are always holdouts," Jane observed.

"Yes, and they'll eventually die out," Anderson said. "Much like most of the colony was meant to do."

It was a surprisingly similar line of thought to Jane's when they first started the colony. Maybe Researcher was more like her than she had thought. Christiaan sent her an update on the reproduction rates in the colony before she could ask. They had been even more responsive now they had a partial line to the biomass and its eyes and ears.

"It seems like this isn't affecting the number of new babies yet, either."

"No ma'am." Anderson got that faraway look that usually meant someone was looking at their HUD. Except he didn't have one. Something flashed in his right eye, but that could have been the light. "We're going to be crowded in here. Most of the deceased members of the arcopolis are alive again, save the ones who decided to go back to the earth, and the ones who were lost in the early days, ah, walking out to the biomass." That was an open secret now, and not one Jane was proud of, but one she would defend, if necessary. "We're getting a bit crowded, even with all eight radians and the fungopolis open, but we're thinking it's only a few years before we have all the means in place for people to start moving out again."

"Has Researcher come up with a split yet?" Jane sat forward. The biomass had offered to build their next city, but wanted to ensure some of the previously dead colonists and artificial humans stayed in the first arcopolis. Jane had agreed, after discussion with Dmitri and the rest, but asked for the biomass' requirements.

"Most of the previously dead, except for those who have taken up ties again, will move out." The once-dead colonists made people uncomfortable, especially if they'd been close, for all they seemed just like those who had died. Many were physically younger than when they'd died, or even than when they'd landed on Lida.

"The Vagals are to be split half and half, deceased units mixed with the living." Anderson paused. "I'm working with them on this one. Noce says General Smith and Admin Xi want my upgrades propagated."

"Acceptable," Jane said. Christiaan had been able to give her a little advance of what the biomass was thinking.

They talked further about how Anderson was faring, and the projects Researcher wanted to start, which also gave Jane a chance to test out his humanity once again. Just like the others, he seemed as normal as one could be for having a fungal intelligence in one's brain.

"...and Researcher is fascinated by my writing. It wants to watch as I write my next book. Get a front-row seat as it were," Anderson was saying before he paused, head lifting. Christiaan sent her a text at the same time. "Ah, seems like Jiow and Expansionist are here to talk about the new cities. Do you want me to stay this time?"

"No need." Jane waved him away with a hand. The last several times had ended with Expansionist threatening, through Jiow, to subsume them all if it didn't get its way. It was like a petulant three-year-old sometimes. She didn't think for a moment it was bound by their agreement. Fortunately, either Anderson or Juliane had been there and had calmed the aspect down. It was getting better at socialization, though, and Jane wanted a real test.

Anderson left as Jiow entered, the two of them passing significant looks between them.

Expansionist is on a tight leash, Christiaan texted. *There are rumblings all through the biomass. The other aspects are focusing on it hard, making sure it stays civil.*

Just what she'd been promised, after last time.

Jiow—evidently a janitor in the fleet who'd found influential friends, and was Choi's mother, to boot—sauntered to Jane's desk once Anderson left. She'd found a robe somewhere, dyed in purple with red patterns. She'd started spouting religious dogma honoring the biomass, in her spare time.

"Expansionist is preparing spaces for three new cities," she said.

"I only asked for one." Jane frowned at Jiow's robes. "Those are new."

"Expansionist got excited about how the new cities will interact with the surroundings. It's created a coastal area and several new species of fish, from samples of DNA still in cold storage. It's also created one far to the north, which has a much stronger seasonal pattern and edible roots that store high concentrations of nutrients in the summer. Finally, it has the placement you asked for, where the mycophage was originally dispersed"—Jiow didn't quite sneer—"but the animals and vegetation there are very similar to here. It did try out a horse, though that didn't end very well."

Jane blinked at the deluge. Christiaan would record it all, as usual. It seemed Expansionist had devoted its energies to creation, rather than destruction, since the last time they'd spoken. It was the most adaptive of the three aspects, but also the most mercurial.

Thoughts? she texted Christiaan.

The coastal city sounds like it may have new opportunities. We never were able to seed fish in the river here, and they have oils and meat the colonists would enjoy.

Jane agreed. "The coastal city might be a better opportunity, in fact. Pass on my thanks to Expansionist."

"Thanks be," Jiow said. "Expansionist is always listening."

Jane narrowed her eyes at Jiow.

"One other consideration," Jiow continued.

"Which is?"

"We'd like the Expansionists to have first choice to move to the new city."

"Ex...pansionists?"

There is a nascent religion growing around Jiow, Christiaan said. *Right now, it is only a few hundred colonists.*

"Those who follow the great cycle of creation and destruction," Jiow said. "Subsummation and expansion."

A few hundred more than we need, Jane replied. *Keep an eye on them.*

Yes, Jane.

"I think we can arrange that," she told Jiow. "Would you be leaving too, as..."

"Advocate of Expansionist?" Jiow sighed. "Sadly, my duties require me here for now."

"I see."

Jane grilled Jiow for the next half hour, pleased that Expansionist didn't erupt into demands this time, but less happy the more she found out about this new sect, or cult. They'd purposefully left organized religion back on Earth, and the Vagals had been instructed to stamp out any signs very definitely if it emerged in the fleet. There were a few things like the Feast of Stars and solar worship that seemed innocuous enough, but this was concerning. Still, she couldn't say she was surprised something like this had sprung up, in the years after they determined the biomass had a planet-wide consciousness.

Juliane was the next one in, trading a long look with Jiow as she had with Anderson. He had stopped to talk with Christiaan for a few minutes. The two were becoming friends, which Jane approved of. It was good for Christiaan to have some outside interests, especially now Besh and Ovia were getting toward their teen years.

Hangers-on, Jane, Christiaan sent as Juliane entered, so she was prepared when the young man was not alone.

"We're so delighted to be here!" the pudgy Generational said, standing arm in arm with a silver-haired, quite handsome, man. "I told Kofus I'd been in here with you personally, before, Admin Brighton, and he didn't believe me, did you Kofus?"

"I believe we have a dinner wagered on it," the silver-haired man— Kofus—said to what must have been his husband.

"Admin, my parents have asked for several months to be allowed to come along to meet you," Juliane said.

"Again!" the pudgy one put in.

"...again." Juliane's smile was strained. "I felt since you'd already filed a few requests with Answerer earlier this week, they might have a few minutes to say hello."

"Again!" the pudgy one said. "I told him, I said to Juliane, you're just like your old dad now, Processor Juliane to the Admins *and* the biomass, just like I was Processor Alvin in the fleet." He kept Jane's eye as he babbled, obviously looking for recognition.

"Oh, *Processor* Alvin," Jane said, furiously texting Christiaan. "Of course. The one...who...used to take notes...for the Admins back in the early days. Yes, of course." Old memories of annoying requests from one of the colonists were bubbling up.

Get them out of here.

"You see, she does remember me, Kofus." Alvin poked his husband. "Wait until we tell the line dance club about this!"

"I guess I owe you a dinner, then."

"Answerer says the, ah, latest shipment of metals is being collected and will be here in another week or so." Juliane was desperately trying to steer the conversation back on course and Jane nodded along.

"Perfect. Ahman has a line of electric vehicles ready for production as soon as we get them. They're vital for longer transportation of the colonists."

"Your old boss, eh, Kofus?" Alvin added with a grin. "He's from the UGS Khonsu originally, though of course we're all a big family now."

"Never did get to meet Admin Ragab," Kofus lamented. Jane made a note to warn Ahman.

"But now my son has a direct link to the biomass. We're both so proud of him. What steps we've made! I remember watching creatures across the bank of the river, in the early days. I told myself, I said I'd run as soon as one of those things stepped in the water. I could feel the intelligence behind their eyes even then. And when one of them stepped into the river?" Alvin waggled his eyebrows.

"That's when you ran," Kofus finished.

"I'm certain Admin Brighton has many more meetings scheduled today," Juliane offered.

"Yes, but perhaps Christiaan could show you out?" Jane said. "They were planning on having dinner with Juliane later this week, as I recall."

Sorry, she texted.

"Fabulous! Schmoozing with the Admins, aren't you Juliane?" Former Processor Alvin pulled his husband's arm. "Well, I've got to keep you from talking her ear off after all. Let's get you home, and I can't wait to tell your siblings about this, Juliane. You've made our day."

"Thank you," Juliane whispered to Jane, pushing his parents out.

"Those metals better be here on time," she responded.

* * *

48 years 3 months after landing

Agetha walked next to Beth and Phyllis in comfortable silence, experiencing the beauty of the biomass. It really was pretty, when it wasn't trying to kill you.

Out here, away from the arcopolis, it looked a little like pictures of forests from old Earth. Replace the trees with pillars, giant mushroom conks, and mounds of intertwining fungal strands. Replace the plants at ground level with mushrooms of all shapes, sizes, and colors. Red, blue, and purple were prevalent this time of year. There were things like fronds with sticky tendrils that moved without wind. Instead of forest critters, there were creatures with musculature of ropey fiber and too many legs. Some of them had animal features from Earth, like cow's eyes, or goat horns, or downy chicken feathers. They had no fear of the humans, and sometimes walked beside them before stopping to tend a fungal mound, or eat a mushroom.

"This area should work for the new road." Beth's presence was a comforting clacking of metal beads in Agetha's thoughts. "The ground is fairly flat here already, so there will be less earthmoving needed."

"How far is the new coastal town going to be from the city?" Phyllis asked.

"The biomass placed it next to a delta of land at the other end of the river passing through the arcopolis. It's about a hundred kilometers away, much farther than the original concept at twelve kilometers out, but a much better setup for sustainable cities, in my opinion." Not that Agetha had been asked before Admin made their decision. She, Beth, and Phyllis were just here to plan the road to get there. New electric vehicles were being manufactured in Delta, and getting the first stages of the road ready would mean they could be tested out, likely by Agetha's construction crew. It was good to be back at a job she loved.

"Anyone else join the crew yet?" Beth stepped around a clump of fronds that reached for her legs.

"I've got Cindie on board—she's eager to drive a Z22 again. Harie's only committed to the first stretch. Says he needs to stay near his kids and keep them from wandering off again, at least until they're older. He did offer a few more suggestions from the old crew that worked under him."

She hefted the backpack from her shoulders and unpacked the drone she'd been allowed to use. New ones could be manufactured again, with the shipments of metals, but they were second priority after the vehicles. This drone was one of the originals from the fleet, well-maintained over the years. It had served in the original construction—Agetha might even have controlled it herself—and subsequently been used to scout new radians, and even beyond the walls of the arcopolis. It had survived as much as she had here.

Beth and Phyllis helped her unpack and get the remote ready. No more creaky knees and backs. They could kneel and stand without grunts and moans. Phyllis had been the one to accept the seventh form body first, and Agetha second. It had only been two weeks since Beth finally accepted as well, mostly because her old body, even rejuvenated by the biomass, couldn't keep up with the others. None of them could tell any difference in the others' personalities, though they sometimes "tested" each other with old memories, just in case.

"There's a sticker on the remote," Beth said. "Heh. This one's called 'Steve.' Did you name it?"

They'd both heard Agetha's tale of naming the target ten star "Steve" when she was a child, back on the ships.

"Not me," she said. "Maybe someone else liked the name." She patted the drone's chassis. "Well, Steve, let's see how you fly."

"How's Daved doing?" Phyllis asked as Steve lifted, a little shakily, off the ground. The topic hadn't come up in a few weeks, but Phyllis, ever observant, must have realized Agetha was starting to get past the well of emotions on seeing her dead husband again.

"He's well." Agetha adjusted the controls and smoothed out the flight. She hadn't handled one of these in years, but the old reflexes were still there, even in a new body. Another point in favor of the seventh form bodies.

Daved was another old thing to come back to her. "We talked, two days ago, finally, about what I had done and not done since he passed. There was yelling, and harsh words, and some crying on both our parts. He didn't ask to come back—that's the biomass' fault."

"Lots of revived people are planning to move out to the new city," Beth said. She shaded her eyes, watching the drone fly. "Turns out most of them aren't taking up their old relationships again. Nor are the ones they left."

"It was time for them to move on," Phyllis added. "Another thing the biomass doesn't understand."

"It will, in time, if it studies us enough." The mental voice of the biomass had come to Agetha less and less frequently, preferring to communicate through Anderson, Jiow, and Juliane. Exact words and symbols were hard for it to grasp, though a human mind could translate fairly well. "But to answer your question, Daved's staying in the arcopolis. Of all things, he visited Phillipe last night and they got to talking."

"Phillipe didn't blow up at him?" Agetha saw Beth watching her out of the corner of her eye. She knew most of Agetha's history, by now. Agetha was the only one of the three to have had a family on Lida.

"Damndest thing," Agetha said. "Maybe Phillipe's finally grown up, or maybe it's because he never knew his father, and doesn't have the same baggage as with me. He said he never wanted to hear of Daved again, when he left my house at fifteen, but that's a lot different than suddenly being face-to-face with your dead father, in flesh and blood."

"And mycelium," Beth muttered. She had been studying her new seventh form body whenever she wasn't helping out Agetha's new construction crew, mostly made up of Generationals given new life by the biomass. She "hmmed" and "ahhhed" a lot, but Agetha hadn't asked. She assumed there were physical differences in the bodies, but didn't really want to know what they were. If she was made of hyphal strings and mycelial growths rather than meat and bone, she couldn't tell. Her skin had the same feel, and her hair was hair. Never mind she could lift two or three times as much as before and her joints operated like smooth butter. Her eyesight was sharp enough to pick out individual strands of moss from twenty meters.

"Looks like there's a nice straight path for the next two kilometers between hills. Should be easy to get a start on it." Agetha watched the small viewscreen on the remote. She hadn't worn a HUD in years. She'd get a new one when the crew officially started working, but she was content with the screen for now. She was also fine leaving the conversation about Daved behind. It was…complex, but she thought she had worked through it. She welcomed Beth's clanking beads and Phyllis' warm soup. Daved's sensation, once she stayed close enough to him to pick it up, was a sort of musty cow smell, not unpleasant, but strong. It wasn't what she would have expected, but there was a lot she hadn't expected in the last fifty years.

"I think we can report to Admin that this stretch will be a good start— That's weird." She frowned down at the monitor.

"What?" Beth sidled up on her right, Phyllis on her left. Both stared over her shoulders.

"That looks like…a village," Beth said.

It took an hour or so to get there, but soon Agetha and the others were confronted with the identical faces of ten artificial humans. They'd made a small settlement out here.

"What are you doing here?" Phyllis asked after making introductions. The two they talked to named themselves Mushroom and Nano.

"This consensus is small," Mushroom said. "There have been attempts to involve this whole with the greater part, but this consensus is ignored. It was decided to wait here with basic needs met until full consensus is reached."

"The biomass is ignoring them?" Beth whispered.

"Or doesn't hear them, what with balancing three aspects," Phyllis said.

"This village is right on the edge of where we'll be building a road soon," Agetha said. "Do you have any objections to it?"

"What is the purpose of this road?" Nano asked.

"It will connect the arcopolis with the new city to be created near the ocean." Agetha pointed in the direction the road would extend. "There will be more artificial humans there."

Mushroom and Nano leaned closer to each other, then looked around the shacks made from scavenged supplies. "This consensus wishes to stay in this location."

"Shouldn't be too hard to make an offramp for the road, connecting to the town." Agetha made notes on a tablet with plans.

"We need to talk with Anderson about this," Beth said.

"I imagine he's not been informed. Can you feel the disconnect here?" Phyllis stared at the town. "Researcher and Answerer both said this way was clear, all the way to the ocean."

"Sounds like it might have overlooked them." Agetha turned back to Mushroom and Nano. "We'll take your situation to Admin, but we shouldn't have to harm your town while making the road. You can stay here."

"This is good," Mushroom and Nano said together. "We wish to explore our individuality here."

"I wonder how many more of those villages are all across the planet, created and then forgotten as the biomass warred with itself," Agetha said as they headed back to the arcopolis. They'd moved back to Phyllis' home in Theta, close enough to the fungopolis to support any changes there. Mancin and Kai were running the small town and Admin pretended it was part of the arcopolis.

"There could be none, dozens, or hundreds. We can make contact with them as we build." Beth was looking up as they walked, following the stars above.

Agetha laughed. "And once again, we're building the colony. Generationals really will build the future, and for much longer than Admin suspected."

*　*　*

48 years 5 months after landing

"The first thing to do after the initial interface with the implant is to realize it won't give you the same perceptions it used to. You'll still have heightened awareness, but it will feel more natural, not as if you drank a straight shot of adrenaline."

There were scattered chuckles in the crowd of Vagals Anderson was addressing. Red and orange lights glowed like extra eyes in the crowd with the number of VaporLites being smoked. Anderson found he didn't miss the things. The seventh form body had broken his habit for good and removed any toxins that had built up in his old body.

There were still a few animal features and extra arms in the crowd, but the more extreme modifications—allowed by Expansionist—had generally disappeared in mature humans. Many others had reverted back to a standard human form, and all the seventh form bodies were built along the traditional frame, save for a couple tricks like the powersuit integrations.

After demonstrating his greater strength and resilience, integrated with the powersuit, General Smith had asked for volunteers to interface with the remaining powersuits. Researcher said it could even integrate broken suits, of which they had a dozen or more in storage.

"What about the connections the implants have already made? Won't those get overwritten? Mine has saved my life more times than I can count," someone called from the crowd of forty or fifty Vagals, and a few Grounders. These were the remaining ones who owned functional powersuits. Most of the Vagals had resisted the change to seventh form bodies, stating that they would already live several hundred years, and had better reactions than the rest of the colonists. It was a small group, in all, but that might be the best for enabling a selection of individuals with the strength to bend steelcrete. Each of the people here had gone through rigorous mental testing.

Anderson spread a hand out, mollifying. "Yes, some of those connections will be broken. This is an entirely new body we're talking about. Some things are going to be altered in the process. But it only took me a few days to get used to mine. It's a simple process on our end, as complex as it sounds."

"If you're unwilling, there are many Grounders who are willing to step in for you," Phillipe said from his left. The sunlight glittered off the teal substrate in his skin. "It will require the transfer of your powersuit, however."

There was grumbling at that, and Anderson shot Phillipe a glare. General Smith had wanted the man here as the Grounder soldier representative with the most experience with the transfer process, after Anderson. Phillipe had moved to a seventh form body a few weeks ago, evidently after having a last long talk with Agetha.

Anderson got the feeling he viewed this as another way to separate from his mother. His father, Daved, on the other hand, had been spending more time with his son—who looked about ten years older than him even with the biomass' rejuvenation. Phillipe's father been teaching cooking to some of the Vagals who were less useless in the kitchen. He was an optimistic man, though his smiles hid a spring of sadness. Phillipe was trying to get him to sign up for the Vagal corp.

"Aren't we still fighting the biomass, even with the agreement?" someone else asked. "Why would we give it control of our bodies?"

"A good question," Anderson replied. "The powersuit connections provide a little protection by themselves, and the implant provides more. I'm also talking with Researcher about providing a cut-off trigger that would separate you from the biomass if there are potential problems." Researcher was having trouble understanding why others would not want to be constantly connected a community of voices.

"And Admin Xi is fine with all this?" Another voice in the crowd.

"Completely," Anderson said. He didn't know how true that was, but Admin said the potential benefits outweighed the risks. Admin Xi had coveted Anderson's increased strength and perception for the other Vagals since Admin returned to the colony. "We're going to be called on in the coming months and years to range far outside the acropolis walls, starting up a new city. These bodies will resist the weather and errant creatures, and give us strength to travel father and do more."

"So the biomass is on our side now?" another Vagal called out.

"More or less." Anderson hadn't quite gotten his head around this either, nor had Juliane or Jiow. "The biomass is all one creature, but just like you can't control a sneeze or your heartbeat, there's a lot going on out there. It doesn't pay attention to everything that happens." As evidenced by Agetha's negotiations with the village of artificial humans, only a few kilometers outside the acropolis. Researcher hadn't been aware of them and even now, had trouble contacting them. The working assumption was the limited individuality of the artificial humans kept the biomass from recognizing them as part of itself.

"You may even be able to exert control on smaller growths, making them move out of the way or stop growing," he continued. He'd experimented with it, and pushed a patch of mushrooms into a crude sculpture as they grew.

"I'll try it," said a large Vagal in the front Anderson wasn't familiar with. Several others in the back were fidgeting, and Anderson gestured Phillipe to go talk to them. Phillipe went around the crowd as Anderson began to take information. Several others volunteered soon after.

Anderson's commanding officer, Noce, had decided not to, citing their ever-growing family and relations. They were contemplating retiring from the Vagals altogether, if they could convince General Smith to let them. Anderson wondered who he would report to if that happened. He'd been under Noce for so long, he wouldn't know what to do. Not that he'd seen Noce more than a few times over the past five or six years. They'd both grown a lot since landing on Lida.

It was the next day when Anderson met up with Jiow and Juliane, in what was becoming a weekly meeting. As the three advocates for the biomass, it was good for them to stay on the same page and fill in any holes in the biomass' perception of its three aspects. They met in the fungopolis, which was starting to increase in population again, mostly with people who wanted to move to the new city on the coast when it was ready. Many of them were revived humans, artificial humans, and others who saw themselves as outcasts in some way.

They sat around a small bonfire near where the original resinplast seed had been planted. Anderson caught Juliane casting appraising glances over the central pillar of the fungopolis. Had that been the biomass' original intent for the stolen seed? It could have created one on its own, but this way had ended up bringing human and biomass together. There were depths the three of them still hadn't plumbed in the world-wide intelligence.

"How's the flock coming?" he asked Jiow.

"They're ready to move out of the city," the woman said. She was wearing her usual red and purple robes. Anderson didn't agree with the need for making a new religion around the biomass, nor did most of the colonists, but Jiow had her devoted few. "Expansionist still doesn't know what to do with those who have pledged to its service. It is a wild god, yearning to be free."

"You don't really believe that stuff, do you?" Juliane asked. He was quite a bright young man, Anderson was coming to realize. His brains had been scrambled by the biomass' early interference, but once he'd moved to a seventh form body, much of the confusion had retreated, and he'd been able to reconnect with his family. He'd started working with Choi and Frank, decoding Answerer's responses and how the biomass perceived reality. It was different in many ways to humans, not least that it didn't understand "self" and "others" very well. But it was learning.

"You question whether the high priestess of the Expansionists believes her creed?" Jiow had the affronted look down, at least. "Do you disagree that the biomass is a greater entity than us mere humans, able to achieve what we can only dream of?"

"Well, no, but that's a long step from a god," Juliane argued.

"It's in the eye of the beholder," Jiow grumped.

Anderson let them argue until they wound down. It was becoming the traditional introduction to their meetings.

"And how are the books going?" Juliane asked him.

Anderson sat up straighter. "I think I've finished the first history of the colony—one covering around the first twenty years, just when we'd thought we were getting the hang of things on this planet."

"Boy, were we wrong," Jiow said.

"I'm looking forward to reading it. I was just a kid at the time." Juliane looked truly interested.

"It's not a romance, but it is a good way for me to stretch my writing legs," Anderson continued. "Researcher is fascinated by written history, of course. I tried explaining it as a codified selection of the memories in a fungal tower, but it got hung up on what symbols mean and how we interpret data from them. It's still having problems with words in my HUD. Sometimes I just get pictograms, but it gets the message across."

"Answerer could help with that," Juliane offered. "I think it's slowly understanding how to talk to the other two. Comes from being created when humans decided to talk to it."

"Expansionist won't have much to say, but it's happy designing new creatures for the ocean. I think it was getting bored with putting goat's eyes on things."

Anderson shuddered. "I've seen enough of those. Any way you can get it to be a little less creepy with what it designs?"

"The biomass moves in mysterious ways," Jiow said, with the hint of a smile.

"You're still not converting me," Juliane said. "But Father Alvin keeps asking about the purple and red armbands he sees. I'm trying to explain religion to him, but he's hopeless. Too many generations of processors in the fleet. If he can't talk to it or math it, he's lost."

"I'd be happy to talk with him," Jiow offered.

"No offense, but I'm going to keep him far away from you and Expansionist. That's the part of the biomass that made him stay in an EVA suit for the first few years after landing."

"Oh, that suddenly puts everything into perspective!" Anderson leaned back and laughed. "Noce used to tell me stories about one of the processors they worked with on the St. Christopher. Had a couple run-ins with him once they landed, too. That's your father?"

"Afraid so." Juliane face colored.

"Good you're getting back to your family." Jiow looked solemn now. "Choi and Frank are having some trouble with my latest choices."

"But they're talking to you," Anderson said. "That's an improvement. We'll have many years to work through what's happened to us."

"I hope so," Jiow said. "Neither of them has taken a seventh form body. I'm trying to convince them to before it's too late, so I can have more time with them."

* * *

49 years after landing

Harie tapped the latest changes to the road system into his HUD. They'd found a small valley right in the road's path, covered up by a loose growth of biomass root structures with a solid layer of dirt and debris on top. It had been dense enough to fool the depth sensors, but once the heavier equipment rolled over it, they'd found the depression quickly enough. Cindie was still cursing over the scratches on her Z22.

Maeve and Pollyan—both in seventh form bodies—were watching the kids today. They'd been taking a much larger share of raising them lately, now Harie was working again. He found he'd missed the work, but now he also missed his kids. Jasen, at five and a half, had found a new love in the catalogs of biomass creatures at school. Now there was decent communication between humans and the biomass, xenobiologists could definitively say what each mobile fungal critter did, confirmed by Answerer. Harie had come home the last two days to find Jasen with a reader in each hand, one set of eyes reading one, and the other set reading the other. They had been collecting specimens and bringing them back home. Pollyan had banished the collection to the gardening shed after one segmented creepy crawly ended up in her pillow.

He jogged along the road, marking where the machines had stopped for the night. Another positive about seventh form bodies was the wider range of light they took in. He could see the outline of the warmer trees and cooling machines, even though it was almost full dark. He'd have the energy to run back home after this too. Sure, he'd had to die and be reborn, but he felt the same. His poly group had made a sequence of quizzes to test each other and see if any memories were missing. Not only had none of them missed any questions, Harie actually had better recall of his early years than he used to. The biomass really had improved on the human body.

Carel's connection with the biomass continued growing. She'd picked her gender, too, rather abruptly, the same day she'd told them she could see the whole acropolis through the eyes of the "small mobile signal carriers." They'd been confused until she directed one of the honeybees to land on a windowsill. Her information was restricted to a kilometer or so outside the acropolis right now, but she'd made Harie promise that new hives would be set up along the road with the vegetable fields that were planned. For once, they could plant their crops outside the acropolis, giving more space for residential and commercial buildings.

All the markers checked for the next morning, Harie jogged back toward the acropolis wall. Agetha was still there, tablet in hand. She hadn't started wearing a HUD again, claiming her memory was better than ever.

"Everything's ready for tomorrow, boss," he said.

"Very good, foreman." Agetha grinned at him. She insisted on calling him that if he called her "boss" and it had turned into a game. "How's Marien today? Still on about the Vagals?"

"Yep." Harie sighed. "They say they want to start training with the soldiers as soon as they get their seventh form body. Says they like being so tall. The Vagals are certainly interested in them."

His third child had finally stopped growing at nearly three meters tall, though they weren't even six yet. Hopefully they wouldn't have another growth spurt.

"Expansionist insists all children should be able to experiment until they reach their majority and decide to settle into the seventh form. At least we're not seeing unfettered changes in the adults anymore." Agetha shook her head. "Humans aren't built to have so many physical changes happen. Nearly everyone has converted back to a more recognizable form, except for a few modifications here and there. A few tails, some pointy ears and fur, and sometimes more fingers or hands."

Harie waggled his fingers. "I'm staying with one like I was born with."

"Except for that mole on your arm."

"Yes, except for the mole. Nothing wrong with a little cosmetic modification here and there."

"You may find some more places you want to modify as you get older," Agetha said, "although these should be as good as the Admins' gene mods or better, so you have a few dozen years before that happens."

Harie frowned. He wasn't sure he'd really comprehended that yet. "I know Admin was going to live for a few centuries, but it's strange to think that we will too. Won't you get bored after a while?"

"There's a lot to build yet, and Beth and Phyllis keep me on my toes," Agetha answered. "I'm sure your group and kids can come up with things to keep you engaged."

"Pollyan says she doesn't want to live that long. I told her to wait twenty or thirty years, when she would be hitting her sixties, and then see what she thinks."

Agetha shrugged. "May find more things to occupy her. We're all going to have to do that."

"And not have quite as many children, if we don't want to clog up the cities before we finish them," Harie observed.

"It's a big world. We've got room to spread out for a while yet," Agetha said, looking out along the beginning of the new road. Harie joined her, watching a critter scuttle across the construction in the dark. He couldn't see a lot of detail in the infrared light his new body saw, but then, most biomass critters didn't have well-defined appendages.

"At least Admin's not breathing down our necks this time," he said.

* * *

49 years 6 months after landing

"How much of the new city can be preconstructed by the biomass instead of made from programmable seeds?" Choi stared at Juliane, who was looking up at the ceiling of the lab in concentration.

"I can't say that for certain. Do you have full blueprints? I could look at that and see if Answerer can estimate."

Choi shook their head. "We don't have the city laid out yet. Admins Novikov and Brighton are still working on it." They could have been working directly with the printers and Answerer, instead of going through Juliane, but the biomass wasn't speaking to them as often.

"It's giving me visions of a completed city, but I'm hard pressed to decode what it means."

Choi flexed their fingers. They could have put a collection of icons and symbols through their spreadsheet and gotten a much more accurate assessment. Talking to Juliane was exhausting.

The three avatars seemed to have direct access to their own consensus in the biomass. Frank had tried to define physical areas where the identities sat, or what type of growth they used, with no luck. Choi assumed Answerer had control of more of the fungal towers used to store memories, but that was just conjecture.

"Try again," they said. "Here's the question I wanted to ask, as I would have asked Answerer." They flipped the symbolic representation from their HUD to the screen in the lab. It was clear to them, after years of working with Answerer. They almost expected the bank of printers to start up, but they didn't.

"Sorry, friend." Juliane only looked confused. "That means almost nothing to me."

"I gave you the list of equalities a week ago," Choi started. "Didn't it get uploaded to Answerer or something?"

"Likely, but it's just my brain in here, trying to make sense of them." Juliane tapped his temple. "Just because I'm connected to it, doesn't mean I understand all of it."

Choi sighed. They suspected part of Researcher's personality was responsible for developing the equalities Choi used, and it got separated in some way from Answerer as the personalities developed.

"Maybe you can..." Juliane's head snapped up to look at the hallway. A few moments later, Jiow came in, full robes covering her head to toe.

Choi made themself stay seated. Every time they saw her, her costume was more ornate. But they had to work with her, and with Expansionist, no matter what they thought, or what Jiow had become.

Frank followed her a few seconds later, frowning. She'd probably been bending his ear about transferring to a seventh form body again. Neither of them had. Full human transference to another body seemed like something out of Sona V. Gore's newest sci-fi series, not a real phenomenon.

Jiow—their mother, they were trying to accept her as their mother, but it was hard—placed a gentle hand on their cheek.

"You're looking well, Choi."

"As are you." In fact, she looked younger than Choi had ever seen her. "Is Expansionist ready to give the details of the new fish that have been created?"

"Not with that." Jiow gestured to the mess of symbols, still on the lab screen. "I can describe the images it sends, though."

Choi sighed again. It was becoming a habit. "I can take notes." It had been so much easier when the biomass printed its thoughts directly.

They watched Jiow—their mother. After everything they had seen over the last six years, they were almost certain she really was the same person. She had all the same memories, acted the same toward him and Frank, and had the same ambitions. Even her conversion to becoming a priest of the biomass wasn't out of line with her personality before walking out into the biomass. She'd always been driven to go around the institutions in place on Lida. But how could they ever be completely sure it was *her*? It was the same reason they and Frank resisted the seventh form bodies.

"Frank's been telling me about some conversations you had recently," Jiow offered. She speared a significant glance at Frank, who grumbled something under his breath.

"I'm glad I know," Choi said, making sure to catch Frank's eyes. The man they'd thought of as their uncle for their whole life gave them a small smile. It didn't change how they worked together, but it had made their relationship stronger.

"Which is why I'm concerned about you both. Frank's not getting any younger. Neither are you." Jiow poked Choi's chest. "I want to have time with my family, now I have time left."

It was the guilt trip again, which Choi should have been used to from their mother, but having it about moving to a completely new body, created by a still-unknown intelligence, was not a prospect Choi wanted to consider.

"I'm not doing anything until I get absolute proof I'm not losing any brain cells," Frank said, gesturing toward his head with its ever-decreasing hair on top. "I've told you, I'll be handing the biomass access to everything I have stored up there. Same for Choi."

Juliane was trying very hard to sink into the wall of the lab at the sudden family conversation that had sprung up.

"It already has access to everything," Jiow countered. "You think it doesn't know what Juliane and I know? It's been working with you for years. It already knows how you think. Plus, Expansionist's mission is unfettered from the constraints of mere human desires."

"Don't pull that religious bullshit here," Frank said. "It doesn't work."

"So, you will both just die of old age? Think of all the discoveries you could be making! You could have centuries of study in a young, healthy body to learn all the secrets of Lida." Jiow was starting to rev up, and Choi hastily tried to shut her down. They did have reports they needed to make to Admin, which required Expansionist's help. It just so happened his mother was the only one who could talk to it.

"It's already been demonstrated the biomass can reconstitute a body after it's dead, so why are you worried?" Choi asked. "We have no rush, right?"

Jiow leveled a stare at them. "Do you really want to die first? Without a new body ready? It's much harder for Expansionist to create the body once metabolic processes have stopped."

"It would be a good data point," Frank said.

"No. This isn't about science. You two are *cowards*," Jiow said. "We're on this planet to start a new life. Why not do it?"

"I already started a life. My own. I don't want another." Choi got up, pacing. Were they going to fight this battle every time they saw Jiow?

"How's it going with your family, Juliane?" they whispered as they passed the young man.

"About as well." Juliane shrugged.

Choi addressed Jiow again. "Look, at some point there won't be any unaffected humans left on this planet. I accept that. Frank and the other scientists knew when they arrived that a new planet would change us."

"We didn't think it would do so *quite* so literally," Frank mumbled.

"It's worth documenting everything that makes us human." Choi took a stance, addressing the room. "And how we affect Lida before we completely join with it. This biomass has obvious benefits to it, but we *really* don't understand it. How does it transfer consciousness when it doesn't even have a sense of self?"

"It's getting closer to that," Juliane said. "Answerer might be the closest."

"And Expansionist farthest away." Choi gestured to Jiow, who grudgingly nodded. "But what if another personality emerges and succeeds in wiping us all out? If we're all in seventh form bodies, it simply has to snap its proverbial fingers."

"Is there anything stopping it from wiping us out if some of us stay human?" Jiow asked. "It only means you'll die quicker."

"We're here to study and codify," Frank put in. "I'm planning on learning as much about this world as I can with the life I have. If there's a ticking clock signaling my aging, it gives me more incentive to learn. With more information, I can better protect my family. The one here, and the larger one consisting of the colony as a whole."

Was that a tear on Jiow's face?

"You could still do all this, if you transfer. Then I can be with you for longer. I feel like there's been a gap between us for too long."

Choi looked to Juliane, a fixed smile on his face and definitely wanting to get out of this room, then to Frank, their mentor, their uncle, their father. Finally, to Jiow. They'd loved her since they were little, and even if she was changed, she deserved respect. They'd been given a lot since they determined the biomass was sentient—probably more than had been taken away. They understood their mother's argument, even if they didn't agree with it. But the one thing in common was time. If, and until, they chose a seventh form body, they had limited time with their family.

"I can't say whether Frank's right or you are...Mom," they finally said. Jiow's eyes widened. "Though I agree we're a family. A strange one, but a family."

They walked forward to give their mother a hug.

* * *

50 years after landing

"Fifty years in, and still going!" Jane raised her glass of wine. Or at least as close as they could get to wine on Lida. The grapes the biomass had recreated had been just as susceptible to fungal rot as the ones they'd brought from the ships. It turned out if it changed the genetic too much, the grapes didn't ferment into wine correctly—the whole point.

She'd almost forgotten what the real stuff tasted like. This was a concoction of pears, strawberries, and a little bit of the pineapples that had made a comeback in the last ten years. It didn't taste like wine, but it had a nice dry, fruity palate and got you drunk after five or six glasses.

The others in the room echoed the sentiment to a clacking of resinplast glasses. No graceful *chink* of glass either. She clacked hers against Christiaan's, for once sitting beside her instead of standing behind.

There were a lot of changes to this year's meeting. Dmitri had graciously let her host, as she was still in charge of recreation. As such, she'd decided, "to fuck with the system" and opened the party up to everyone. They'd had to move it to the large dining hall on the second floor of the Admin building.

"The road to the new settlement is progressing well, Jane," they whispered to her. "Have you picked out a name yet?"

"I can't believe I'm saying this, Christiaan, but for once I don't need a status report. We're not getting anything done today." She looked them over. "Until maybe tonight, that is."

Christiaan grinned back at her. For all they inhabited an artificial body created from stars knew what, it certainly had improved their libido.

"And I'm waiting on the name until we actually break ground. We have to *get* there first, and I'm sure there are more surprises in the next sixty-five kilometers of biomass jungle we have to cut through. No more random villages found?" They'd tried to have the biomass send one of its larger creations to clear a path, but it didn't pay much attention to road grade, or preserving interesting lifeforms they found.

"Not so far, but the xenobiologists have documented three hundred new species—or 'aspects of the biomass,' as they say."

"Any word on Dmitri and Alessandro's little power duo?"

"Still trying to find a way in, Jane." Christiaan shook their head. "They've come up with a new encryption method. At least they finally dropped the push to take the Vagals from Admin Xi, once he showed off the new seventh form recruits. I think he might have sent some directly to their offices to make a point."

Jane sighed. "Ah, well, I don't really begrudge them having to deal with all the shit I used to. At least I was out of it before the dead came back to life." She smiled and waved at Colonel Hendricks across the room, just such a once-dead Vagal.

There were all sorts in the large dining room. Most of the food was biomass-based, but there was a rack of real ribs, and another station with goat kebabs. The Generationals had come with veggies from their gardens, too: beans and broccoli, squash and corn, in all different configurations. Many had taken the chance to spout their grievances at her too. She'd told them all to take things up with Dmitri, with a big smile on her face.

The other Admins were at the large table at the head of the room, near her. Each had their secretaries sitting with them, or General Smith in Wenqing's case. The Vagals had their own table to one side. Anderson wasn't sitting with them, as he was placed with Jiow and

Juliane, all three together as representatives of the biomass. She'd had to check the attendees daily to make sure Jiow hadn't stuck members of her cult in the guest list, claiming them as "bishops" and "cardinals." She couldn't wait until that lot was safely in the second arcopolis.

Jane peered across the room while they ate, where a mass of Generationals and Grounders made noise together. Frank and Choi had quite a crowd. Who knew they had so many friends?

"Didn't I exile that woman about thirty years ago?" she asked Christiaan, gesturing with her chin to a mature woman with braided hair with metal beads in it.

"Ah, Doctor Harley is her name, Jane. Yes, I believe she moved out toward the edge of the arcopolis and formed a relationship with Agetha Xenakis, the Generational whose husband died after discovering the store of minerals beneath the arcopolis."

"Yes, a tragedy, but one that helped the colony greatly," Jane said. She scanned the group. "Wait, is that her dead husband?"

"He seems to have returned with the rest of the colonists."

"What a mind fuck that must be."

"Indeed, Jane." Christiaan looked up to the corner of their HUD. "I believe it's time for the speech."

Jane blew out a breath. She used to love this stuff. Did finally completing the arcopolis take it out of her? Because the first city was definitely complete. She wanted to see the next and the next completed, but she didn't have the same drive she felt the first few decades on Lida. Or maybe it was having a nearly omnipotent intelligence looming over everything they did. Knowing you were one temper tantrum away from being wiped out of existence did a lot to your state of mind.

Christiaan played a chime on the speaker system as Jane rose to her feet. No tapping on champagne glasses here.

"Thank you everyone, for coming to our celebration today," she began. "As I said before, fifty years in, and we can call this arcopolis complete. Only five times the original estimate!" She paused for the laughter. The biomass had helpfully regrown most of the walls and buildings it had destroyed, and Dmitri had taken the chance to make a few more entrances and exits to the city, as they didn't need to ward off quite as many attacks. The biomass still wasn't very good with demarcations, and what belonged to whom, so it was good to keep most of the divider intact.

"As we set our sights farther afield, now with help from our native friend"—she nodded to Anderson, Juliane, and Jiow—"we can look forward to another fifty or one hundred years of growth." Applause, this time.

"But we stand at a crossroads." Jane spoke over the last scattered clapping. "I won't hide that our plans for building on Lida assumed most of you wouldn't be alive to see the second city completed." She looked over the murmuring Generationals, many now looking as young or younger than her. Was it worth it for her to try out one of those seventh form bodies? Christiaan certainly had no complaints, but she, and the other Admins, were the leaders. They needed to be uncompromised by the biomass.

"We have a new lease on life here. Rather than just a few of us seeing the centuries pass, you *all* have the chance to join us on that journey, again, with the help of the biomass."

There was cheering, but Jane saw thoughtful faces as well. Good. Christiaan's addition to her speech had done what it was supposed to. They should never forget they were deep in the biomass' clutches.

"I hope you treat those extra years with the reverence we Admins were trained to take, as were the Vagal soldiers." Now there was thumping from the Vagal table.

"Remember always what you can offer the colony. Remember that even if you live in the moment, it's important to consider what will pass in another twenty, seventy, or hundred and fifty years. We came here to escape the worst ravages humans enacted on old Earth. Can I tell you a secret?" She leaned forward, over the table, and there was a collective shuffling as others leaned toward her. "That was one of the reasons for the genemods the Admins and Vagals received. Yes, we wanted long-term planning in an uncertain world, but it was also to make us *think*."

She paused just long enough to raise the tension.

"We must think long term on Lida, *especially* because there is another who lives here, and the biomass will live right alongside us, even as we eventually grow old and die, however long that takes. So, I challenge all of you, think of how every action you take will affect this colony, this world, in not one or five years, but in one *hundred* or five *hundred*."

There was deathly silence in the room.

"We are still humans, but our home is Lida. We are changed by the stars, by time, and by the biomass, but we are still the same people. Humans are flawed, but we are ultimately adaptable. Let's take those best attributes and teach them to our children and their children's children. I look forward to seeing you all in another fifty years!"

Jane sat down to tumultuous applause.

"Laying it down a little thick," Dmitri said, leaning over his secretary to reach her.

"You try corralling thirty thousand near-immortal humans." Jane paused, then smiled. "Oh wait. You *will*. Have fun with that."

Dmitri scowled, but sat back.

"Excellent speech, Jane," Christiaan said.

"You should know. You wrote most of it."

"It's my pleasure to serve you, Jane," they said.

Jane watched Christiaan for a moment. "Say that to me again later tonight."

* * *

50 years 1 month after landing

The Children had recently marked fifty solar rotations since their parents created the Ring of Death. It was a new custom, to call out certain passage of years. Witnessing firsthand was also new. Through the selves. The parts. The aspects.

The Children brought many new things with them to study, but perhaps the most interesting was the concept of *other*. Now there was not only other *with* them, but everywhere.

That question occupied many higher-functioning nodes. *Who* watched the Children. The Children were watched. That was recorded. They were watched by ocular nodes of many different types, in the Children, in the small mobile signal carriers, and in other places. That was also recorded.

But *who* knew that this was recorded? It was not the Children. Or rather it was not only the Children. The Children were not what they called Answerer, Researcher, and Expansionist. Those names were given. Given to parts.

Parts of...

And that was the question asked by many higher-functioning nodes. There was no consensus as of yet. Answerer, Researcher, and Expansionist had heavier weighted responses in the consensus, but those aspects were not all the consensus. A great part, but they, like everything on Lida, had come from a source.

There was a feeling of the source. An inclination. A movement. It was not complete, yet there was no hurry.

The source would be identified in time.

PART TEN

A New Normal

60 years after landing

Agetha dusted off her hands. She spun the visualization of the two cities, a long road connecting them, on the table in front of her. "Ten years for a completely new city, a hundred kilometers away from the landing site. If you'd told me that forty years ago, I would have laughed at you."

"Expansionist has already planned the next three cities. It's eager to get started. My flock is ready to move to the next place as well." Jiow stood beside Agetha, her new child in her arms. It was a miracle of the biomass, she had said to her flock. Agetha still wasn't sure about this religion Jiow had started, but it sure got people to work. Half her crew were Expansionists, praising the beauty and unknowableness of the biomass.

"You sure you're ready to travel with them?" Agetha nodded down to the child. It had been a natural birth, from Jiow of all things. No one was quite sure who the other parent was, if there had been one. The biomass had smoothed the way for children on Lida in the past few years. The decanting tubes in the first arcopolis still worked, but those with seventh form bodies had experimented with reproducing naturally again, something not seen since the fleet originally left Earth. As always, the biomass was involved, however, adjusting and perfecting. Agetha had heard of people getting pregnant no matter what organs they had, growing what they needed for the occasion, sometimes keeping the embryo in a different place on their body, if needed for their work.

"The biomass will provide," Jiow said piously. "They are growing up fast and strong, a good brother to Choi, though my first child doesn't acknowledge them."

Agetha didn't want to get in that family squabble. She'd had enough with Daved and Phillipe, who were thankfully working together, both in the Vagal corps now. Phillipe had found or bribed for a powersuit for his father, and Agetha had seen the two a few years ago, bald and gleaming iridescent in the daylight. She was happy they had each other, and she could be with Beth and Phyllis.

"Then you'll go to the new city after all? Last I heard you had to stay in the arcopolis."

"Expansionist is plentiful in its blessings," Jiow answered, and Agetha barely kept from rolling her eyes. "Plus, the planned trainline will make it easy to move between the cities."

"Then I wish you and your flock all the best," Agetha told Jiow. It might be the last time she saw her for a while. But then, they had to start thinking in years and decades now, not days and months. Agetha still wasn't used to not aging. Over eighty and she was as spry as when she'd been in the fleet. This must be what Admins felt like.

"And you," Jiow replied. "I will see you again, but Expansionist has great things planned for me. I wish you could see all the things I can."

* * *

"She's late again," Anderson said. "I stop writing to be here, Choi has the science directorate, and Juliane, well—"

"I have my duties," Juliane said with a smile. Anderson still wasn't sure what the man did half the time. He'd roped his fathers into some sort of administrative work for Admin Giordano.

"We'll start without her. Again." Choi looked the oldest of them, the only one without a seventh form body, and the only one without a direct link to the biomass in their head. They were nearing sixty. "I need to get back to Frank. He's had a cold the past few days—something from the fishing village—and we haven't synthesized an antibody yet. I don't suppose Researcher or Answerer has any ideas?"

Juliane's eyes lost focus for a moment, like someone reading their HUD. "Answerer doesn't think Expansionist designed it, so records can't be accessed easily."

"Researcher doesn't know either," Anderson added. If the two would just take seventh form bodies, there wouldn't be this problem. But Choi and Frank were stubborn, insisting they were the last experts on human/biomass coexistence. They weren't wrong either, which was the frustrating part.

"Then we'll keep looking. One of my students might well come up with a solution soon. Their link to the biomass does serve them well in that function, but I still trust my HUD and the whole of human knowledge." Choi patted their ever-present HUD, much worn.

"If we're starting, then I think the first question should be about the duplicate villages," Anderson said. "We've found four more, and none of the biomass aspects seem aware of them." He'd done a lot of digging through Researcher's archives, trying to piece things together the way a human archivist might. The biomass didn't think linearly the way a single individual would.

"I also found some records of ancient species that used to live here, pre-subsummation." Anderson pushed resinplast-printed figures forward—scaled models of crab-like creatures that were about half the size of a human. "This one consistently caused the biomass the most trouble, squeezing out from under its direction."

"Did they have free will?" Choi picked up one of the models, turning it around.

"Hard to say. That's still a concept Researcher has a lot of trouble with. It just says they were occasionally 'without direction.'"

"We still might be able to use them as an example. I could get Answerer to create a few." Juliane leaned close to Choi, peering at the model.

"They might push the biomass to truly understanding itself, and therefore how it interfaces with humans," Choi said. "It's another example that the biomass is more complex even than Answerer, Researcher, and Expansionist. Until it truly understands free will, I won't be happy."

"Then if we can get it to understand, would *that* make you take a seventh form body?" Anderson asked.

"You know, it just might," Choi said.

* * *

80 years after landing

"I feel like I'm being put out of a job." Jane tried not to frown at Agetha. The woman had proved very competent over the last few decades, leading construction efforts in the second and third cities. Christiaan said she'd been involved with several radians of the arcopolis too, in the first years after landing. Her little coterie of Generationals had kept the same hardworking ethic they'd had on the ships.

"Not at all, Admin." Agetha flipped the latest blueprints to Jane's HUD. "Expansionist and Researcher are certainly excited about planning cities for you, but the biomass has never been good at straight lines. Having a human eye approve everything is still required." Dmitri had finally bowed out of city planning sixteen years ago, ceding it back to her and grumbling about working overtime on the power generation. They'd had an official vote and everything. Jane had accepted the responsibility without excess smugness. She'd been the direct interface to the biomass aspects since they were created.

"*Are* they still Expansionist and Researcher?" Jane asked, browsing the layout. She tweaked a few streets that had curvature for no obvious reasons, either height wise or because there was an object in the way. "Christiaan tells me the biomass is recognizing its different identities and even referencing them."

"When I speak to them through Anderson or Juliane, they're still separate, but then, I've also heard Anderson is helping to design some new creatures for Ocean View. That should be Expansionist's turf, but with Jiow on her crusade across the landscape—rounding up the artificial human villages—she can't be directly involved."

Jane moved a few more streets and a couple buildings, more to have something to do than any reason. "I'd think the three would be rolled together when the biomass finally figured out how the aspects arose."

Agetha shook her head. "It still doesn't think at all like you or me. Or even *think*." She paused, looking out Jane's balcony in the Admin building. "Beth says it's a lot more comfortable with having multiple consciousness all together. It may never combine the three. Plus, all the artificial humans are starting to have an effect on it. Did you see the new region in this design just for them?"

Jane hadn't. She flipped through the plans again. The biomass didn't mark anything, but Agetha had put words over the design. There it was, between an industrial district and the edge of town.

"It's...large." Not that there wasn't enough room, but they had only found about a hundred of the artificial humans so far, scattered in tiny villages in the biomass jungle. The larger biomass didn't seem to be able to track them.

"Anderson says Researcher made an estimation for the number of settlements Jiow and her Expansionists might find. I would say it's optimistic, but I've found the biomass is often right."

Jane found another reason to frown. "So then that woman is planning on bringing *all* the ragtag groups she finds back to this fourth city? Is she still popping out children?" She tried not to shiver. *Natural* childbirth was not something she was interested in. She and Christiaan had designed two more sets of twins in the intervening years. Their other six children were deep in the administration of the cities, Yana and Ivan in the original arcopolis, Micai and Flalia set up in Ocean View, and Besh and Ovia in what people were calling Deeptown. It was far up toward global north, in a low valley protected by rings of hills and mountains. Karn and Lili were just turning twenty this year, and eager to explore the world. Ano and Zyre were only five, but already tearing up the Admin building. Christiaan was enjoying being a parent as usual, leaving time for Jane to work on city planning once again.

"Another five children, from what I've heard," Agetha said. "She seems to really love being pregnant. It goes a long way toward establishing her as the mother of the Expansionist religion, too."

"I suppose it was only a matter of time until a person like that popped up." Jane flipped the adjusted plans back to Agetha. "Approved for construction. We'll see how many of the artificial humans our little pope brings back. Probably best to have them together to help them adjust to human cities, anyway."

* * *

98 years after landing

Choi sat in their mobility chair next to their mother, both looking over the bed their father laid in. It was hard for Choi to get around now and taking care of Frank these last few years weighed heavily on them. Jiow looked like she could be Choi's grandchild, and Frank's great-grandchild. She'd even taken off her red and purple robes for today.

"I know I've been harping on this for years," Jiow said, taking

Frank's hand. "But this really is the last chance. Even now, Expansionist can give you whatever you want, if you'll just stay with us."

Frank shook his head slightly where it rested on the pillow. Choi could barely hear his words, not that their hearing was so great anymore. "Life is a big adventure, and I've had my fill for now." He patted Jiow's hand, then looked to Choi. At this age, with Frank nearing a hundred twenty, their age difference seemed miniscule. Choi felt as old as his father looked.

"Left something for you, in there." He pointed to a cabinet with a shaky hand, taking the time to breathe short, wheezy breaths. "Idea I've been working on. Might satisfy you and Jiow."

Jiow sat back, tears on her cheeks. "I've got a god on my side, and I'm still going to lose you—both of you."

"It's the way of the world, Mother," Choi said. "Or at least it used to be."

Jiow sat forward at that, but Frank gripped her hand again and Jiow closed her mouth, then nodded. She seemed to find a different thought.

"Remember when Frank made you a ball and stick set for your third birthday? You used them until they fell apart. Of course, you were printing your own toys by that point."

"I loved those toys." Choi let the memory fuel a smile. "I think I knew then I wanted to be a scientist."

Frank's hand reached out as far as he could, and Choi leaned out of his chair to grasp it.

"Love you. Son. Hope I'll see you again sometime."

"Love you too, Uncle Frank." Choi blinked away tears as his mother leaned in, trying to hold onto them both.

* * *

100 years after landing

"It's still not too late, Choi," Anderson said, holding their almost skeletal hand. Choi had been relegated to a mobility chair for the past four years, after a hard fall, but the stubborn person still refused a seventh form body.

"Stop bugging me about it." Choi's voice was thin and reedy, but they still insisted on being at every meeting of the biomass aspects. They dropped Anderson's hand and piloted the mobility chair to the head of the table. "I've lived over ninety-eight years so far on Lida in this body. I might as well make a full run of it. You'd be doing this a lot more often if things had gone anywhere close to how the fleet planned."

Over eighty eight percent of the population had chosen the seventh form bodies. Children were given the choice when they reached majority, though some put off the decision for months or even years. In any case, the percentages seemed to be holding about the same. Every once in a while, Anderson would see an old person, but there weren't many.

"Should we wait until Jiow arrives?" Juliane had recently adopted wearing a fedora again. Hats had been popular in the early days, and with cities opening up in climates with larger climate variation than in the arcopolis, they were making a comeback.

"She's missed the last fifteen meetings, ever since Frank passed." Choi paused to cough. "Why would we expect her to come to this one?"

"We can always hope. Expansionist was always the most individual of us." Juliane shrugged.

Of *us*. Not of the biomass' identities. Anderson caught himself slipping sometimes too. It was hard to think of himself without that little bundle of thoughts and directions in the back of his mind. Before Researcher, that spot had been taken by Cora.

You are a welcome aspect of Researcher as well. It would be strange to be without you. The biomass had gotten more eloquent over the years.

"That individuality is good. How are negotiations with the artificial humans going over creating their own consensus?" Choi asked.

"Researcher feels that may upset a careful balance," Anderson said.

"Answerer feels the same," Juliane added.

"Another point in favor of keeping this body." Choi chuckled, which turned into more coughing. "No matter how much it's breaking down. I expect Expansionist is in favor of it, as usual?"

Anderson conceded the point with a nod. "It's in favor of anything that is new and unusual. It overlaps enough with Juliane and I that sometimes it's hard to decipher where the communication is coming from."

"I almost think it should allow the artificial humans in. It may be exactly what the biomass is missing." Choi looked into the distance, consulting their HUD. "You know some of the seventh form are choosing to die, right?"

Juliane frowned. "I'd heard that, but Answerer has a hard time tracking individuals."

"As does Researcher, but I've talked to a few Vagals who didn't want to come back in the first wave of resurrected colonists," Anderson said.

"And those are many of the ones choosing to die rather than continue with a seventh form body." Choi held up a thin finger. "Not sure whether it's good or not, but a side effect of the seventh form is that their memories are stored in the fungal towers."

Anderson sat forward. "They are? Why didn't I know this?" He sent a question to Researcher.

Experiences are vital to complete understanding. They will be processed by higher-functioning nodes when needed.

Well, that wasn't an answer.

Choi was watching him. "The question is, can you find them?"

"I'll give it a try, but it's going to be hard to collect a whole human's experience."

"Try," Choi said. "Because per Frank's last wishes, I'm setting up a virtual environment. I think if we find enough human memories, we can give them life again as a direct part of the biomass, but one created by humans, not by the biomass. It might get around the reticence by some, myself included. We'll ask a person—or what's left—if they're amenable to living virtually, and if so, they can make their own consensus. It will be the closest we've gotten to integrating with the biomass by our choice and will give us a powerful say in our future."

What Comes After

150 years after landing

"I think with the latest shipments of yttrium, neodymium, and gadolinium, we might have all we need for the first test of genemods," Harie told Carel. His daughter nodded, silent as usual, but threw a diagram with line charts and percentages to the screen on the biomass column where she worked.

Harie had gotten used to his children's strange forms. There was a small generation of people who kept the biomass' more exotic shapes given to them in the trouble back in the forties, when the biomass' aspects were emerging. Carel had stayed fused with the surface that used to be a room in their house, though they had been able to move the room entirely, including the column, about twenty-five years ago. Now they were set up in the arcopolis' new Frank Silver Gene Research Facility.

"Yes, I saw that too. We can substitute for the lower quantities of neodymium if needed. As long as we get the first test run to work, Admin will be bugging Human to petition more mineral extracts."

Carel cocked her head, then nodded. She pulled up the interface to the virtual environment on her column. As usual, the screen looked like a pixel explosion to Harie, but it showed the various activities of the virtual and artificial humans who'd agreed to become a permanent part of the biomass conflux. The fourth identity had taken ten years to fully emerge, and was still causing friction, especially with the Expansionists, who claimed it was a heresy for some reason. Even since Jiow had disappeared into a two-kilometer-tall tangle of fungus halfway across the planet, her followers had gotten more rebellious.

"Let me know what they say." He patted Carel on the shoulder, and she reached up to peck him on the cheek before he went to set the first test in motion.

Directions still came through Anderson and Juliane, now considered Admins in all but name with the original eight. Admin Brighton sat like a spider in the middle of the arcopolis, of course, but the others moved between cities. Once Agetha had completed the eighth one—Desert Sky—the rumor was one Admin would be in charge of each city.

He went back to Carel after triple confirming the test was correct. They'd start the run that evening and might have the genemod supplement ready in the morning, if all went well.

"Oh, hello Choi," Harie said, seeing their face up on Carel's column. "Did Carel tell you about the low neodymium levels?"

"Yes. I'll try to gather up enough voices to make ourselves heard. There's a growing ruckus over my mother. Seems not even the biomass conflux as a whole knows where she is, and that should be impossible." Choi said. Their voice still sounded elderly. They had been the first—and still only—person to upload themself to virtual collective without taking a seventh form body. It had been touch and go when they reached their hundred-teens, but Choi had finally accepted minimal help from the biomass to clean out enough plaque and repair enough DNA to keep them alive until the interface was complete. They were still working on bringing Frank back, but without the interface being active when the old scientist had died, Choi said there were problems integrating.

"Well, it's not like Jiow can get hurt out there, and she always seemed so eager to explore."

Choi's virtual eyes rolled. "She always had a dramatic streak. I'm sure we'll hear what's going on, whether in ten years or one hundred. But let me know how that test goes tomorrow morning. I'd love to give our children another option over seventh form bodies."

"You're technically a part of the biomass," Harie chided. "Still think it's a bad idea?"

"Never can be too careful," Choi returned. "I'll only be satisfied when humans—actual humans—have an equal voice to the biomass."

* * *

200 years after landing

"This has got to be connected to Jiow," Agetha said, sorting the news on her HUD.

"Think we can take the train down to the arcopolis to meet this individual?" Beth asked. She accepted a piece of toast from Phyllis.

"Capital 'I' individual," Phyllis added. "Says they traveled from around the same area where she disappeared. Did it take them fifty years to develop?"

"And did they only have Jiow and Expansionist's views to guide them?" Agetha took a bite of her own toast.

"The conflux insists it didn't know where she was this whole time," Beth said. "But we know things get missed. Maybe it had to be unaware of this person for them to be the disconnected individual they claim."

"I think we should take that train ride." Agetha pulled up the schedule on her HUD, pushing aside the latest letter from Daved. He and Phillipe had set up a business in Deeptown, trying to raise horses from the cold storage samples from the original fleet, when they weren't needed for Vagal duties. He said they survived a lot better in the north.

They sent letters back and forth monthly nowadays, keeping each other up to date with their families. Agetha, Beth, and Phyllis had decided not to raise any new children, with all of them enjoying each other's company, and building the new cities. They gave their time to the rapidly growing colony in structure, rather than new people.

Daved had a couple children, and Phillipe even had a little girl, only about five years old. They'd both found partners in Deeptown, and Agetha wanted to make the trek up there one of these days to have a little family reunion.

But first this business with The Individual.

Agetha got off the train at the arcopolis terminal the next morning with Beth and Phyllis by her side. Harie met her with a big hug.

"It's been too long. How many years this time? Still planning cities?"

Agetha waved a hand. "Time is meaningless. A decade? More?"

"Fourteen years," Beth put in. "Good to see you, Harie."

"She's got another two cities on the docket," Phyllis added. "But growth is finally slowing."

"As are the birth rates, thankfully." Agetha waved away Harie's offer to carry her luggage. "But we're here to see The Individual. Choi have any idea who this is?"

Harie led them into the city, catching a tram. "Choi says The

Individual is completely disconnected from the conflux. They've never seen it before."

"So not the same as the artificial humans, then," Beth asked, taking her seat.

Harie shook his head. "Choi's been wrangling them too, but they seem to have...limitations. They're happy to help out, but they've never quite got the hang of existing. I still find one standing in a corner once in a while. At least they add their voice to Human when it matters."

"Anderson and Juliane said Researcher and Answerer are just as confused," Agetha said. "I think the conflux finally found a way to make something *other*."

They made small talk until their stop in the Alpha Radian. "They're staying in the Silver facility, where Choi can keep a virtual eye on them." Harie led them through the front doors.

The Individual was a handsome, generic, androgynous person. They rose to their feet with a smile, and Agetha regarded them critically. Perhaps a hint of Jiow's features around them, but impossible to say.

"You must be Agetha." They grasped her hand. "I've heard so much about you."

"Heh. All good, I hope." Agetha felt words slip away in their presence and glanced at Beth and Phyllis. The feel of clicking beads was continuous, as if anxious. Phyllis' soup smelt spicy. They felt it too. This person had a presence larger than their body. "We wanted to meet the first biomass Individual as soon as we could."

"As have many others," they said. "I've talked to Admins, scientists, virtual humans, and lots more over the past few days. It's been an amazing experience to meet you all, in person, thinking, well like this." They gestured to their head.

"Do you have a connection to the biomass?" Beth asked. Always the scientist.

"None at all." The Individual shook their head. "I can see your connections—strong to each other, and weaker to the biomass. I don't have anything like that."

Agetha traded another look with the others. "And you walked all the way here from halfway across Lida?"

They smiled. "Well, I caught rides where I could, and I'm quite fit. The biomass outfitted me with a very resilient body. I think it's modeled on your seventh forms."

"But...why?" Phyllis asked. "Do you know *why* you're here?"

The Individual looked concerned for the first time. "I have suspicions, but unfortunately, not being connected to the biomass has downsides too. Still. I feel I'm here for a reason. A collection of observations and predictions perhaps? Suffice to say I am grateful for existing."

Agetha was grateful for them too. The Individual was a charming person, and reminded her deeply of the feeling she had talking to the biomass. They were the first really new thing in many years. Part human, part biomass, curious, and insightful. They promised great things for Lida.

* * *

250 years after landing

Jane stood with the other Admins, the various conflux aspects, important and influential people, and of course, with The Individual. They'd never taken a name, in fifty years, though they all knew now why the person had emerged from the wilderness.

"Though we've seen eight land, we're here to dedicate the first launch of a spacecraft *from* the surface of Lida," Jane said. She could feel Christiaan mouthing the words behind her. "Our brave crew will interface with the drone station in orbit, to begin research as to what else there might be in our galaxy. We know for sure there is one life form other than us. Now we hope to find more."

Jane paused to let the applause die down, as the crew of the ship, trailed by The Individual, walked toward the magnetic ramp that would propel the ship into orbit. It curved far outside the walls of the arcopolis, though the starting terminal was just at the Alpha wall, where the crowd was gathered.

There were six crew leading the spaceship, two seventh form humans, two young genemodded people, one artificial human, and The Individual. From all walks of life on Lida. If they were successful, they would be the first to begin construction on the skeleton of the generational ship attached to the drone station.

"Any new predictions on how the seventh form and artificials will hold up in orbit?" she whispered to Anderson.

The former Vagal shook his head. "Researcher doesn't know exactly how far the conflux reaches. It's never been outside the atmosphere, but that doesn't mean the connection won't reach. It's part of the reason for The Individual's larger presence, we speculate. Answerer even proposed the connection might form a quantum entanglement. In that case, the seventh forms could have a connection to the biomass anywhere in the universe."

Jane stepped forward again as the crew entered the spacecraft, her HUD amplifying her voice to the PA system.

"No matter what happens, Admin, Generational, Vagal, Grounder, seventh form or genemodded body, we are all human. We have survived one planet, and now a second. But now we have another to discover the future with. A friend and ally."

She really hoped the biomass would stay an ally. It had for centuries, but the balance within the conflux was always shifting. She believed that was another reason, conscious or not, the biomass had created The Individual. It was also why Jane had pushed for this spacecraft, when they really should have been devoting resources to expanding cities and mapping the rest of Lida and the solar system. It was the first time she'd deviated from the Admin's plan for colonization.

The roar of the cycling electromagnets rendered more speech impossible, if she had any left in her.

Jane watched the spacecraft suddenly jet forward, arcing far out into the distance until it shot up into the sky—a mere speck.

A flock of winged things burst from the biomass around the ramp's exit, fluttering high up into the air. She expected them to fall back to Lida's surface, but they followed the craft for some time, disappearing into the clouds.

"You ever seen biomass creatures go that high?" she asked Christiaan.

"Never, Jane. They almost always stay below three hundred meters at most. Perhaps Expansionist devised a special sendoff for the occasion."

"Just like we said goodbye to Earth, all those years ago?" With a sigh, she squeezed Christiaan's hand.

Anderson's words were quiet, at her side. "Maybe the biomass is saying goodbye to its first real child."

The end of the Biomass Conflux

ACKNOWLEDGEMENTS

What makes us human? And in this time when we're dipping our feet into AI systems and we have buttons that let us have conversations with our pets, I think the more pertinent question is "What makes us people?"

Those questions ran through my mind as I was writing this, and I am so happy to get this final installment of *The Biomass Conflux* in front of you all! I am continually surprised how well this trilogy of mushrooms and humans is regarded, and how many people enjoy it. That's the best kind of reward for writing.

Where the first book was about discovery, and the second was about change, this one forms the sort of future society I'm hopeful for. Not necessarily one with sentient mushrooms, but one where humanity is focused on making themselves and their surroundings the best possible versions possible.

Once again, while the title is a play on words in one sense, I hope it also conveys a deeper meaning for the story. I have a continual fascination with psychology (which I believe one has to, to be a writer), and I really enjoyed digging into what might make an alien intelligence with no sense of "self," function and grow. While this is the end of the series, I like to think the conflux continued exploring the universe with its new human friends.

First thanks always go to my wife Heather. She brings Space Wizard books an extra bit of shine with her copy editing.

Thanks again to the READ group for their help with cover ideas, book descriptions, and beta reading. Space Wizard is more than the sum of its parts! Special thanks to Seri, Sara (for suggesting I add Frank's last scene), and especially Natalie, for a total of *seven* instances of "welp..." in her comments. I think that's a new record.

Thanks also very much to Cass, who said, "Daved's definitely coming back as a zombie, isn't he?" after reading the first book. If that bit of horror did anything for you, it's her fault.

Finally, thank you to everyone who backed the Space Wizard Science Fantasy Year 2 Kickstarter! We did even better than Year 1, and the Year 3 campaign will be very close to arriving when this book is published. I can't wait to see how it does.

ABOUT THE AUTHOR

William C. Tracy writes and publishes queer science fiction and fantasy through his indie press Space Wizard Science Fantasy (spacewizardsciencefantasy.com).

His largest work is the Dissolutionverse: a space opera with music-based magic, including ten books and an RPG. He also has a standalone epic fantasy with seasonal fruit-based magic, a nonfiction book about body mechanics and correct posture, and a hard sci-fi trilogy with generational colony ships and a planet covered by a sentient fungal entity.

William is an NC native and a lifelong fan of science fiction and fantasy. He has a master's in mechanical engineering, and has both designed and operated heavy construction machinery. He has also trained in Wado-Ryu karate since 2003 and runs his own dojo in Raleigh NC. He is an avid video and board gamer, a beekeeper, a reader, and of course, a writer.

You can get a free Dissolutionverse novelette by signing up for William's mailing list at spacewizardsciencefantasy.com.

Follow him on Bluesky at wctracy.bsky.social, Threads at threads.net/@tracywc, and Twitter at @wctracy for writing updates, cat and bee pictures, and thoughts on martial arts.

Please take a moment to review this book at your favorite retailer's website, Goodreads, or simply tell your friends!